Praise for
Camille Claudel, a Novel

Psychoanalyst Dr. Alma Bond knows how to get inside people's minds, & in this fictional reminiscence, she recreates the passionate life & times of one of the most powerful artists of the early 20th century, who became the revered Rodin's apprentice & mistress. As with *The Autobiography of Maria Callas: A Novel*, Dr. Bond has breathed fresh life into a forgotten giant in her field of brilliance, & written a fascinating memoir of what drove a woman to break through the glass ceiling in a world ruled by men, & take the dire consequences.

> – Rebecca Brown
> publisher and editor-in-chief of Rebeccasreads.com

A rave review for Dr. Alma H. Bond's brilliant new novel, *Camille Claudel: A Novel*. Dr. Bond gives us an intriguing account of the juicy affair between the young, innocent Camille (a budding and genius sculptor in her own right) and the older distinguished and very married Auguste Rodin. We are treated to their love affair as well as a glimpse at her early years, her rejection by Rodin and ultimate decent into madness and life in an insane asylum. Dr. Bond's psychological twist on this age-old story makes this beautifully written novel a read that is truly impossible to put down. Bravo!

> –Janet Brill, Ph.D.
> instructor University of Miami, author of *CholesterolDown*.

Dr. Bond has written a tour de force! *Camille Claudel: A Novel* is a beautifully sculpted work, filled with appreciation, insight and craft."

> –Feather Schwartz Foster
> author of *LADIES: A Conjecture of Personalities*
> and *Garfield's Train*.

In the art world, we are familiar with the photograph of Camille Claudel in old age wearing a coat and squashed down cap sitting with her hands, those wonderful, now motionless beautiful tools, folded outside Montdevergues asylum. In reading Alma Bond's novel, I feel I am sitting across from Camille Claudel on a fall day. She is looking at me with those intelligent, indigo blue eyes. Eyes that are filled with a certain amount of resignation and wistfulness and she has chosen me to tell me her life story.

As a woman sculptor, I feel an overwhelming connection to Camille Claudel. The shared passion for all things related to sculpture, the smell of the clay, the fingering of the tolls, the movement of the muscle, the push and pull of the medium, the power to extract the truth and soul from a lump of clay or a piece of stone, the sheer physical exhaustion that is part of the work. Claudel believed that sculptures of women would be best done by women, because of the deeper understanding of our emotions, sensibilities and soul. I too believe this.

Camile Claudel does not regret the passion for the work she chose to pursue, dos not regret the intensity of her love experience. Her regret lies in the gender discrimination she was plagued with in the artistic and social setting and the unjust years at Montdevergues.

Camille Claudel was a sculptor of genius. Alma Bond, in this book, sheds an unforgettable light on a truly deserving Claudel.

– Maria Trapani, award-wining sculptor.

Alma Bond has done it again! Another passionate love story of two illustrious artists, Auguste Rodin and Camille Claudel, one whose life ended in glory, the other in madness. Combining meticulous research with finely honed analytical skills, the author immerses herself in her subject, leading the reader through the development of an artist from childhood; her emotional and artistic life as a woman; and into the creative process itself.

Dr. Bond takes an imaginative leap into the life, mind and work of a woman sculptor and restores Claudel to her rightful place in art history.

–Mimi Weisbord, artist and writer.

Camille Claudel

a Novel

Alma H. Bond

PublishAmerica
Baltimore

First printing

At the specific preference of the author, PublishAmerica allowed this work to remain exactly as the author intended, verbatim, without editorial input.

ISBN: 1-4241-1670-8
PUBLISHED BY PUBLISHAMERICA, LLLP
www.publishamerica.com
Baltimore

Printed in the United States of America

Dedication

To Mme. Madeleine Rondin
Secretary General
Association for Camille and Paul Claudel
Tardenois, France

Acknowledgements

I would like to thank the following people who helped in the researching and writing of this book, whose caring and going the extra inch turned a difficult project into a work of love: Alyson Matley, Lola Hoffman, Zita Walsh, and Vicki Lawrence, who read early versions of Part One, and enthusiastically encouraged me to proceed with the book. Rebecca Brown, publisher and editor of RebeccasReads.com, who readily took time out from her busy life to serve as first reader of the final draft. I am particularly grateful for her wonderful suggestion of the fictional contribution of William Barrett, Professor Emeritus, French Literature, University of Paris. Kathryn Lance, who did a brilliant job of editing the book. Lois Barrowcliff, Interior Designer, who supplied the description of Marie Antoinette's bed in the Petit Trianon in Versailles. Dr. Thomas A. Godwin, the benevolent stranger who explained the concept of Epiploic Hernia. Leslie, of the Surfside, Florida library, who in all humility, would not give me her last name, who has been helpful beyond the call of duty in researching this book. The late Eugene Canondé who helped find knowledgeable literary sources in Paris. Bianca Bacalar, Celia Roberts, Patricia Mervelce, and Sylvia and Eric Cheval, who assisted in the translation of difficult French material. Terri Parise, for her wonderful stories about growing up a sculptor. Thomas Streeter, Director of the U.S.

Streaming Media Project of the University of Cincinnati, for the CD of *Clotho,* an opera about Camille Claudel. Danielle Arnoux, for the gift of her award-winning book, *Camille Claudel, l'ironic sacrifice.* Le Musée d'Art & Archéologie, for their pamphlets on Alfred Boucher. Jeff Kempe of the University of Washington Libraries, for material on Jessie Lipscomb. Robert Wernick, for sending me his article, *Camille Claudel's tempestuous life of art and passion.* Mme. Christiane Sinnig–Haas, of the Musée Jean de La Fontaine, who on her own time allowed me to view sculptures of Camille Claudel not available elsewhere. Sophie Gauthier for her gracious French hospitality. David Chauvet, co-author of *Montdevergues, Les mémoires d'un hôpital* who cordially squired me around the grounds of the hospital where Camille Claudel spent the last thirty years of her life, and presented me with a copy of his book.

But most of all, I would like to express my gratitude to Mme. Madeleine Rondin, the Secretary General of the Association for Camille and Paul Claudel in Tardinois, France, for her encouragement, her unbelievably kind hospitality, and her inclusive tour of Villeneuve in Tarendois, where Camille Claudel grew up and created her first magnificent masterpieces. Mme. Rondin helped Camille come alive for me.

Camille Claudel, a Novel is a work of fiction. Although it is based upon historical facts, the events described have been greatly embellished by the author's imagination. All the characters are historical figures doing and saying pretty much what I think they must have, except for the psychiatrist Dr. Brunet who treated Camille for a while, and Prof. Barrett, both complete fabrications on my part.

Contents

Foreword   11
Prologue   13

Part I
THE EARLY YEARS 1864–1881   17

Part II
THE RODIN YEARS 1881–1912   61

       The Love Affair 1882–1892   63
       The Breakup 1893–1901   132
       The Downhill Slide 1902–1912   177

Part III
THE ASYLUM YEARS 1913–1943   195

Addendum   239
Bibliography   241
Glossary   243

Foreword

As translated by William Barrett, Professor Emeritus, Classic French Literature, University of Paris.

I was an American French Literature post-graduate student when I was drafted as an interpreter of war documents in the army that liberated the area near Avignon during WWII. There, in the chaos the Germans left in the hotel rooms where they had their headquarters, I was deciphering thousands of files and pages when a young nurse came in and thrust an old cardboard suitcase at me. She darted away with no explanation. Upon opening it I found bundles bound in silk thread of hundreds of sheets of yellowed, splotched foolscap paper on which had been scribbled in red pencil an unending passionate stream of memories by someone called Camille Claudel. Amidst the flimsy fabric that once might have been a night robe were nestled three little soap figurines, carved in exquisite detail. As they had no bearing on my war work, I simply stowed the baggage in my personal gear, and forgot about it.

After the war I returned to the States to marry my childhood sweetheart, and become a professor of Classic French Literature. I helped raise our four children, outlived my dear wife, became a great-grandfather, and upon retiring, was enticed to fly to France to be the recipient of a medal at the 60th anniversary of the Liberation. As I was viewing an exhibit at the Rodin Museum I came upon a sculpture that entranced me, and seemed strangely familiar. On the bronze plaque was the name Camille Claudel, and with a shock I suddenly remembered that long-forgotten, battered piece of hand luggage up in my attic in the trunk where I kept my uniforms and war mementoes.

I am an old man now who is almost blind, and must beg the reader to excuse my poor attempts at translating this soaring spirit's handwriting, and for any of my errors in bringing a semblance of order to this passionate plea to be remembered.

I hope you will enjoy reading these memoirs as much as I have transcribing them, and that her manuscript will bring Camille Claudel into the consciousness of the present-day world as a great artist, the muse of Rodin, and an unfortunate soul who surely deserved far more from life than she received.

Prologue

Montdevergues Asylum, 1943

*T*hey say I'm crazy, and have me locked up in this dreary dungeon where I live without a face, without a soul, without a name. I've been here for so long I've lost track. I'm so old I forget my exact age. I've been writing this memoir to get things straightened out in my own mind before I die, and to leave my true story behind for future generations to puzzle over. It's the tale of what fate had in store for the child Camille Claudel.

My life has been a romance, a mystery, a poem, an epic, a novel, an elegy, a historical treatise which would take a Shakespeare to describe. But since no Shakespeare is available, at least to me, I shall have to do the best I can to convey the magnificence and the horror of my sojourn on earth. I hope it will illustrate the heights of passion Rodin and I reached and unravel the mystery of why they were transformed to vinegar and ashes.

Even more important, this may illuminate the reasons why Auguste Rodin is known and adored worldwide for work done largely by my hands, while I fester away in this dungeon of despair. And it may even help me to discover why my genius brother Paul is rich and famous while I, a far more gifted artist, am locked up here forever.

You might wonder why I don't ask Paul to write this for me. It would make my life simpler, not to mention be a much finer work of art. He is, after all, a great poet and playwright. But deeply as I love Paul, he and I look at life very differently. Paul is a dedicated Catholic, some might say a man obsessed with his religion. We see eye-to-eye only on my talent, and have completely different explanations for the course my life has taken since we were so close as children. If Paul were to tell my story, I'm sure he'd create a brilliant book, but it would not be me.

It was Sister Sylvie who suggested I write down the story of my life. All of it? I thought. Like a confession? All of it? All of it! And then I remembered the seltzer and jelly Maman would give me when she was in a good mood, and how, when I'd burped, the flavor came back. What a grand idea!

"And this will be good for what ails me?" I taunted the good Sister.

"Very much so," she said with conviction.

"On what?" I challenged her, looking around my miserable cell.

She said, "Perhaps we could persuade your brother to supply you with pencils and paper?"

And I scoffed, "Perhaps you could persuade my brother to get me out of this hell hole!"

She actually smiled, shook her head, and said, "That we cannot do."

And there it was, in the very next parcel of supplies from Maman, which she sent in a sad, old cardboard case. A ream of the loveliest foolscap paper with six yellow pencils with red lead and pink erasers, all wrapped inside white butcher paper. Of course the nuns had to sharpen the pencils for me as no one would allow me the possession of a knife!

And in my solitude of waiting for who-knows-what I did begin to write. Not my metiér, of course, but as I progressed the memories took over me, and I wrote and wrote and wrote, just as I'd sculpted. And the reams arrived year after year. Even when no one ever visited.

It's funny about being independent in France. One would think people would admire individuals who carve paths through the unknown or create beautiful works of art. But this is not so, particularly in small towns like Villeneuve in Fère-en-Tardenois, where I was born on December 8, 1864. An independent person—and especially a woman—is often considered rude, rebellious, insolent, and a troublemaker unfit for social life (like you-know-who). I cannot imagine why people prefer such ways of thinking. Why go into society at all if only to hear viewpoints you already know?

The tragedy is not only mine, but that of many talented women of our times who find it impossible to achieve anywhere near the recognition bestowed on men artists of lesser ability, and either drop out of the art world like my friend Jessie Lipscomb, or remain in it like me and starve. Our fate is not only that of female artists, but of all women in France and England, and probably all over the world.

The difference in the education and treatment of men and women has caused innumerable tragedies in the relationships of many couples, including my own parents. It has separated parents from their children and siblings from each other. It has imprisoned intelligent women as surely as I've been sequestered here at Montdevergues. It's too late for me, but perhaps my memoirs will help bring capable women of the future the acclaim that our own generation cannot or will not grant, and make the achievement of happiness a greater possibility for women of all sorts.

Tell me, Reader, am I crazy, or is the story of my life one of the great catastrophes of our era? You decide.

Camille Claudel

Part I
The Early Years

1864–1881

When I was little, I loved playing in the mud and shaping tiny people out of it. I made a mama, a papa, a little girl, and a little boy that looked just Paul, curly hair and all. One day it suddenly began to pour torrents, the way it always rains in Villeneuve, and all my little people began to melt. I stood there watching as they grew smaller and smaller and finally flowed away in the flood. It made me cry so hard I couldn't stop, and I was glad when Maman pulled me away from the mud, even if she did send me to bed without any supper. As I lay in bed and seethed, I determined to make new little people the first thing in the morning. It had felt so good I wanted to do it always.

Before anyone one else was up I crept into the back yard. It was spring. The rain had stopped, and the smell of the sweet green grass of Villeneuve lingered in the air. I discovered that the thick red dirt was harder than it had been yesterday and had changed color. Now some whitish streaks showed through it. I knelt by the mud hole I'd made the day before and grasped fistfuls of dirt in both hands. It felt chalky and stuck together. I rolled it between my hands until it became a solid ball, and joyfully clutched it against my woolen jumper, forgetting what Maman would say about dirtying my clothes. I held the ball up to my nose and sniffed its fragrance all the way down to my tummy, and held my breath as long as I could. The rich red earth smelled so fresh I wanted to lick it, but I didn't because I was afraid of what Maman would do if she found out.

Then I dug into my mud ball with a frenzy and began to mold the little figures again. I pressed here and there, now indenting it to form the eyes and mouth, now building it up to make the nose and forehead, smoothing it with my fingernails or a flat stick I'd saved from the fireplace. Suddenly I saw that the figure I called Maman had large, sad eyes. It amazed me that she looked stern and duty-bound, just like she really does.

I, Camille Rosalie Claudel, had made a real little person, all by myself! I couldn't get over how true to life she looked. First there was nothing but mud, and then there was a real little person. If there is a God, I'll bet he felt like that when he made Adam.

But I wasn't as satisfied with the Papa character. No matter how hard I tried, I couldn't keep him from looking angry. Maybe that's because he always is. I liked my figure of the little boy better; he was handsome and serious, like the thinker Paul always was. While even to my biased eyes, the image of my little vacant-eyed sister was beautiful.

The sun was now overhead and drying up the mud until it turned the color of chalk. I spit on my people so I could keep on working. I was so absorbed with making the little figures come alive that I didn't hear Papa come up behind me until he shouted, "Camille!" I started shaking because I was scared he'd lecture me like he always does. But he didn't. Instead he stopped short with the strangest expression on his face, kind of screwed-up as if he'd tasted a lemon, like the time when I drew a picture of the ocean and he said I was a little Rembrandt. Then he knelt by the mud hole and reached out with both hands for the Maman. Lifting it up as carefully as if it were one of her precious champagne glasses, he turned it from front to back and side to side over and over again. His eyes filled with tears.

"Camille," he said, swallowing hard, "these are very good. I'm going to try to find you some real clay to work with. I want you to do the best you can with it."

"Oh Papa, I will! I will!"

"Good. If you do as well with the clay as you have with this mud, I'm going to show your statues to Alfred Boucher, the famous sculptor in Nogent-sur-Seine. Would you like that?"

"Oh Papa, yes! Thank you! I'm so happy!" I threw myself into his arms. He hugged me back, slimy hands, muddy boots, dripping dress, and all.

I ran into the house singing a strange chaotic melody I'd made up, a kind of prayer of thanks to the universe that came into my head when life pleased me, only to find Maman sitting by the window with her head in her hands. She was crying. She's always crying. I knew it was no time to tell her about my little people and Papa's plans for me. She never had any feeling for what I thought was important; she just didn't want me to mess up her kitchen.

"Maman, what's the matter?" I asked dutifully, even though I already knew.

She sat rocking back and forth in her tapestried chair and moaning. "My baby, my baby."

"Maman." I said impatiently. "Henri died a long time ago, before I was in your tummy."

"It doesn't matter!" she shouted. "I will never get over him! He was the love of my life, my first child. He was only fifteen days old when he died."

"I know, Maman," I said grumpily, "when I was born the next year you were so disappointed I wasn't a boy that you called me Camille, a name that can be given to either a boy or a girl."

But she continued as if she hadn't heard me. "And then Louise arrived fourteen months later, before I had a chance to..."

"...be a mother to me. I know all that," I sighed. "She was the daughter you always wanted. Your beautiful, obedient Louise!"

"What are you saying, Camille? You speak this way to your *mother*? How dare you talk to me like that! You don't deserve to be in this distinguished family. Henri would never have behaved like you. I had hoped you would be like him, but you turned out to be a violent, vicious child! It is *your* fault this family is always fighting. You know just how to set everyone against each other. Hold your tongue, or you will go to bed without your supper again!"

She was being unfair, as usual. What I said about my little sister Louise was one hundred percent correct, as any sensitive child would have picked up. She was born when I was only a year and two months old. I don't remember it, of course, but I've been told and told and told the story. Maman loved her right away. If she could have picked a personality for her daughter, I'm sure she would have chosen Louise, who was named after Maman, and seemed to know from the start she was destined to be her carbon copy. She was completely dependent on our mother and had no mind of her own. I loved to taunt her with it, and said to her once, "What will happen to the copy when the original is gone?" Louise was what Maman valued above all else, a *good* baby. On the other hand, I'm told that I cried every time she came near me, as if I knew in the womb that Maman didn't want me. I didn't take to her the way babies usually attach to their mothers, or let her comfort me. To make matters worse, when *la bonne* Hélène or Papa came into the room, I was all smiles. I think Maman has never forgiven me for that. In retaliation, she made it quite clear from her nasty comments that she couldn't stand me. She got a sullen, pinched expression on her face whenever I came near her, as if she suddenly smelled a skunk.

I used to watch Maman and Louise with their heads together talking like girlfriends. Why didn't she ever talk with me like that? Whenever I came near her she'd move away. She never had two words to say to me that weren't a criticism. She ached for Henri, adored Louise and Paul, and skipped me altogether. Sometimes I wonder how much she would have loved Henri had he lived.

Another reason she never loved me, although she'd deny it from now to Kingdom Come, is that I was born with one leg a bit shorter than the other and I walk with a slight limp. Even though people say they don't notice it, I don't believe them. My rhythm is a bit off, so that my gait goes ump-up-ump-up, instead of ump-ump-ump-ump, like that of normal people.

I've always been self-conscious about my walk. When I pass people on the street, I check to see if they notice my limping. If a cart stops to let me cross the road, I think they're being nice because I'm lame. I wonder if anyone ever can really love a cripple. I used to believe that if only I walked like everybody else, my mother would love me. That must be why I'm so fascinated by balance in my work. My figures, like those in *La Valse*, manage extraordinary feats of equilibrium, even if I myself stumble all over the place. I believe one reason I was a perfectionist in my work is that if I didn't have a completely intact body, I could always try for perfection in the bodies I sculpted.

I guess that's why I really never liked my perfect sister. My feelings are obvious in the statue I did of her when she was twenty. I call it *Jeune fille aux yeux clos* (*Young girl with closed eyes*). She looks beautiful, but her eyes are closed, because she really sees nothing. Her expression is benign on the surface, but if you study it closely, you'll see stubborn hostility underneath her faint smile. That's not so strange, for she was jealous of me from the moment she was born. Unlike my other work, looking at this piece gives me nothing, just like Louise.

The story in the family is that soon after she arrived, Papa said, "Camille, shall we keep her or send her back?" I said, "Send her back." He thought that was very funny, but of course Maman didn't, and has never let me forget it.

The birth of Paul, which is my first real memory, was quite different. Papa put this sweet-smelling little bundle on my lap and said, "You have a little brother, *ton petit Paul*." I put my finger in his hand and he closed his tiny fist around it. My heart pounded and my eyes teared up. I fell in love with him right then, and have loved him ever since.

Another thing about Maman. She hasn't had an original thought in her whole life, and can't stand anybody who does. She's just like all the other women she knows. Paul and I got the giggles when our tutor told us that her maiden name was Louise-Athanaise Cerveaux. As everyone knows, "*cerveau*" in French means brain, mind, or mastermind, which Maman certainly is not. If I believed in God, I would think he had a great sense of humor and selected her name as a celestial joke. Being so conventional, she objects whenever I show any imagination or think anything that has never occurred to her. Maman is a perfect example of someone who values good form above all else and has no use for my way of thinking or my art. And of course Louise has never had an unconventional idea in her life.

*I*t's a good thing for me that we had Hélène, or I would *really* belong in this den of iniquity I've lived in for thirty years. I learned a lot about maids when I eavesdropped on the weekly chatting circle of my mother and her neighbors. When they weren't disapproving of me or their husbands spending all their free time with buddies at the cafes, they mostly complained about the impossibility of getting good work out of their servants. I learned as the women sat at their embroidery and chitchatted away that they thought the *bonnes* were good-tempered and well-mannered, but insensitive to the subtleties of French cooking and the fine care of a household. Because the *bonnes* came from peasant stock (Hélène is Alsatian) they understood nothing about the art of maintaining a lovely home. They could not be taught to cook, except when constantly watched, nor could they be trusted to handle china or glass such as Maman's fragile crystal ware without breaking it. They burned the food Maman nursed along for hours to reach the required state of perfection. Even if a maid had done something well a hundred times, let the mistress turn her back once, and the *bonne* was sure to do it wrong the hundred-and-first time. Most important of all, the housekeepers whispered over their stitching, when there was any refinement in the house, it was certainly due to the intelligence and knowledge of the lady of the house, namely the woman doing the complaining, (usually Maman). It's true that these women were scientific house administrators and able to run their households with far more skill than their servants. But the *bonnes* were very clean and excellent at hard work like digging in the garden, cleaning the outhouse, fetching water, fattening up poultry, washing down the buggy, harnessing the horses, making butter, and carrying heavy logs. They were a delight to have around because the harder they worked the louder they laughed and sang. What a contrast to Maman's grouchy griping! Hélène had gentle, far-reaching eyes that took in everything and a quiet, amused smile. Whatever the season, she tied a kerchief around her shoulders and wore a grey bonnet, a petticoat she had spun herself from the wool of sheep and dyed red, and an apron over her long woolen skirt. She was naturally polite and kind, and did things like saving me the heel of the bread and bringing me nice soap and *Calisson*[1] when she went to visit her family.

I only saw her upset once. When I was about seven years old, I heard a sobbing in the back of the kitchen. I ran in and it was Hélène crying bitterly. I knelt at her feet, saying, "What is it, Hélène? What's wrong? Did Maman scold you again?"

Papa must have heard me and came in and put his arm around me. He said, "Let her alone, Camille. Something terrible has happened."

"What is it Papa? What's the matter with Hélène?"

"You know we've been at war with the Prussians. France has lost," he said sadly. "Hélène's home in Alsace isn't part of France anymore. The government says she's now a German. Her nieces and nephews won't even be allowed to talk French in their school after today."

I didn't understand how Hélène could be French like us one day and German the next, and began to cry too. But in a few days she was back to her pleasant self and nobody ever talked to me about it again. Except sometimes at night I heard her crying in her bed.

I really liked my bust of Hélène. Every time I looked at it, my first impulse was to laugh, but when I looked again it made me sad. It's as if she were smiling her warm crooked smile to keep away the tears. It said she knew what life was really about, and had no need to blab about it all the time like Maman and her accomplices. Although Hélène understood that life can be awful and lonely and sad, she loved it anyway. Strong and wise like the giant stones on the moor, she never fooled herself. I learned from her how to be direct and honest, and I would not trade those lessons for all the degrees of the Sorbonne. Hélène was a wonderful woman. How I wish she were with me now.

It was a good thing for all of us, not just me, that we had Hélène. Everyone in our family was always fighting: Maman with Papa, Maman with the children, Papa with the children, Louise with Paul, Paul with me, and worst of all, Louise and me. We fought over everything, which one got a larger slice of pie, who sat next to Papa at the dinner table, whose dress was prettier.

I remember once my godfather brought me and my sister some candy. The two pieces were wrapped festively in colored paper and were identical, except that the paper around one was pink and the other blue. Would you believe we both wanted the pink one? Or maybe it was the blue, I don't remember. I only know we wanted the same piece. We fought for an hour over which one would get the coveted candy, slapping and kicking each other until Maman took both pieces away. We never saw them again. (Did you eat them, Maman?) When we kept on fighting anyway and knocked a dish to the floor, she said, "If you're going to kill each other, do it outside. I've just finished cleaning."

Hélène was the only one who could get us to stop quarreling. She had only to look at us firmly and crinkle her forehead to make us stop. With her tranquil personality, she was our shelter in a stormy household.

As usual when Maman hurt my feelings, I rushed outside to my favorite spot in the whole world, *Le Geyn²*, a stunning moor filled with huge weird rocks that had been left on the outskirts of Villeneuve by glaciers eons ago. It was known as *la Hottée du Diable, The Devil's Basket*. According to local myths, the hill of rocks had been formed by the devil who agreed to build a convent overnight in return for the soul of the contractor. The devil crammed a huge basket with gigantic stones and proceeded to build *Le Geyn*. We never heard what happened to the contractor, but the rocks remain like frozen giants throughout eternity. They formed fantastic animals for us to climb upon, marvelous caves to curl up in, and mythological beings like in legends and fairy tales. Paul and I had a fairyland for a playground, and I had the finest sculpture *maîtres* in existence to teach me the basics of my art.

I studied the lines, the forms, and the contours of the rocks. I noticed the way the light fell upon them and how the shadows changed as the sun rose and set in the sky. They were my first teachers and only friends, except *le petit Paul*. They would soothe me when I was hurting from Maman's nasty words. They would tell me all the gossip of the village, which Maman and her neighbors spoke of in whispers, to make sure I wouldn't hear them, especially when they were talking about me. To the rocks I poured out my pain that Maman didn't love or understand me, about my love for my little clay people that Papa encouraged, and my hopes for the future. They told me what I wanted to hear, that some day when I grew up I would become a great sculptor, perhaps the greatest in the whole world.

Often when I needed solace I went there alone, and sometimes I took

Paul with me and told him what the stones were saying. His huge blue eyes opened wide as he listened. Even when he was very little, he understood a lot of what I said.

When he was three years old, as we sat upon the lap of *Le Géant*, I taught him to read three words, *dire* (to say), *apprendre* (to learn), and *lire* (to read). From those three words he figured out how to read everything else. I knew then he was a genius. I think I am, too, but a different kind of genius. He's a genius in thinking and I'm a genius in knowing things in my heart. That's what I wanted to put in my sculptures, the truth I see in people's eyes, not the way they show themselves to the world.

I could always talk with him about things that mattered. I said, "*Mon petit Paul*, what would you like to do when you grow up? Would you like to be a farmer, or maybe a fireman like most little boys your age?" I should have known better. Paul didn't do anything like other boys his age.

He answered slowly and thoughtfully. "No, Cam. I want to do— thinking."

"Thinking? What kind of work is that? What do you mean, Paul?"

He screwed up his face. "When we were dipping our bread into the wine at supper last night you made a face as though the wine was sour. It tasted sweet to me. I thought that wine tastes different to you than it does to me. Maybe it does to everybody, sugary to some people and bitter to others…I like to think up things like that. When I grow up I want to do thinking work."

"Well, I guess you can find some kind of work like that," I said, although I was not sure there was any such thing. We were quiet for a while, as I thought it over and decided if that was what he wanted to be, I would help him become it. So I said solemnly, "Paul, I want us to make a promise to each other. Let's vow that when we grow up, you won't become just any old thinker, but will measure yourself against Aeschylus and Shakespeare, and I will take Michelangelo's work as my standard."

"I promise," Paul nodded, his great blue eyes wide in awe. "We will be the great ones of our time. I'll be the great thinker and you'll be the great artist."

"Swear to it?"

"Yes. You swear too."

27

He put his hand on my heart and I put mine on his. We looked straight into each other's eyes and swore on our lives to make our vows come true.

Le Geyn had as profound an effect on the grown-up Paul as it did on me. The third act of his play, *La Jeune Fille Violaine*, was set in a similar locale, as were *L'otage, Pain dur,* and *Père humilié.* He formulated *La Tête d'Or* on the lap of *LeGeyn* and it was there that he first realized he was destined to be a poet. For both of us all of our lives, Villeneuve was to be home.

I learned very early that people were not always the way they showed themselves to the world. For instance, everybody thought Maman was humble and simple, but I knew that's not how she really was. Underneath she was arrogant, and believed that because her father, Athanase Cerveaux, had been a well-known doctor in Fère, and had left her some money and the house in Villeneuve, she was better than everyone else. But she wasn't. She was stupid as a goose and had no sense of what art is or any understanding of the creative personality. She couldn't really believe that anyone could feel different from her about anything, or have other tastes or beliefs. There was only one way to think, and that was her way. "I cannot imagine why you like to mess around with dirt all day long," she always said. "Nothing could induce me to spend my days in filth!"

To be fair, I have to admit that neither Paul nor Louise felt the way I did about Maman; nor did her grandchildren later, who adored her. But nobody knew she behaved very differently to me than to anyone else.

Neither was Papa what he seemed to others. He was nice as could be to his friends at his club, but raged and ranted at home. He was much smarter than Maman. He had a wonderful library which he stayed in a lot, and I was allowed to read anything in it I wanted. I read all the classics from the time I was very little. I devoured the books on mythology, and drew upon them later in my life when I sculpted two of my greatest works, *Clotho* and *Perseus and the Gorgon.*

A myth I read over and over again was the story of Camilla. I used to imagine that Papa named me Camille as her namesake, because he wanted me to grow up as brave and strong. Camilla was the daughter of Metabus, the king of the Italian tribe the Volsci. Metabus was driven out of his city of Privernum by the Volsci, and took his baby daughter with him. When he came to the river Amasenus, he had no way of getting across with the infant. So he bound Camilla to his spear, and with a prayer to Diana, hurled it across to the other bank. (Yes, Papa would do that for me.) He then swam across and found Camilla safe and sound in the arms of Diana. He fed Camilla mare's milk and taught her to fight and hunt. She grew up to become a virgin warrior and queen of the Volscians, and she rode like an Amazon with one breast bared to give freedom to her bow arm. A girl after my own heart!

My absolute favorite myths, however, were written by Ossian, the Gaelic poet of the third century, whose scenes of wild grandeur and haunting melancholy reminded me of my beloved *Le Geyn*. I read the poetry over and over, especially when I was confined to my bedroom by you-know-who because of some fancied misbehavior. Some of my first drawings were illustrations of Ossian's poems. I wish I knew where they were. (Note to Maman: Did you throw those away, too?) Then, when I got tired of reading, I spent hours in front of the frosted windows, reciting the poetry out loud and outlining the giant rocks of *Le Geyn* with my fingers through the ice.

Maman never punished us physically, as she said only peasants hit their children. Heaven forbid that she act like a peasant! She said I was an incorrigible, because I wouldn't do what she wanted. Why should I do something I knew was stupid? So I was sent to my bedroom a lot. It would have felt better to have been slapped.

One winter evening, Maman sent me to bed without any supper. It was so cold in my room that the frost froze my breath. I was lying in bed sobbing, when I thought I heard her at the foot of the stairs.

"Maman…Maman?" I called softly, as her footsteps gradually got louder. A surge of joy washed through me. "Oh, Maman is coming to see me! Maman is coming to see me! She has forgiven me for making a mess on the kitchen table." Slowly, slowly, her heavy footsteps resounded as she reached the top of the stairs and continued down the hall. I held my breath. "She really is coming! She really is! She is!" But it was not to be, for the footsteps passed my door and then faded as she made her way up the stairs to her bedroom. I lay in desolate stillness. Did she hear me and was just being mean? Or was she so wrapped up in her malaise that she really

29

didn't hear me? I'll never know. I said out loud, "Who needs that ugly old frump, anyhow?" I yanked the ribbon off my heavy, unruly curls (which Maman hated and was always trying to restrain) and shook them loose. Then I leapt out of bed, ran to the window, and traced the grotto of *Le Geyn* on the windowpane, under the light of the moon.

She's been angry about my drawing ever since I was five. I'd just gone to the top of *Le Geyn* for the first time, and was so enthralled that I came home and drew huge pictures of him with a red crayon all over the dining room walls. Maman has never forgiven me for ruining her eighteenth century wallpaper, even though I told her Paul did it. I was always a sensual child, who loved to know what everything tasted and looked like. But when she saw me sniffing my crayons or watching Hélène putting on her underpants, Maman acted like I was crazy.

I love the taste and feel of seltzer and jelly, which Maman served on the rare occasions when she had to entertain quests, like the time the rector and his parched-faced wife visited, to try to bring us into the church.

Maman would carry in tall, fluted glasses of seltzer with a silver spoon resting on top of each, dripping with the jelly she had made herself. She would smile as she handed a glass to each guest. I sat in tense anticipation. Would I get one, too? It depended on her mood. If she was in a good one, there would also be one for me. But if she was unhappy, and she often was unhappy, my heart would sink as she walked by my chair without even looking at me. But oh the joy of joys when she would stop by my chair and hand me a frosty glass! It was the treat I had been dreaming about, and I seized it with glee.

I can still remember one of the first times I received that delectable treat. I hold it up to the window. The jelly is the color of raspberry wine. Translucent and shimmering, it dances in the sparkles of sunlight.

I slowly taste it. It's smooth, except for the little lumps of fruit in it, which I seize on like jewels. My tongue is covered with sweetness. I roll it to the back of my mouth until it is alive with sensation.

I lick off the remaining drops of jelly until the silver is cool to my skin. I run my tongue over the hollow of the spoon, then up and down the curve of its back. Then I pull the spoon through my closed lips. I hoard the sugary flavor until it disappears. Then I do it all over again.

When the sweetness becomes so strong I can't stand it, I hold the graceful glass beneath my chin until the bubbles spray in my face. They feel frosty in the humid French summer. I look deep down into the glass and the bubbles look like tiny fishes leaping through crystal waters.

I put both hands around the coolness, rub my wrists against it, roll it over my face. The moisture leaves a fresh feeling which lingers through the heat. Now I roll the glass back and forth over my lips, until I get a dirty look from my mother.

I take a huge guzzle. The bubbles fizz up and tickle my nose. It's so strong it makes my tastebuds smart with a pleasure that stops just short of pain. I roll it around in my mouth and keep from swallowing, to hold on to the sensation. Then I take a big gulp again. The feeling is so strong I shiver. I stop and lean into the fizz again. Then I take a little sip and whirl it around my gums. Anything to extend the sensation, which seeps down my gullet until my stomach, too, is sparkling like the sunlight.

I feel pleasure up and down my throat, as if the drink is dancing in my mouth, and take a lot of gulps to see if more feels better. It doesn't. To the belly, a little or a lot of seltzer are all the same thing. I no longer am thirsty, but go on drinking anyway because it makes me feel so good.

I burp. I'm surprised to find that it brings back the seltzer, and the glow starts all over again. I read in one of Papa's books that a cow brings up its cud and chews it over and over. I smile. I am a cow.

I smack the inside of my lips and make a sound like a cork coming out of a bottle. It's fun so I keep on doing it, until I hear a disapproving clearing of her throat from my mother.

I look up with a sharp jolt of my neck. I see everyone in the room staring at me with a peculiar, questioning look, as if they can't quite believe what they see. The rector's wife laughs a nasty laugh and exchanges a look with her husband. Maman stamps over and pulls the glass away from me and ships me off to my room again.

The sunlight has stopped streaming through the windows. The glass is just a glass; the spoon is just a spoon. They would never taste as good again. Those were the times I wanted to rush out to the great stones and sit in the lap of the huge rock shaped like a lady and rub my hot face against the cool granite.

I suppose I shouldn't be so hard on Maman. Besides losing her first child, she had an angry husband who was eighteen years older and a daughter she couldn't stand.

I can feel her essence now, taking up more space than she has any right to. Even if she doesn't say a word, she has a heavy presence that makes you know she's there. She moves awkwardly and laboriously, and although we children are talking together, we grow silent when the squeaking floorboards announce her approach. She wears cumbersome dark clothing and is stiffly corseted, even in summertime.

A distinctive smell about her, kind of like dead flowers, permeates the room. She sits down as if she were a queen on her throne. Naturally, we are allowed to sit only after the queen has taken her place at the head of the table. Surrounded by her offspring (Papa's off at his club), she glowers at me for some minor transgression like grabbing a chunk of bread before she gives permission. We sit there stiffly awaiting her next rebuke, each one hoping this time the criminal will be someone else. As she perpetually watches for some infraction of the rules, especially by me, I doubt if she could taste her food, let alone enjoy it. No wonder I would often skip a meal and pluck an apple on my way to *Le Geyn*!

What I can never forgive is that she *never never* showed us any affection. I don't believe she ever kissed me, not even once. She never took me in her arms and cuddled and comforted me. I would have liked to be able to hug and kiss her, and hold her hand in turn to console her when she was needy.

Once, long ago, when she was slumping in her rocking chair with her head in her hands, I reached out and touched her knobby hand. She yanked it away. I never tried it again.

I know Maman's mother died when she was only three years old. Sometimes when I was feeling generous because I had a good day with my clay, I would think she never had anyone to teach her how to be a mother, and that was why she was so cold-hearted.

I've spent my lifetime yearning for human touch. We really don't touch other people much, you know, even our friends. It's a very intimate thing to do. Perhaps that's one reason why molding clay with my hands was so important to me. I could touch my little people all I wanted. There was a feeling I got sometimes when sculpting, however, which made me uncomfortable. The figure could become so real to me I felt uneasy about putting my hands on her body. It was like I was taking liberties Maman would not allow, and the person I was sculpting would be angry with me and shout, "How dare you put your filthy hands all over me?"

Since I knew very early that Maman was no comfort to me, I found an even better remedy against her cruelty than the stones. When I was five years old, I discovered a secret tool that could always make me feel better. Just before falling asleep every night, I would make up a story in which a great artist flew down from the heavens and picked me up in his arms. He would hold me closely and tenderly, telling me how much he loved me and stroking my hair back from my forehead. Then he would soar away with me to his *atelier* and teach me to become a great sculptor...I mean a great artist like him. I would continue the story until I fell happily asleep.

I picked up the fantasy each night for many years, adding and changing the characteristics of the "great artist" as my knowledge of the field (and sex) expanded. When I got to my teens, the scenario became one in which the great artist seduced me. The details changed slightly over time. In one version, I would be molding a statue and he burst into my studio, saying, "I've heard about your marvelous work, Mademoiselle Claudel, and I just had to come see it for myself." He would look over the sculpture and say, "I have never seen such wonderful work in so young a sculptor! It's better than I did at your age. You're a great genius!"

Perhaps he would give me a point or two I hadn't known, and in so doing brush his hand across my breast. I would righteously pull away, although I secretly liked the feeling. That of course set him on fire even more, and he would grab me and begin to kiss me passionately. I fought off his embraces like the good girl I never was, but he always won out. I would then imagine every step of the "seduction," according to how much I knew about such things. When I first began the fantasy, I would stop at the passionate kisses. Then I began to add new details as I learned about them in Papa's books. Sometimes my fantasizing got me so excited I couldn't fall asleep for hours, especially after I advanced to the part where he ripped my clothes off and ravaged me. I didn't mind being awake at all, as it gave me more time to elaborate on the story. It was much

more interesting than sleeping. I continued the saga until Rodin and I
became lovers. After that, no matter how hard I tried, the fantasy didn't
work for me anymore. It was just too tame, after experiencing the real
thing.

Although Maman always discouraged my sculpting, Papa felt
otherwise about it. Even though he had a terrible temper and fought with
Maman all the time and was a very practical man, he liked that I wanted
to sculpt and believed that someday I would become a great artist.

Once when I was a little child, perhaps four or five, Papa had to go to
Le Havre on government business, and took me with him in our small cart
and little grey mare on the all-day journey. We left before sunrise, and
when dawn arrived it was almost too magnificent to bear, with the sky
pink and blue and green, lit up with flashes of orange and deep blue, the
color of my eyes. Every jolt of the wheels reminded me of how thrilling
it was to be alone with Papa on an outing. I was half mad with pleasure at
the sight of the huge overhanging trees, the cows and horses grazing in
the meadows, and sniffed the sweet springtime air until I thought I would
burst. Papa was happy, too, the happiest I'd ever seen him. I was filled
with a terrible inner gladness, as I understood how special I was to him,
away from the cruelties of Maman.

When we got to Le Havre, he said, "I'm going to show you something
you will never forget, Camille," and swung me up on his shoulders. I was
high in the air, so high I was the tallest person in the whole world! I held
on to his hair and screamed with delight as he walked me down to the
open sea. The water flashed in the sunlight, glorious in its kaleidoscope of
colors, and the immense vault of the sky loomed overhead. Sailboats of
all sizes glided by, their sails swelling up like the new rubber balloons Papa
told me he had read about in the newspaper. The tranquil waves broke
upon the beach, which stretched out as far as you could see, and the sound
of the surf splashing on the sand echoed the beating of my heart. When
Papa put me down I buried my feet in the cool sand and shouted with joy.
A musical laugh poured out of me like an endless song, until he had to
sooth me by running his hand over my forehead.

I could have stood there forever staring at the movement of the waves
and the rainbow of colors in the water, especially all the different shades

of blue. I started sobbing when Papa said we had to leave. Pulling me away by the arm, he said, "We have to leave now, Camille. It's a long way home." I kept yelling, "It's not fair, it's not fair!" all the time he was yanking me to the buggy. As the grey mare trotted home, it dawned on me that if I could draw a picture of the scene I could hold onto it forever.

Papa had brought me some drawing crayons in Le Havre, which smelled so good I almost took a bite out of one. (I didn't because I didn't want to waste it.) At home, I took out the crayons and the heavy white paper that came wrapped around the butter and eggs Maman bought for our Sunday dinner, and danced the crayons and the paper around the room. I was very particular about the colors. I had to have two shades of blue, not one, because I wanted to draw them in layers. Fortunately, there were two blue crayons, one light and one dark. I was very careful to take the two shades of blue and draw the ocean with one color over the other, so that it looked like the waves were moving on top of each other. Then I drew a few little fish and an eel that you could see through the water. At the very bottom of the picture I drew beige sand.

When I finished, I stepped back and pointing at it with the crayon in my hand, studied the drawing in detail. It passed my inspection. Even better, it brought back the mad ecstasy of Papa and me at the ocean. I had found a wonderful secret that was to change my life. Papa looked at me and the drawing with a peculiar expression on his face and said, "You're a little Rembrandt, Camille." I said, "Is that good, Papa?" He laughed merrily. Papa never even smiles, so when he laughed, I decided to be an artist when I grow up.

I guess I was born an artist. When I was only five, Maman's uncle Nicolas Cerveaux, the pastor who baptized me, stomped into the house in a terrible snowstorm, and said, 'Camille, can you make me a snowman in a blizzard?' He was joking, of course, and I'm sure he thought the whole drawing would be pure white and would only look like an empty page. But I've never been one to give up before a challenge. I took a piece of white paper which Hélène had unwrapped from around some plums and drew a snowman wearing a hat like Papa's blue tam and a red woolen vest like

Louise's. I gave him two black coals for eyes, a slice of potato painted red for his mouth, and an orange scarf like Paul's. Then I tore up hundreds of little white papers and glued each tiny piece onto the background paper. Paul wanted me to play outside with him and make a real snowman, but I wouldn't. I only wanted to sit there and finish my drawing, no matter how long it took. When I showed it to Uncle Nicolas he couldn't believe what he saw. He said, "Camille, I didn't think you could do it, but it's truly a picture of a snowman in a blizzard!"

My earliest memories are of drawing, sculpting, and sketching. Materials were scarce and to be treasured. I used to draw the faces and beards of people in the village when they passed by our house, on paper the butcher wrapped meat in. They were primitive sketches which I rubbed with my finger to make shadows. Papa was very proud of them. When company came, he would say, "Go get those pictures." He showed them to Uncle Nicolas, who presented me with a box of numbered pencils after he saw the drawings. I loved the woodsy smell of the twelve colored pencils and the gummy pink erasers on their tips, and the way all twelve fit so neatly into the box. They came in a yellow wooden case and were my greatest pleasure for years. I was tempted to chew on them, but was afraid leaving teeth marks. I didn't draw with them much, either, because I didn't want to use them up. I was saving them for some masterpieces of the future, which, unfortunately, are lost to posterity. Maman threw out those sketches, too, during one of her endless spring cleanings.

Those pencils were even more precious to me, as they were the last gift my dear Uncle Nicolas ever gave me. He died shortly thereafter. I think of him sometimes when I feel discouraged, as I do more and more these days. His was the first death I ever experienced, and the pain of the loss has never gone away.

I said to Papa, "Where's Uncle Nicolas? He hasn't come to see me for a long time."

He sighed and answered, "I'm sorry to have to tell you this, Camille, but Uncle Nicolas has died."

"I know he's died, Papa, but when's he coming to see me?"

Papa sighed again and pulled me down on his lap. "Camille, when a person dies it means that he…he…isn't with us anymore. He has…uh…gone away."

"But where has he gone, Papa?"

"Nobody knows that, Camille. Remember when your pet frog died and you wondered why he couldn't jump or croak? All the life went out of him. It's like when you blow out a candle and the light isn't there anymore."

"Can I go see him?"

"No, Camille, I hope you won't go where he is for a long, long time. But you know he loved you very much."

I began to cry. "Does that mean he can't bring me any more pencils?"

He answered, "I'm afraid so, Camille. But tell me when you need some and I'll get them for you."

As always, Papa stuck to his word. When he had to go to Paris a few weeks later, he found an artists' store and bought the clay he had promised me. From then on I spent every waking hour I could steal from the rest of the day modeling my sculptures. When I wasn't molding figures from life, I studied anatomy from his books. Like my great predecessor Leonardo da Vinci, I was fascinated by the size, weight, and composition of bones. Since, unlike him, I had no access to human bodies, I studied the bones of the sheep that Hélène roasted for us, and cut them crosswise to see what they looked like inside. Then, following the illustrations in Papa's books, I carved myself a complete set of human bones out of wood, and carried a rhinoceros skull around with me like a purse, to get the feeling of bone in every aspect of my body.

Another thing I had to do was prepare the clay to my liking. Before using any kind of clay, it has to be pounded so that every tiny air bubble is kneaded out. If not, the piece will explode in the kiln. There's nothing more heartbreaking than working for months on a statue, only to have it blow up. One of my first sculptures was a quarter-sized torso of a nude woman, for which I myself was the model, since of course nobody else would pose in the nude. I worked on it months and months and really fell in love with it. I called it *Torso of a Nude Woman*. I kept looking at it from every angle, in every light of the day, throwing off my clothes as I ran time after time from my bedroom to my *atelier* in the attic, in a state of excitement that grew with every viewing. Each repetition uncovered something I hadn't noticed before. One time the skin of the figure looked slightly pink. Another time, her body position appeared shy and vulnerable; still a third time, she looked like a very sexy lady. I simply couldn't believe that I had made her, she was so life-like and lovely. I didn't want to start on any new work, because it would mean giving up my beautiful sculpture. Long after it was finished, when I couldn't find another detail to change without ruining her, I laboriously carted the statue to the *fondeur*. To my great disappointment, he couldn't work on it then, and insisted I leave it there.

I kept badgering him every day for weeks until he could find the time to fire it. Finally, he said, "Stop bothering me, Camille! I'll let you know when it's done." I don't know how I got through the eternity it took him to get to it. Then, weeks later, he sent his assistant to tell me to come see him. While running to his foundry, I kept repeating out loud with each slap of my boots, "I hope…I hope…I hope…I hope…" When I got there he opened the door solemnly and flushed and examined his feet. I took one look at him and knew that the statue had exploded in the kiln. "I'm sorry, Camille," the *fondeur* said sadly. "But that happens sometimes. There was nothing I could do. The next one will do better."

Without answering him, I jumped up and hurled myself outside into the bitter wind. Gasping for breath, I ran until I reached the top of *Le Geyn*, where I shouted to the giant, "God did that! I hate God! I'll never make another sculpture again!" But of course I did. Nor was the catastrophe all in vain, for it taught me to be painstakingly careful in kneading out unseen pockets of air.

Nevertheless, I still miss my *Torso of a Nude Woman*. I mourn for her almost as Maman grieved all her life for the lost Henri. I tried many times to sculpt the figure again. My best effort was the *Torse de Femme Debout (Torso of a woman standing up)* in 1888 when I was twenty-four years old. But like Maman, whose attempt to replace Henri with me failed, I never succeeded in recapturing the quality of the creation I loved most. Sometimes I dream I find her in a secret pocket at the bottom of the kiln.

A few years later, I told Rodin the story of my broken statue. He described a similar experience of a statue he lost which he said took with it the last of his youth. He had spent many months in his freezing cramped studio molding a sculpture celebrating youth and beauty, called *Bacchante*. It was his first life-sized figure, radiant with youthful passions, desires, and dreams.

Rodin was so poor that his landlord threatened to evict him the next day unless he paid the rent. Fortunately, he sold a plaster statue to a secondhand dealer for twelve francs. Singing happily on his long walk home, he stopped to visit his friend, the Belgian painter, Albert Williams. There he beheld a scene that would have fit into *The Gates of Hell*. William's wife Renée was lying in bed cringing in pain from tuberculosis, while Albert sat dejected in a chair holding his head in his hands. His seven-year-old daughter looked up at Rodin with tear-filled, reddened eyes, while the little two-year-old girl greeted him with screams. Williams lethargically handed Rodin a marshal's order for the eviction of the family and the sale of their furniture at eight o'clock the next morning. "How much do you need?" Rodin asked. "Eight francs," the painter listlessly replied. Rodin knew that unless he turned over the twelve francs he had earned to his own landlord, he too would be evicted, so he kept two francs to lease a coal-seller's cart to move his belongings and handed the rest of the money to Williams. Rodin hurried out the door to hide his embarrassment at his friend's profuse thanks. Then he hired the cart to move his scant possessions to a temporary shelter at the home of a friend. As the cart rumbled down the dirt road, a rut below the cart wheel tilted a piece of furniture and knocked it over onto his favorite statue. To Rodin's despair, it was smashed it into bits.

Unlike me, he never tried to reconstruct the statue, although he felt it was his best work to date. He simply said, "God must have been displeased with me, because I shouldn't have withheld the last two francs from my friend."

Another statue I sculpted when I was quite young had a better fate than the *Torso of a Nude Woman*. I called it *Giganti*, and had it cast in bronze a few years later when I got a little money. *Giganti* is the bust of a laborer who did some work on our house, who I later was told was a brigand. He was always so nice to me I didn't believe the story, so it didn't change my feeling about him very much. I thought he was magnificent looking. I loved the strength of the man and used to watch him pick up stacks of wood as if they were a plate of the blackberries that grew around our house. I especially admired the sense he had of liking who he was. In the statue, he seems to be daydreaming about a lover, as I always do. It makes a wonderful contrast to his manliness. Whenever I look at the bust, it makes me feel like a giant myself.

*P*eople always ask me how I work. I usually think, "If you have to ask, Madame or Monsieur, nothing will help you!" But I politely answer that a great creative force seems to come out of nowhere and take me over. I rarely tell them of what goes on before "the great creative force comes out of nowhere"—that all my life I studied every person I saw, whether I was staring out the window at passers-by or walking around the lime tree-shaded square in my beloved town of Villeneuve.

To me each face is a library, and has engraved on it the past, present, and future of its owner. By reading it intently, I could learn each person's story. The body, too, is a historical record that inscribes the lives of the models in the lines and wrinkles of their flesh. There I found their joys and triumphs, their losses and their sorrows. If I wanted to sculpt a likeness of a townsperson, I concealed myself behind a building, a door, or a tree, and sooner or later he or she would go by. Sometimes I was lucky and the person came right along, and I would run up the hillside singing. But even though Villeneuve is small, it might have taken weeks or months until the person passed by again.

A great many aspects must be studied in order to understand the subject on the most profound levels, which is why it takes so long to shape a fine piece of sculpture. The sculptor must search for the deep structure of the muscles and bones that lie beneath the skin, and must construct the play of sinews and the soft swellings of human flesh. The creation of a great sculpture requires as much time, thought, and energy as the formation of a great book. In fact, the process is very similar. Besides intelligent planning, knowledge, and careful research, both arts require time for the development of the fruits of the unconscious. Of course, there are hastily written, superficial books, just as there are poor sculptures, and none are worth the time it takes to view them.

I have to be in love with a subject before it's worth the total investment a great work of art demands. Then no discipline is necessary, any more than being in the company of someone you love. I remember years ago I decided to accept a commission to do a bust of someone I couldn't stand. With the best intentions in the world, I never got to it. Now I understand why. The head is not the womb of creation, the heart is.

My sculptures usually began with a little feeling of excitement at the bottom of my belly. I would gouge out a huge hunk of clay from the covered barrel which kept it damp and useful, and hastily lug it onto a stool at about the height of my eyes. At this point the clay revealed absolutely nothing about the people that were locked inside it. It was just an inert lump. I feel it, pound it, caress it, plead with it, whisper to it like a baby, knead it, probe it, clutch it, cuddle it, squeeze it, and stretch it, before deciding to model it into a definite shape. The spirit cannot be rushed, no matter how badly I want to move on. As Leonardo said, "Where the spirit does not work with the hand there is no art." I've been preparing for this moment for days and days, fully conscious of the efforts it takes to reach it. For a long time my disembodied hands hesitantly order me to pat here and press there, to mold a flat plain into a curved slope, to claw away a chunk and put it back again.

Sometimes the mass looks like nothing so much as a grotesquely shaped stump of a tree, and I can only throw the clay back in the barrel and start all over again. Perhaps it's because I've studied the human body in every way open to me that I'm sure of my métier. I feel no sense of mystery, trouble, or suffering in the gestation period, as I know from experience that sooner or later a figure or figures will suggest themselves.

After hours, days, or even weeks, an image seizes hold of me and I attack the clay in a frenzy. It's as if I have a fever. I know the instructions are coming from somewhere and I must carry them out. I remain in a daze for hour after hour and hardly know where I am. Bodily needs pass unheeded. Sometimes I look up and am shocked to see the sun setting. The action frees me, although I have yet to pummel my vision into the clay. I have to let it remain free for a while, to enclose the idea in all its emotional force and at the same time to liberate it. During this period, everything seems possible.

Of all the moments of my life this is when I'm happiest. Without stopping for an instant, I jump to the stool, walk around it, step backward and forward, attack the clay in the delirium of getting started, stop and glance out the window, laugh raucously about everything and nothing, and spin around until I'm face-to-face with the mound of clay. Exhilarated, I again take a few backward steps, examining and measuring the lump with my eyes as if I were seeing it for the first time. Suddenly, miraculously, I submit to the will of the clay, and cut away, refill, hollow out, add another pellet, and know with absolute certainty what form it will take. In one moment the fruit has ripened, the mystery is resolved, and the inorganic lump has taken on a life of its own. The physical, psychological, and spiritual transformation of the clay has been launched in the frenzy of creation. The baby is born and the ecstatic flight begun. It's as good as soaring to the heavens in the arms of my phantom lover.

After I had done good work, there was nothing I liked better than to relax in our hot tin tub in the kitchen and think about my creation. Of course Maman objected, because I was "wasting good hot water and heat." But I did it anyway.

Once when I was lying back and daydreaming about showing the sculpture to my "great artist", I happened to notice the white ring around the inside of the tub. I remembered reading in one of Papa's science books that scum is formed by a combination of chemicals. So I said to Maman, who was helping Hélène cut up vegetables for dinner, "Maman, do you know the ring inside the tub is caused by chemicals and not dirt?" She answered, "I don't care what it is. I don't want it in my bath tub!" Some mother I had!

The family sensed how important the work was to me, and finally even Maman gave in and left me alone to sculpt. All of a sudden, I was no longer just a little girl playing in the mud, but an artist immersed in her art. Soon my people grew larger, and I went on to create busts of everyone who would sit still for me for a few moments. Before I'd had my first lesson, I got Maman to pose for me, along with Papa, Paul and Louise. By the time I was fifteen, besides the ill-fated *Torso*, I had molded figurines of Napoleon 1, David and Goliath, and Bismarck. I've always loved Bible stories, so I particularly liked my statue of David and his noble stance. I guess he reminded me of Paul. And myself, when I stood up to Maman.

Speaking of the Bible, my parents are atheists. I received the usual sacraments up until my First Communion, but my parents didn't seem very interested. Nor, I must admit, was I.

One Sunday, the rector insisted Maman bring us to church, if she didn't want us to go to Hell. I doubt if that visit will be of much help in getting me into Heaven. I sat there during the whole sermon looking at the statue of Jesus on the cross and wondering how the sculptor put the wrinkles in his loincloth.

Nevertheless, I read the whole Bible through in my early teens, to try to make up my own mind about whether or not there is a god. I didn't find any answers, but I found it very beautiful in spots. My favorite section is Psalm 139³. I first read it one night right before bedtime. I was so enraptured by it that I couldn't fall asleep and started reciting the Psalm aloud. To my surprise, I found that I remembered every word. It was truly a miracle, as that has never happened to me before. It makes me feel that if there is a god at all, he is *Le Grand Sculpteur du Ciel.*

O Lord, thou hast searchest me and known me!
Thou knowest when I stumble and when I rise up.
Thou discernest my thoughts from afar.
Thou searchest out my path and places of rest,
And are acquainted with all my ways…
There is not a word upon my lips
But thou, O Lord, knowest it first.
Thou hast beset me before and behind,
And covered Thy hand over mine.
Such knowledge is too awesome to bear;
Too high; I cannot attain it…

If I fly with the wings of the morning,
Or dwell in the bottomless depths of the sea,
Even there Thy hand shall find me,
And Thy right hand hold me fast.

The darkness is as light to Thee,
The night shines like the day,
Thou, who shaped my innermost being,
And molded me in my mother's womb.
Yea, I am fearfully and wondrously made
And marvelous is Thy craft.

Thou knewest my essence,
In secret Thou formed it,
Skillfully cast from the rich fruitful earth.
Thine eyes envisioned my unformed being,
When I was yet a void.

Thy thoughts of me are precious, O Lord!
How vast is the sum of them all![4]

Like God in the Psalm, I could never know enough about my subjects, and had to understand them "behind and before," indeed from every angle. And like God, I understood my people best when I laid my hand upon them and held them inside of me. Sometimes I think it was through my hands that I learned to love. When I was sculpting someone, I thought about that person all the time, until his essence was revealed to me and I understood him in my heart. God did this in boundless silence, taking the essence of Adam from the dirt on the ground, as I did with my clay. Yes, God is the greatest sculptor of us all. Although I didn't like to admit it, I could not hope to attain His heights. That job was already filled.

I guess I was a believer for a little while. I liked being one, and it comforted me while it lasted. The feeling is best communicated by *The Prayer*, which I sculpted when I was a young woman. A few years later, Matthias Morhardt wrote that it was "tender, humane, alive, sincere, simple, and truthful, in the way that the masters of the sixteenth century had shown us." I don't know about that, but I do know that it reminds me of how it felt to pray. A young girl with closed eyes is deep, deep inside of herself, as if she were alone with her God. She looks ecstatic, and appears to be in a State of Grace, almost like Joan of Arc. I wish I felt that way now.

When I look at it carefully, I realize that I was twenty-five years old when I sculpted it, and Rodin was breaking my heart.

Here's the girl's prayer:

"Please, please, O Lord, give him to me. Make Rodin love me and not that chintzy Rose. If you do, O Lord, I promise I'll be good. I'll control my temper. I won't say nasty things to anyone, even Louise. I'll stop torturing Paul. I won't answer Maman back. I'll even go to church and pray to You and the Lord Jesus. I'll try to listen instead of drawing when the priest is talking. Listen, Lord. I don't ask You for much, I'm always too busy with my art to bother to communicate with You. But now I need to fill this cavernous hole inside me. It gnaws at me twenty-four hours a day and hurts bad, O Lord. It won't let me sleep, it won't let me eat, it only makes me crave more wine. Please, O Lord, just let me have him and I'll believe in You forever." But He didn't. And I didn't.

Presently I came upon the philosophy of Ernest Renan, apostle of the scientific approach to religion, literature and history, who said, "Nothing proves to us that there exists in the world a central consciousness—a soul of the universe—and nothing proves the contrary." After reading his works, I became a rabid agnostic like my parents.

If I needed further discouragement about religion, the quality of the church sermons I attended provided it. The French clergy lack knowledge and intellectual culture, even the better ones like Maman's uncle, who was the pastor of Villeneuve when I was little. The Church demands so much of their time that there's little left for intellectual growth. They have Mass every morning, daily service to attend as well as the reading of the eternal breviary, and special readings for the religious days that are always coming around. Also, a priest who has a large country parish like Villeneuve often has a lot of walking to do, for the parish cannot always afford to supply them with a horse and buggy.

The magnificent organization of the Catholic Church has produced a monumental instrument for influencing mankind, which would produce glorious results if it were really used for their enlightenment. But sadly, that's not the case. It's tragic that the Church doesn't make use of its power to benefit humanity. Instead, it encourages superstition and perpetuates ignorance among its parishioners. Unfortunately, it had no answers for me. Instead of solving moral dilemmas through religion as most people do, I believed that I could work them out for myself. But it has been a terrible loss.

Of course, toward the end of my life, my agnosticism, like that of many people, has begun to waver. But that's getting ahead of my story.

Papa was born in 1826 to an old established bourgeois family from Bresse, near Gerardmer, that dated from the seventeenth century. He never talked about them much, but then he rarely talked to us about anything else, either. He was a thin, almost bald man with a long nose, deep wrinkles around his eyes, and a sparse grey mustache and mutton chop beard. He dressed neatly, like the official Registrar of Mortgages he was, and smoked his pipe a lot, filling the room with the heady smell of tobacco. I've always loved that smell, no matter who's smoking it. When he was in the room, I was always aware of his presence, even when he was perfectly still. He often assumed a thoughtful, faraway expression, as if his eyes were used to looking out at the windswept, rainy foothills of the Champagne district, which Paul later called *Wuthering Heights*.

Sometimes I think Papa was dreaming he'd become an artist. Educated by the Jesuits in Strassbourg, he was graduated with a barrelful of prizes. He was very intelligent for a provincial functionary and read all the time. In 1864, the year I was born, at least a quarter of the people in France spoke *patois* and didn't speak or read French at all. Only "high society" habitually spoke French. But the Third Republic had made the *format d'école* a prerequisite for upper level civil service jobs. Since Papa had learned French in school, he qualified for the job of registrar, which gave him a sense of superiority that remained with him until his death.

Like many French country people, Papa saved money by spending it only on what he pleased, without caring one whit what anybody else thought. Although he was stingy about spending his income needlessly (he would call unnecessary spending "the fruit of disorder and misdeed"), he didn't hesitate to splurge in matters of importance, such as financing our vocations, getting me important materials like crayons and clay, or supplementing his extensive library. But there never was enough money to buy me an apple cider or a ready-made dress at the Whitsun or Trinity Sunday in June, where everybody gathered to exchange news as much as goods. Not that we were poor. He earned more than twice as much a year as the average clerk or teacher in our town, and we owned the house Maman had inherited from her father. In addition, we always had a *bonne* and kept a horse and cart. But Papa believed in the old proverb, "The fatter the kitchen, the thinner the last will."

Papa was not alone in his conservative ways. Most of the French workmen and farmers we knew were incredibly stingy with money, probably because they rarely had any. I guess his stinginess didn't hurt me, as I loved my clay people more than I would have the apple cider, and I myself made most of the few clothes I had. I'm like Papa in that respect. I preferred to save what little money I had for models, who didn't come cheap.

We often puzzled over why Papa hadn't made more of himself professionally, and suspected that he hadn't wanted to spend the money further education would have cost. Or maybe he'd been afraid to risk a job without a guaranteed income. But I think the most important reason is *la vie de petite ville,* a kind of life which is said all over France to be damaging to men in that it arrests their professional development and stifles their ambition. It doesn't produce spendthrifts (ha) but it has a strange effect that makes men stop short of their abilities. The long balmy summers and the pleasant ambience of our rural towns helped to form these habits.

I'm talking about the small town clubs of educated men who were either independently wealthy, or who, like some doctors, lawyers, solicitors, and civil servants of Papa's ilk, had professions which kept them affluent without demanding much of their time and energy. The clubs provided good food and drink and interesting talk, leaving the men to sink into their comfortable lounge chairs and give up any ideas they had of gaining wealth, fame, and the desire to travel or learn a new language. The main evil that came from this perpetual lounging was a tremendous waste of time. As I know from my own total absorption in my art, it's utterly impossible to pursue a profession seriously without limiting one's contact with a society of this nature. To my knowledge, no great artist or philosopher has ever come out of the mens' clubs of rural France. Which is too bad for Papa; I believe he had the seeds of greatness in him.

Small town ladies, and Louise-Athanaïse Claudel in particular, loudly objected to the *cafes* and clubs as an outrage, as it deprived them of the company of their husbands. Yet the interests of the women were largely confined to their housekeeping and families, and totally outside the concerns of educated Frenchmen like my father. These men liked to talk about politics, law, business, and perhaps science or philosophy, which were completely out of the realm of the average French housewife's interest. It's understandable that the men sought out a place they could relax without anticipating immediate contradiction. In the case of the Louis-Prosper Claudels, it's even more understandable. Not only did he and Maman argue all the time, but she was stupid and he was intelligent. What else could the poor man do but seek out others of his kind where he could speak up and not be contradicted every time he opened his mouth?

In my little bed at night, Paul and I also dared to question why Papa had not married a woman as intelligent as he. If Paul and I inherited our genius from anyone, it had to be from Papa. It certainly wasn't from Maman! Besides having an ordinary mind, she was insensitive to anyone's feelings, and said whatever she wanted, no matter how much it hurt.

Maman was also quite plain looking, to the point where she offended my eyes. I used to wish I had a beautiful mother, like the portrait I drew later of Marie Paillette. Instead I had a mother who reminds me of my sculpture of a decaying Clotho. My mother had straight dark hair that she wore severely parted in the middle and pulled back tightly behind her ears. I often pleaded with her to let it hang loosely around her face, the way it did as she was brushing her hair getting ready for bed, when it was quite pretty. Her face didn't seem as beefy when surrounded by her beautiful hair. But of course she saw to it that I never got what I asked for. She had a large mouth, which drooped like an over-fried sausage, and contributed to her missionary look. She usually sat with her hands crossed on her knees, like a woman who had never had a bodily need in her life. I think even dirt was afraid to come near her. I once had a dream that her wheels didn't have any grease in them.

It's strange she was an agnostic, for she reminded me of nothing so much as the wife of a Protestant minister. People often wonder why I didn't do a portrait of her, like the one I drew of Papa. Well, I did. It showed so much of the real Louise-Athanaïse Claudel that I slashed it to shreds. Can you blame me?

It's a good thing I love beauty in nature, in art, and in my books, for neither Maman nor Papa were beautiful people. Paul and I often wondered how all three of us children turned out to be so good looking. Paul was a proud and beautiful little boy who became a handsome man, at least while he was young. I'm afraid the years have not been kind to him, and he's not so attractive any more.

As for my looks, people seemed to think I was beautiful, too. Everybody always raves about my eyes of deep midnight blue, especially Paul. I'd rather believe they're the color of that rich indigo blue you see in the great stained-glass windows of centuries past, whose secret formulas have long been forgotten. Paul wrote that I had "a splendid brow above magnificent eyes of that rare dark blue you hardly ever meet with outside the covers of a novel." Dear Paul! He never mentioned that one of my legs is shorter than the other. I'm afraid, however, that my looks didn't hold a candle to Louise's. Even though I disliked her I have to admit she was the real beauty of the family, with wavy hair like Paul's, large wistful eyes, and perfect features.

A family photograph taken on the terrace of our apartment on the Boulevard de Port-Royal tells much about our family. It was taken on the day the engagement of Louise and Ferdinand de Massary was announced. Maman looks stern and homely, Papa resembles a Jewish rabbi (which is not a bad analogy), Paul is shyly smiling, and Louise of course is beautiful as ever. It's as if the family is divided in two. Louise and Maman are apart from the rest of us, especially Louise, who is facing away and hardly seems part of the group. She was only nineteen at the time, and perhaps she was having second thoughts about marrying de Massary. I was never too interested in Louise except to hate her, so I really don't know what she was thinking. I'm surrounded by a cluster of people, including Papa, Paul, my sculptor friend Jessie, and Ferdinand, the groom, who is standing near me, even though he's looking at Louise. In this photo, I look pretty and even happy. I guess I liked being encircled by men, with Maman and Louise practically out of the picture. And no one could tell from the photograph that one of my legs is shorter than the other.

When Papa showed my sculptures of *Napoleon 1, Bismarck*, and *David and Goliath* to his young sculptor friend Alfred Boucher, the artist was astounded to see so much talent in a child of fifteen. To tell the truth, I didn't quite understand his accolades. I was only sculpting the people around me, my family, our servants Eugénie and Hélène,, our friends, their children, and the villagers. But if Papa needed any confirmation of my potential as a sculptor, he certainly received it from his friend Boucher, who raved about my work and said I could use his studio when I came to Paris.

I was so exhilarated by Boucher's praise I knew I had to live in Paris where I could take advantage of his kind offer, and where everything important in sculpture was happening. To get there I had to turn to Papa, the great supporter of my career as an artist. I ran into the library where he sat reading as usual in his battered brown leather chair, and knelt at his feet with my head in his lap. I sat there for a few moments, as he gently stroked the hair back from my forehead. Then I excitedly said, "Papa, I need to live in Paris! I just have to! Can you help me?"

"How can I do that, Camille?" he said.

"Let's move the whole family there."

He gave me a peculiar look and said, "Move the whole family to Paris? Are you losing your mind?" I begged and pleaded with him, as I knew he always found it hard to say no to me. This time, however, he was more difficult to reach.

"How am I going to make a living for you and the family, if I leave my job?" he asked in a flat tone of voice.

"Oh, Papa," I begged, "you know they think you're wonderful at the office. You practically run the place. They won't want to lose you. You can ask them to move you to Paris. Please, Papa, please? That would make me very happy." I peeked up at his face and saw him considering the move, and knew he was weakening.

"What about Maman?" he said after a while. "You know she has no interest in your being a sculptor and certainly won't want to leave this house that belonged to her father. And how about Paul and Louise?"

"Paul can go to the Lycée Louis-le-Grand, where all the brilliant young Parisian boys go. You know he needs the very best school. The one here is not good enough for a boy of his abilities. And any school will do for Louise, because she's a girl and not too bright a one at that."

Papa weakened even more. "You have a point there," he said with a sigh. "And Maman? She says you have me twisted around your little finger."

I tried to hide a smile. "You know you want me to be a great sculptor, Papa." I said, brimming over with joy at the thought of going to Paris, to say nothing of winning the argument. "You want it as much as I do. But to do that I have to be in Paris. Maman will have to move," I said, fiercely shaking my head, "whether she wants to or not. We can't let her hold back her genius children!"

"Ah Camille, you know I cannot resist you!" he said. "I don't promise, but I'll see what I can do."

You may wonder why it was so easy to argue Papa into moving to Paris. One might think it would be difficult to persuade a career man of advanced age to pick up his family, pull up his roots, and begin a new life in a strange city. I believe Papa was amenable to the move partly because he'd been encouraged about my artistic talents by my educators even before Boucher came along. In 1870, Papa had been transferred to the little town of Bar-le-Duc and moved the whole family there. From my sixth to thirteenth year I attended the school of the Sisters of the Christian Doctrine in the nearby town of Epernay. The nuns, especially Mère St. Joseph, were most enthusiastic about my work. They told Papa I was a genius and insisted I study art. They pinned my drawings on the wall where anyone coming into the room couldn't miss them, and made sure the other students saw them (which was a great way to make those children hate me and treat me even more like an outsider. But I got even by ignoring them). That was my last formal schooling.

When I was twelve years old, Papa was again transferred, this time to Nogent-sur-Seine, a small town about sixty-five miles from Paris. There we were given private lessons by Monsieur Colin, a tutor who saw to it that I got the same education as my brother. He was a remarkable and inspiring teacher, although I always felt he preferred Paul to me. He taught us a lot about history, spelling, mathematics, and read to us from wonderful books like Aristophanes' *La Chanson de Roland,* which were rarely taught to children. He loved the statue of *David and Goliath* that I sculpted when I was thirteen, and raved to Papa about it. So I was grateful to the nuns as well as to Monsieur Colin for confirming Papa's appraisal of my talent. Then when Boucher corroborated the praise of my teachers, it was easier than I expected to convince Papa I had to study in Paris. In fact, I suspect he was only waiting for me to push him into action, because he'd chosen me to live out the genius life he had always wanted for himself.

Unfortunately, the Mortgage Registration Bureau could not transfer Papa to Paris, but they did assign him to posts in Rambouillet and Compiègne, from which he was able to commute to Paris. The rest of us moved to a rented apartment, selected by me, of course, at 111, rue Notre-Dame-des-Champs, in a quiet, inexpensive area artists were just discovering. Poor Papa had to be satisfied with visiting us whenever he could. Maman added that to the list of things for which she would never forgive me. But I didn't care. I was in Paris! I was going to be a real sculptor!

The first thing I had to do in Paris was to find a good art school that taught sculpting. This was not an easy thing to do for a serious woman artist, as the best school, L'École des Beaux-Arts, did not accept female students at all. Many artists took on students in their private *ateliers,* but to enroll in them was risky, as their quality was just as likely to be poor as good. I didn't know what to do, so I asked Papa to take me to see his friend Boucher for advice.

Boucher lit up when he saw the pair of us, and kissed us both on each cheek. He seemed pleased to be able to help, and got right down to business.

"There is a private *atelier* Rodolphe Julian runs which accepts women students," he said. "The school is a big improvement over most of the others. Julian hires well-known artists to visit twice a week and monitor the work of his students. He also provides nude models for both sexes," he said, looking intently at me. I smiled.

"But," he continued, "it is extremely overcrowded, so you have to fight to get a good spot to see the models." I stopped smiling.

"What good is it to have models, nude or otherwise, if you can't even see them?" I said with exasperation.

Boucher added, "Now don't be angry when I tell you this, Camille, but there's worse to come. Julian's fees are quite high, and he charges women students twice as much as he does the men. This is so his school can compete with L'École des Beaux-Arts, which men can attend free of charge, and where women are not admitted at all. Since female artists like you have little choice if they want to go to an art school, many pay Julian's higher tuition."

Papa said, "That's outrageous! How dare he charge me more for the same classes, simply because you are a woman? I refuse to pay it!"

Boucher nodded in deference to Papa, and looked at me again. He understood me well; I was seething. I clenched and unclenched my fists. Then I bellowed, "Papa is right! How dare a school charge more, simply because we are women? Is there no justice in the world? Why would any woman go to Julian's? I wouldn't stoop so low if there wasn't another art school in all of France!"

Boucher looked at my glum face and got serious. "There is a second possibility which might suit you better," he continued mercifully. "A private school with a good reputation is run by Phillippo Colarossi, a former model and sculptor who exhibited several plaster busts during the '80s at the Salon des Artistes Français. The school was founded in 1815 as the Académie Suisse, but he changed the name to the Académie Colarossi when he took over. An excellent business man, Colarossi decided to follow Julian's philosophy, only to do it better. Like Julian, Colarossi hires experienced artists to teach his students, but he allows more flexibility in scheduling, and pupils can enroll for any amount of time from one week to ten months. The school is quite informal, and students can drop in and sculpt or draw whenever they want to. In a nice touch for out-of-doors painters, Colarossi arranges expeditions to the countryside, so those students who wish to draw or paint out-of-doors have the opportunity to do so. But more important for you, Camille, as a sculptor himself he emphasizes sculpting more than Julian does, and hires well-known sculptors to teach. Also admission is more equal. An equal number of women students are enrolled as men, and both sexes pay the same fees. Women and men sit side by side in the classes, and nude models are available for all students." This time the smile remained on my face. I looked at Papa and saw he was smiling too.

Boucher went on. "Well, what do you think, Camille? Are you ready to make a decision?" The rascal knew very well what I thought, and had known all along where I would wind up. He just likes to be dramatic: he should have gone on the stage. It was a simple matter for me to choose between the two schools. As I liked the emphasis on sculpture at Colarossi, and would never pay double the price paid by male students even if Papa let me, I soon was enrolled at the Colarossi Academy. I felt better about myself as soon as I had matriculated, for I find it humiliating to be treated as a second class person. Will there ever come a day when artists are judged by their work and not their gender? I wanted to become the greatest sculptor in the whole world, better than any man. I didn't see why I couldn't do it.

I took private lessons for a time from an Italian sculptor at the Academy whose name I've fortunately forgotten. I don't know how much I learned from him, but I wasn't too happy with his teaching. I can only take so many curlicues and angels before I get disgusted. I told Papa about my dissatisfaction. He came to my rescue again and immediately called on his friend Boucher, who this time insisted that Papa bring me right over to his *atelier*, where I would work as his student.

When Papa first took me to Boucher's studio, I was struck wordless by the large whitewashed *atelier*, strewn with fascinating tools and magnificent blocks of Carrere marble wherever you looked. It was totally unlike the cramped dreary maid's room that had been my first Paris workshop, that I had stolen away from Eugénie, making her move to the attic. (She was so angry about it she quit the job and left!) Boucher's *atelier* was filled with bustling assistants, and resounding with the striking of mallets on chisels. The studio was covered with an open skylight through which the sunlight poured in light of honey yellow that was speckled with marble dust. Boucher's exquisite marble sculptures posed all over the room dazzled my eyes. I stood frozen in front of *The Runners.* I've always admired the poise of athletes, and believe their bodies in motion are as beautiful as those of dancers. I hadn't seen any sculpted figures in action as superb as *The Runners* since I found a picture of a Greek sculpture from around 450 B.C. in a book of my father's when I was a little girl. It was called *Bronze statuette of a youth finishing a jump.* The athlete is leaning as far back as he can as he lands, and holding himself on his feet by superb muscular control. Since my short leg makes me incapable of that kind of balance in life, I vowed right then to sculpt a figure like that some day. A similar grace and equilibrium and the sense of a single movement drawing a number of figures toward the same goal were what I wanted to capture in my work. One moment of beauty was enshrined forever in the magnificent sculpture.

I watched how Boucher moved and copied the way he paced himself, never hurrying and never stopping. I used what I learned from him all of my sculpting career. The motion of the dancers in *La Valse* reminds me of the movement he sculpted in *The Runners.* I was carried away too by his *Danseuse espagnole,* whose lovely movement and balance also brings to mind my sculpture, *La Valse.* And then there was his exquisite statue of the little boy *Enfant* which has a bit of the quality of my first sculpture of Paul.

Boucher was the perfect teacher for me. If he liked a statue I was molding, he would look at me and slowly nod his head. There was no "Cover up that girl's nakedness, Camille," or "Make that boy's head less arrogant." He left me free to develop my art in my own way, so that I could ripen as sweetly as a melon under the sun. In this manner I set and mastered my own style, as can be seen in my sculptures from that period, *Paul Claudel at thirteen years of age (Jeune romain)* and *Old Hélène (La Veille Hélèn).* I'm a person who needs inner solitude in order to create. I couldn't have grown as a sculptor in any other way.

I absorbed each bit of information in the studio with every bit of my body. I was fascinated with the way they mixed clay, the melding of earth colors, the delicate strength of tools for molding and carving, and the way they extended the sensual beauty of the hand. I loved their utility and beauty and the feel in my fingertips of what they had formed. I learned to understand tools there, so that later I could make my own scrapers, scribers, flats, curves, and such exactly as I wanted them at practically no cost. Which made me feel like another hero of mine, Leonardo da Vinci, who not only made tools but constructed a lute in silver in the shape of a horse's head.

I loved everything about Boucher's *atelier*, even the discomforts of sculpting. At first my arms ached after a day and evening of modeling and couldn't stop shaking, but I soon got used to it, and much preferred being there to anywhere else. My blouses increased by a full size as the muscles in my shoulders developed. I liked that my whole center of gravity changed. Despite my lameness, I learned to move from a core of strength and balance in the center of my body, so that I could touch the surface of clay as gently as the flutter of a leaf in the springtime.

I think Boucher liked me, too. Of course I was disappointed that he never followed the "great artist" scenario, although I secretly kept daydreaming that he would. He made up for it by sculpting *Camille Claudel lisant* (*Camille Claudel reading*), which he dedicated "To Camille Claudel in memory of A. Boucher." I felt honored to be chosen to model for him, and now in my old age I like to think that I once was as pretty as he saw me, although it's hard to believe I was ever that young.

Soon after our meeting I rented my first *atelier* on the fifth floor at 117, rue Notre-Dame-des-Champs, right next door to our family apartment. I loved the area, which was filled with artists' studios, many of them rented by famous painters such as Whistler, Bonheur, and Corolus-Duran, whose ranks I dreamed of joining some day. I shared my *atelier* with three English girls I had met at the Academy. One of them, Jessie Lipscomb, became my best friend, who remained a faithful friend for much of my life. In a gesture that was typical of his generous nature, Boucher dropped by the studio from time to time to see if we needed any help.

When I was seventeen, he was so impressed with my work that he introduced me to his teacher, Paul Dubois, the famous director of L'École des Beaux-Arts. Dubois had sculpted the delicately modeled bronze effigy of Louis Pasteur, and was working on the elegant *Florentine Singer* which later won the Salon's medal of honor. I excitedly rushed around his *atelier*, devouring one beautiful statue after another. Here was a sculptor after my own heart! He was a pioneer who broke away from the desexualization of the nude practiced by the École, and portrayed the naked body *au naturel*. Personally, I've never understood why it's permissible to show shoulders and male chests unclothed, but not to exhibit buttocks or genitalia. (Does anyone really believe a fig leaf is much of a cover?) Such thinking says to me that the artist and/or the state consider those parts of the body to be pure filth that must be kept away from the eyes of "normal" human beings who, incidentally, have the same equipment as the nude statues. It makes no sense to me whatever! If some bureaucratic idiot decided that exposed fingernails are obscene, my sheeplike compatriots wouldn't be found dead without gloves on. Come to think of it, we're not so far away from that situation now. No "lady" walks out of doors without wearing gloves, even in the heat of summer. The next thing you know, people caught with bare hands will be put in prison! Needless to say, I don't share such sentiments, which is why I could pose in the nude for Rodin. I've never regretted it, and even though he's a cheat and a liar in his personal life, I'm proud to be part of his art. To me the whole body is sacred, even our fingernails.

I also could see that Monsieur Dubois was a perfectionist like me, and made many wax models and drawings of each of his sculptures before finishing them. I knew right away that I owed him a great debt and subsequently listed him as one of my teachers. Monsieur Dubois was quite taken with my work, too, and asked me if I had taken lessons from Rodin. Of course I hadn't. I'd never even heard of him.

Boucher and I were getting along beautifully, and I looked forward to his visits as to nothing else in my life. Joy flowed through me like a river on the days he came to our *atelier*. Fool that I was, I thought it would go on forever. But what good relationship in my life has ever lasted? I should have learned. This one was to prove no different from any of the others.

After several months of gloriously working together he came up to me, and looking down at his shoes, said, "Camille, I have something to tell you that I feel bad about." I looked up from my modeling in surprise. He didn't usually talk about his feelings.

"What is it, Monsieur Boucher? I hope nothing is wrong."

"No, Camille. In fact something wonderful has happened. I just don't think *you* will be so happy about it."

"I can't imagine. Tell me what it is and we shall see."

He blurted out, "I just found out that I won the Prix du Salon with my sculpture, *La Piété Filiale.*"

"But that's wonderful, Monsieur Boucher!" I said, smiling. "I'm sure it's for your poetic statue of the young girl giving her breast to the old man." I can understand loving an old man enough to do such a thing, and make him young and vigorous again. After all, I was to do that with Rodin. "Why would I object?"

"You don't understand, Camille. To accept the prize I have to spend six months in Florence, and won't be able to continue with our lessons."

I felt my lovely little world sliding down the sewer. "You mean…you're going to leave me?"

"I'm afraid that *is* what I mean, Camille."

I stood there frozen in time like one of his sculptures. I wanted to congratulate him but the words stuck in my throat. To have so much and then to lose it all in one brief moment! How cruel life can be. Of course I was proud of my teacher and wanted to tell him so, but I didn't want to show him how betrayed I felt. After all, I have my pride. I thrust out my hand and ran out of the *atelier.*

Then the blood stormed into my veins. I couldn't wait to get back to Villeneuve, where I raged and screamed in the grotto of *Le Géyn* for hours, shouting "How come he's leaving me, if he thinks I'm such a great sculptor?" 'My so-called sculpture teacher,' I labeled him, to anyone who would listen. The real pain was that it became quite clear he was not going to be the artist I dreamed about. How could he be, when he was abandoning me for a mere prize?

But it turned out that I underrated his feelings for me and my work. Before leaving, the dear man came to our *atelier* and said, "Camille, I've asked Auguste Rodin to replace me in my visits, and to pay particular attention to the work of Camille Claudel. That should make you feel better about my leaving."

I had heard of Rodin by this time, as he already was known to many as a great sculptor. To tell the truth, the trade-up soothed my hurt feelings, although I wouldn't admit it to Boucher. For there was always the chance that Rodin would turn out to be "the one."

I was nineteen years old when he took me on as his first female student. He was forty-three.

Part II
The Rodin Years

1881–1912

The Love Affair

1882–1892

What a joy to experience the freedom of Paris, after living under the roof of my dear old mother! I could think as I liked, do as I liked, use nude models if I liked, eat, sleep, and yes, drink when I liked, with nobody to make nasty comments like, "Louis-Prosper, can't you do *anything* with that daughter of yours? She never listens to me and opens up her big mouth whenever I say a word. Mark my words, Prosper, that girl will come to no good end!"

I have to admit she wasn't wrong about her prophecy, although it didn't happen the way she envisioned. Maman was probably no worse than all the other women we knew, but that didn't make it any easier to occupy the same house. I thought day and night about getting my own apartment, and daydreamed about the time when I could.

Soon after the meeting with Boucher, I woke up one morning with a novel thought in my head. "I'm a big girl now! I don't have to take her overbearing ways or her insults anymore. I can live in my *atelier* and sleep on the couch. There's no reason why I can't. Papa's helping me with my share of the rent, and the English girls are paying the rest. I'm going to move in *this very day!*" Then singing loudly, I tucked my cat Tabasco under my arm and lugged my sparse wardrobe to where Papa was waiting to drive me to my new home. I proudly ignored the tongue-lashing from you-know-who that followed me all the way to the horse and buggy. As it clattered away on the cobble stones, I looked back and stuck out my tongue at her.

It was a great time to live in Paris! I was glad it wasn't eleven years earlier, when the French army was defeated by the Prussians in 1870 at Sedan, and Emperor Napoléon III had been forced to surrender under conditions so humiliating that partisans rebelled against their own government. Many people, like Hélène, deeply mourned the loss of Alsace-Lorraine. It had been a terrible time for Parisians, as the revolutionaries of the Paris Commune destroyed and set on fire many buildings like churches, libraries, and theaters. Some of the destruction was still evident, like the ruins of the Palais of the Tuileries, which depressed me every time I walked by. One good thing for sculptors came out of the downfall of France, however: In a great surge of patriotism, many monuments symbolizing the indestructible spirit of France were commissioned.

I didn't know it yet, but it was to have a great effect on my future life as a sculptor and a model for Rodin. But being only seventeen and an apolitical person, I didn't think too much about such things. I was much more concerned with the wonder of being a young sculptor in Paris, where every block bustled with artists and studios.

In my new home, I felt like a real sculptor for the first time. I wasn't lonely, because I had Tabasco with me. When I was a child, we had a family pet named Crapitoche who looked just like Tabasco (maybe it was his father, I don't remember), but I always felt at home when I had my beloved cat with me. I sculpted *Le Chat* once, which was a figure of Crapitoche stretching his beautiful back high into the air as if he were ready to spring. I took money Papa had given me for food and had the statue cast in bronze. It looked so much like Crapitoche that I wanted to scratch his head. I liked my sculpture almost as much as the real cat. I've no idea what happened to it. I wish I had it now.

I couldn't believe I had my very own place, that no one could come in any time she felt like it to check up on what I was doing and to clean up when I didn't think the room was dirty.

One of the three English girls I shared it with, Jessie Lipscomb, became my best friend. At the beginning of our friendship we were together practically all the time, and shared the *atelier*, food, work, and study. The other girls, Amy Singer and Emily Fawcett, were friends of Jessie's who were pleasant to have around, even though they weren't the world's greatest sculptors. The *atelier* consisted of only one room, which we used both as a studio and a sitting room, as none of us had enough money to afford a larger place. To make it as attractive as possible, we hung colorful Persian rugs supplied by our mothers, which served as backdrops for the models. We also added many creative touches, like paintings, copper pots, and even a parrot made of plaster that Jessie had brought back from her travels. It was quite comfortable at first, and we enjoyed many an afternoon tea in it during our rest periods, when we dared to try our first cigarettes. My first was also my last. I didn't like it. It made me gag.

All three girls had come over from England because Victorian society considered female artists the next thing to fallen women. The "protective" art schools dutifully looked after the morals of women students and wouldn't allow them to attend classes where models posed in the nude. Nice of them, wasn't it? Even though the South Kensington Museum, which Jessie attended, was considered one of the more liberal art schools, it only admitted women to separate classes, which served as a kind of finishing school for debutantes or prepared them to be art teachers. It still makes me furious that male students worked primarily from nudes, while females were allowed only alternate weeks of naked models. Even worse, the fall classes on modeling were completely closed to women. Can you imagine me sitting around for half a year waiting for classes to begin? Fortunately for Jessie, her father, like mine, was very supportive of her wish to learn sculpting. When she told him about our *atelier*, he allowed her to come to Paris, the most celebrated art center in the world. Thank goodness for fathers! Where would we women artists be without them?

Despite our efforts to make it attractive, the *atelier* was still cramped and dark, and soon became cluttered with broken and discarded *maquettes*, so that the four of us could hardly find enough working space when we were all there together. (Guess who had the best and largest space by the window!) But none of us complained, as we felt lucky to be there at all. We were supposed to share the rent equally, although I was the only one who lived there. Seeing that I slept on the couch, I thought the arrangement was fair enough. But more often than not, I didn't have any money, so Jessie paid my share.

I'm afraid I had Jessie under my spell, because she let me treat her the way I used to treat Paul and Louise, making her run errands for me, clean up the *atelier*, and get supplies for me when I needed them. Unlike Paul, who once said I was so controlling and mean to him that it scarred him for life, Jessie was very good natured about it. She knew who I was, and allowed me to have things my own way. She was one of the few people in my lifetime who genuinely loved me, and was happy just to be around me. Jessie even kept us in food, as her rich father sent her a weekly allowance. I told her I would pay her back some day, but unfortunately, that day never arrived.

All three girls admired me and did my bidding, as it was clear I was the best sculptor in the group. Although the way they gave in to me made me feel important, I must confess I sometimes felt disdainful when they submitted to my tyranny. I like a person to have more gumption. If the girls had stood up to me instead of behaving like *bonnes*, I would have treated them better. I myself will not accept being bullied, and demand respect at all times. In my opinion, what you put up with in a relationship is what you get.

As the most experienced sculptor, I felt I had the right to make all the major decisions. I selected the work spaces for us, giving Jessie the second best spot, and putting the other two way back in dark corners. It was I who decided when we needed models, picked them out, and hired them. They treated me very badly, showing no respect for me as an artist, and were openly contemptuous because we were women. I often heard them laughing at me behind my back. When I told them to take a position for modeling, they would argue with me and say it was too uncomfortable.

They insisted on frequent rests and refused to hold a pose until we were finished. They demanded more money from us than they charged the men. When I wouldn't give it to them, they shouted curses at me and walked off. Sometimes they just walked off for no reason at all. Even more often, when I didn't like their behavior, I fired them, leaving us with incomplete work that had to be thrown out. They would never have treated men sculptors the way they did us. It was so hard to be a woman artist, and a young one at that. Sometimes I wished I were a man. It would have been much easier to get ahead. Now I suppose it wouldn't make any difference what sex I am. The men patients here are just as miserable as I am.

Besides being a lot of trouble, models were very expensive. One session with a good model cost as much as a whole week's food money, so we often posed for each other instead. The girls wouldn't take their clothes off, even though I asked them to, but that didn't matter, because at that time there was much else I was eager to sculpt. I love the bust I did of Jessie. She looks kindly, loving, and accommodating, just as she was in real life. She was a good friend. I was to find out how good when I decided to leave Rodin, but that comes later in my story.

Jessie and I were real pals. We loved the same sights and beauties of Paris. I'd never had a friend like her before. We went to all the museums of course, the Louvre, the Luxembourg Palace, the Cluny, where we sat and sketched to our hearts' content. We even took a day trip to Versailles, where I had a great time imagining myself a queen. There was an elegant bed in Marie Antoinette's bedroom in the *Petit Trianon*, with an upholstered headboard and footboard brocaded in a light and delicate pattern. The canopy over the headboard was draped with damask and taffeta, embroidered with roses, bouquets, and Cupid's bows, darts and all. As if that wasn't fancy enough, the headboard was trimmed with ribbon bowknots with flying ends and fringe. To top it all off, the elegant wood was edged with gold. I could sculpt for a solid year on what the wood alone must have cost. Carried away with my fantasies of being a queen, I flopped myself down on the bed, eagle-spread my arms and legs, and lay there ecstatically until an irate guard chased me away.

We often took the lengthy Boulevard Raspail to the Boulevard St.

Germain, which led all the way to the left bank of the Seine. The architecture of Paris is so rich that walking around it was like reading a history book in buildings. It was fascinating to see how the materials used evolved over the centuries, as the artisans learned to use different kinds of stone in their work. The wonderful carvings of the gargoyles of The Cathedral de Notre-Dame made us feel close to the hearts and souls of the long dead artisans, who dedicated their lives to the perfection of their work. I was especially interested in the earliest medieval sculpture in the Saint Anne portal of the west façade. The twelfth century columns include a statue of David, which I compared to the one I had sculpted at age thirteen. I must admit I liked mine better. It is much more real.

A favorite spot of ours was the lush green square behind the Cathedral, where we sat beneath the trees and lunched on bread, cheese, and wine. When we had a few extra francs, we sat at an outdoor café across from the Seine and sipped wine as we watched the people go by. I said, "Jessie, some day I'm going to do nothing but observe people like these as they promenade by and sculpt them all." And that is just what I did, near the end of my sculpting career. It is nice that at least one of my dreams came true.

We delighted in the charming little bridges that crossed the Seine, but the walk we cherished the most was beside its banks. One morning the rising sun cast a silver sparkle on the river. We held hands and stood enchanted at its beauty, and vowed that every time we saw shimmering water we would think of each other.

There isn't too much glistening water in Montdevergues, and I don't know about Jessie, but on the rare occasions I was taken on trips near a river (even when I was mad at her) I kept my vow. I suspect that she does, too. Remembering our fun together makes me miss Jessie. I would gladly trade the rest of my life (such as it is) to return for one hour to our wonderful days in Paris.

He was a bulky, bow-legged 40-year-old, with a thick red bush for a beard. When he first dropped by our *atelier*, I thought, "No! Rodin is not going to be the artist I dream about." I liked a man to be slender like my father, but Rodin looked more like my mother. His head was too big for the rest of him, like hers, and both were lumpish. His posture was stooped, as if he were about to keel forward. "NO!" I thought, "THAT MAN IS NOT MY ARTIST!"

For a man of his height (he was five feet-four inches tall, the same size as me), he did have an enormous head and a hulking body, with the muscular shoulders of a peasant. His gargantuan hands looked like those of a powerful young man, and he was always rolling or squeezing a pellet of clay. He had reddish-chestnut hair and a huge forehead. His nose was thick, bony, and aquiline, like a statesman of ancient Rome. He had small blue eyes which were always half-closed, with two dents on the sides of his nose that had been gouged out by his glasses. Because he was very near-sighted, he wore the glasses all the time, except when he went to sleep. His floating reddish beard, heavy-lidded eyes, and gait, which rolled from the hips, reminded me of a lion in the jungle searching for his prey. He even had the lively, penetrating gaze of a great cat preparing to jump. When I saw Rodin's sculpture, *The Crying Lion,* a few years later I guffawed, because that's exactly how he first appeared to me.

To my surprise, Rodin's voice was gentle and rather monotonous. Actually, he sounded more like a pussycat than a lion. He spoke seriously and slowly and seemed uncomfortable with talking, except when he mentioned sculpting. Then an immense energy radiated from him, like the sun flashing through the sky after a storm. Every time it happened I stood there mesmerized. Despite his occasional transformation, however, he struck me as a gloomy person. In fact, he appeared almost beaten. "No, no, no, no, no " I reassured myself. "I don't need an ugly old gloompot. I want a handsome young man like Paul. Auguste Rodin is definitely not *the one* I'm looking for!" Ah, shades of Shakespeare. "Methinks the lady doth protest too much."

Rodin came into our *atelier* acting as if he'd rather be anywhere else. He kept on his big shabby beret that half covered his head. He walked around indifferently, glancing here and there, passing Jessie's work without pausing a moment. I didn't blame him. Jessie was my best friend and I loved her dearly, but her work, which some people like and she even got prizes for, really didn't come up to my standards. It was relatively stiff, without the naturalness that is the mark of a real sculptor. Except for her statue, *Day Dreams*, a lovely bust of a woman lost in fantasy, which Jessie said was of her future sister-in-law, she lacked the imagination one needs to become a great sculptor. (Incidentally, the bust reminds me of me. I think she caught me daydreaming about Rodin one day, and sculpted it, even though she denied that I had anything to do with the portrait.) The famous critic Mathias Morhardt apparently agreed with my assessment of Jessie's talents. When he wrote an article about me and the *atelier* a few years later, he didn't even mention her. As far as the work of the other two girls was concerned, nothing need be said. Rodin didn't even see it, as I kept their pieces way in the back.

When Rodin came to the bust of our family maid, *Vielle femme (The Old Woman),* he gave it a brief look and started to move on. I thought sadly, "He's putting me in a class with Jessie!" Suddenly, he did a double-take, and whirled around and stood in front of it. He took off his beret and dropped it to the floor. Then he bent so close to the statue he could have kissed it (he is myopic). He closed his eyes and began to move his fingers up and down on it. I had an urge to throw myself against him and do the same to him, but of course I didn't. I just stood there motionless, as he kept on feeling the bust. He began to breath heavily, and I wondered if he was sick. But he looked fine, so I dared to wonder if he was breathing so hard because he was moved by my work. I decided I had to be wrong, for a great sculptor like Rodin couldn't possibly have been affected by the work of a young girl like me. Jessie and I looked at each other with raised eyebrows and shrugged. After a long while, he moved to the left side of the bust and remained there for a full five minutes, when he went around to the right side for another five, and around to the back, where he hungrily ran his huge hands up and down over it. Then he looked deep into my eyes.

"Mademoiselle Claudel?" he asked sternly, "did you copy this from someone else's sculpture?"

"I did not! Of course not," I answered indignantly. "It's the bust of our family servant, Hélène. That's exactly how she looks. She has deep wrinkles on her forehead, cheeks that look like apples, and a chin that sticks way out! Well, maybe I exaggerated her traits a bit, but it's definitely Hélène." Then I wondered if he thought that I had copied the sculpture because he himself was not above copying someone else's work, but I put the thought aside as unworthy of a great artist.

Rodin looked at me incredulously and then moved on to the bust of *Paul at the age of thirteen*. I've always loved that bust, although I had a terrible time getting him to pose for me. I had to keep promising him my desserts at dinnertime so he would stay seated. Sometimes no matter how much I pleaded he would run away and hide under the bridge, and I had to go looking for him. It put me in a rage, losing all that time from my work, and I had to drag him by the arm back to my workshop in the attic, hollering loudly all the way. Although I didn't work for it consciously, the statue has a very domineering expression on its face. But then, so does Paul.

Although I liked the bust of Hélène very much, I liked the one I sculpted of Paul even more. I can see it before me now. His neck and back are bare and he has an ancient Roman tunic draped over his shoulders. I love the way his short boyish-smelling hair curves around the back of his neck, just as it did in real life. His profile is straight and trim, like a Roman emperor's. He has an aquiline nose, with slightly extended nostrils that look like he is really breathing. His dear little ears are shaped like a cocoon, and stick out a little. He has a serious expression and the inward-looking eyes of a dreamer. His erect posture has a certain nobility about it, which was apparent to me when he was thirteen years old. I think this work shows I was clairvoyant about Paul, and knew somewhere inside of me that some day he would become a great statesman. Although I was to do many other busts of Paul, I always loved this one the most.

Continuing his tour of our *atelier*, Rodin stopped in front of the bust of Paul and gasped. Then he explored the statue as he did Hélène's, rubbing his hands against it even longer and grasping it all over as if he wanted to swallow it up. When he left it, his eyes seemed to take me inside of them, although he said only, "Come to my studio tomorrow morning, Mademoiselle Camille. Come tomorrow, Studio J, door five." He walked to the door, where he suddenly stopped, looked over his shoulder at Jessie and said, "You come, too." Then he opened the door and left without looking back.

I chased him up the street. "Monsieur Rodin! Monsieur Rodin!" I shouted after him.

He turned around and smiled at me for the first time.

"You forgot your beret," I said, handing it to him.

"Thank you, Mademoiselle Camille." He said kindly. But I thought he looked disappointed.

When I returned, Jessie and I looked at each other as if *Pâques*[4] had come in the dead of winter, and rushed into each other's arms. We jumped up and down together, shrieking, "He likes our sculptures!! He likes them! He likes them!" And danced uproariously around the statues. No wonder I was happy! In one instant the horizons of my life had expanded from a little girl's make-believe workshop to that of a real artist working with the greatest sculptor in France. It wasn't until I licked the salt water off the sides of my mouth that I realized I was crying.

I was up all night, worrying that the great man would change his mind, or wouldn't like my work or me, or oddly enough, that he would. The next morning I was at his studio at daybreak, shaking so hard I had to keep my hands in my pockets, even though it was summertime. I strode around the courtyard many times to relax myself, and then waited impatiently on the thick grass under the old chestnut trees until Rodin arrived half an hour later and unlocked Studio J, door five. He greeted me quietly, as if it were the most natural thing in the world for me to be there, and motioned for me to follow him inside. Jessie came a bit later, and I was happy to have her to hold on to and keep me from being swept away with excitement when Rodin showed us around the studio.

After all the lifeless sculptures I had seen drearily stacked up against the walls of this or that exhibition, I knew as soon as I approached the entrance of his *atelier*, where *L'Age d'Airain (The Age of Bronze)* was standing, that Rodin was a magnificent artist. I suspected right then that he would be known someday as the greatest sculptor in France. I must say that my atheism got a bit shaky at that point. "How could it have happened?" I marveled. "That I wind up on the doorstep of a genius sculptor? It *can't* have been a coincidence, because he's just the teacher I need. Was our meeting predestined by some benevolent Fate that wants me to be a great sculptor, too?"

I was too overwhelmed to take in much more, however, until he gave me the hand of one of his statues to work on. Hands to Rodin were the epitome of the human body, a little miniature self that stood for the whole person. He kept drawers and drawers full of hands he had sculpted over the years; large hands, small hands, wrinkled and weatherbeaten hands, beautiful, graceful hands, deformed arthritic hands, the hands of lovers, the hands of field workers, artists' hands, hands with beautiful fingers, hands with no fingers at all. He believed that one could reveal the complete individual through observation of a fragment of their body. Sometimes if he needed a hand for an ongoing work, he would simply go to his drawers and select one of the proper category.

I agreed with him on the unique significance of hands. I hoped he would not forget that I had sculpted the hand, and stick it in his drawer with all the others. But I was happy that he had assigned me to model one, and immediately became so absorbed in sculpting it that I forgot where I was. Being entrusted to work on a hand by the master was very special. "Life is movement," he frequently said. "Hands and feet are the foundation of all action, and demand commitment and concentration." I realized he preferred my work to Jessie's when he assigned her to work on draperies, which I must admit made me smile. We were also put in charge of getting the master's work ready for him, enlarging the small models he had made, and sketching whatever he happened to need at the moment. My panic soon dissipated and was replaced with exhilaration. Then the hairs on my arms stood straight up as I wondered if Auguste Rodin might turn out to be *my artist* after all.

I went to his *atelier* every day, sixteen hours a day, seven days a week. I hated to leave at night, and would have stayed longer if he had let me. I loved being surrounded by half-formed works of beauty, and the marvelous pieces of Carrera marble which had the seeds of their future concealed inside them. There were no warm Persian carpets or tea pots in Rodin's *atelier*, but who needed them? I was bewitched by the sounds of the workplace, the plaster casters, the marble carvers, the bronze founders, the fascinating models and the way everyone joked around together. I loved the feel of the damp clay, and the chalky smell of the wet linen that covered the work and preserved it for another day. I even loved the dust, because it was proof that we really were sculpting. I didn't mind that it made me sneeze. I loved learning exciting new techniques, like the time one of the workers taught me a method of polishing stone with a mutton bone that was used in Bernini's time. I showed it to *le Maître* and was thrilled when he said it worked well. Best of all, I never tired of watching Rodin's massive hands kneading the clay at lightning speed, uncannily transforming inanimate earth into a living creature that seemed to stir with every breath. He was the only person I knew who shared my passion for transposing the truth into a clump of clay. For a little while, at least, I wasn't alone in the universe.

We all loved to watch him at work, to study the way his eloquent hands and sensitive eye packed the clay in place and rapidly outlined the figure in its proper proportions. All this time, the models walked freely about in the nude. At first I tried not to gape at the size of a woman's breast and the fullness of her bush, but I soon got used to naked women parading around and reacted to them as if they were part of the furniture. The naked men took me a little longer.

When Rodin finished drafting the figure in clay, he began a more personal kind of modeling. He seemed to have memorized the appearance of the model, for he would cut here and there and back again, scarcely looking at him or her. After that he would climb a ladder and study the top of the model's head, which he would then reproduce in clay. Next, he would cut off the head and place it on a pillow. He would then ask the model to lie face down on a sofa and examine the spot where head and neck met, the depression of the neck, and the surfaces behind the ears. Later the model would sit facing Rodin, at the height of the clay on the modeling stand. With a small knife, Rodin marked the highs and the lows of the model's face, the eyebrows, the eyes, the eyelids, the nose, the nostrils, the outline of the lips, and the size of the ears on the clay. He then had half-a-dozen proofs made, on which he experimented with various expressions until he found the one he preferred. But he always left one untouched, so that he could return to the original if the work left him unsatisfied.

Before closing the studio at night, Rodin would make one final check of his work, lighting a candle and circling the new statue to search for flaws. If he found any, he would take his knife and carve a little cross where he needed to attach or remove clay. I learned from him to do the same with my sculptures, so I always knew what I would return to the next morning. On those days, I looked forward all night to the start of a newborn day. Sometimes it set off a dream about the statue I was working on, which gave me a whole new slant on the piece. Once when I couldn't get the expression I wanted on the face of a head I was sculpting, I dreamed Rodin appeared and said, "Camille, turn her so that the light shines out of her eyes." I did as he said, and like magic she came alive.

Rodin devoted himself as much to teaching his assistants as he did to his sculptures. Often when I was sculpting, *Le Maître* came and stood over my shoulder and watched me work. If he walked away without a word, I knew he approved of my craftsmanship. But occasionally he would have a suggestion for me. Shortly after I came to work at his studio, he came and stood behind me as I was having trouble finishing the nose on my bust of *Diane*. I was overcome with his musky smell and could hardly concentrate on the statue.

"Mademoiselle Camille," he said after a few moments (he called me Mademoiselle Camille, I called him Monsieur Rodin[5]), "when you sculpt a portrait, always work from the profile. When you finish one side, go around to the other. You'll find that the rest of the portrait takes care of itself."

"Yes, Monsieur Rodin, thank you," I answered. I was so charged up with being near the great sculptor that I couldn't say anything more. (I certainly changed later, when absolutely nothing was too frank or direct for me to say to him. He liked that about me and said that was what made me different from any other woman except his dead sister, Maria.) But the truth of the moment was that I had known the technique of what he said since I was six years old. I remember copying a photograph in a book of Papa's about Egypt that was called *The Book of the Dead*. I was sketching some hieroglyphics from the facade of an pharaoh's mausoleum. The straight, stiff images of the Egyptians were painted in red, and faced frontward, as they staunchly guarded the tomb. I wasn't satisfied with the images I drew, as I thought they looked like figurines from *La Galette des Rois*.[6] I said to myself, "I'll bet I can get a better likeness of their faces if I draw them from the side." So I made my figures face sideways and drew them in profile, and was much happier with the result. Nevertheless,

Rodin was right about my bust of *Diane*. I got her nose done more to my satisfaction when I approached it from the side.

I had my first real success soon after I began my work with Rodin. My *Bust of Madame B*, which I'm happy to say I'd begun before I met Rodin, was accepted for the yearly exhibition of the Salon of the Société des Artistes Français in 1883. I was proud of this sculpture because it was a whole new type of work for me. I loved *Madame B*'s compassionate, affectionate, intelligent look. She was the kind of mother I'd always wanted. It was good to learn once more that what I couldn't have, I could create. Having the piece selected by the Salon was a great honor for so young an artist. Besides that, the Salon served as a market where winning pieces were purchased by the State, and the government awarded commissions to those selected for first place. No women had ever been granted awards by the Salon, but I was so thrilled about being selected that I didn't much care. I thought I had plenty of time to win awards. I was so happy when Papa came to Paris especially to see the exhibition and, of course, I was delighted to be a winner in the eyes of Rodin.

He soon developed an endless fascination with my face, examining every little bump and crevice as if he had never seen a face before. When we were together he never took his eyes off it. As he was myopic, this meant he was always a foot closer to me than other people were. I wriggled a bit under his fierce scrutiny, but not too much, because I couldn't help a feeling of pleasure creeping down my body. He never lost his intense absorption in my face, and molded statues of it again and again. Among them were *Camille Claudel* (1884), *L'Aurore* (1885), *Camille au bonnet* (1885), *L'Adieu* (1892), *La Convalescente* (1892), *Masque de Camille dans la main gauch de Pierre de Wissant* (1900), *La France* (1904) and another *Camille au bonnet* (1911). Within this list of the many faces of Camille Claudel lies the history of our love.

Sometimes I think I loved Rodin before I even knew of his existence. When I first met him, it was as if the role had been written for him in my fantasies every night and I was just waiting for him to come along and fill it. The night between his first visit to me and mine to his *atelier*, I wrote a poem to him called *Camille in Love*:

In the grey-white light
of waiting day
When the sun's twin sister to the moon
I saw him,
Saw him with his back
against the sky

Against God and nature
Sky and man
Twixt the miracles of sun and moon
Twixt and of the silver twins
Facing me.

Oh space, time, stars,
And all the universe
yet holds
to pray to,
Let me spill
the bursting vessels of my heart
That he who dwells
with the bodies of Heaven
Squaring his back
against the sky
Should yet
Face me![7]

I never showed him the poem, but locked it up inside of me along with my sweet fantasies. In fact I feigned a complete lack of interest in him and pretended to concentrate doubly-hard on my work when he came near me. When we were together with the others in the *atelier*, I made sure to talk to one of them and not him. My mother taught me well that you should never show your love to anybody or the person will pull away.

But little by little, even the naive country girl that I was had to recognize that he was singling me out from the others. In the beginning, he would give me little sideway glances, stand closer to me than he did to anyone else. A half-shy warmth shone from his eyes when he looked at me, a warmth that made my stomach turn somersaults. I didn't know whether it was because he liked my work or he liked me. Once he gently guided my arm on the clay, and it tingled afterwards for hours. I felt he was *aware of me* even when he wasn't looking at me. I don't know how, but I can always tell when someone is aware of me. Beams of energy seem to shine out of the person in my direction, even when he doesn't seem to know I'm around. When Rodin was near me, the rays poured out of him like shafts of sunlight. That's when I grew certain he wanted something more from me than help with his sculpting. To be sure, he sometimes had another sort of look, a stare really, an artist's scrutiny, as if he had never seen such a being before in his life. But I'm not talking about that type of gaze, which is really an examination. This kind was a thirst that was very personal and intense. I recognized it because I often felt the same way. I thought, "This man looks at me as if he wants to drink me in." You'd think I would have been happy about it, but I wasn't; I was terrified. I don't know whether I was more scared that he *would* care for me or that he *wouldn't*.

One day as the *practiciens* were preparing to leave, Rodin came up behind me and began to stroke the back of my neck. I stood there as if paralyzed. This was too much like my "scenario." I didn't know yet how I felt about it. After all, even though I had fantasied about such a relationship most of my life, I was my mother's daughter, and although I was not a practicing Catholic I had taken Communion and been educated by the Sisters of Christian Doctrine.

Rodin turned me around like a puppet, looked me straight in the eyes and said, "Mademoiselle Claudel, please remain in the *atelier* after the others leave." Then even a country girl like me knew what his look meant. My head began to swim, and I knew I couldn't be alone with him. So I muttered something about my parents needing me, and putting out my hand, thanked him for everything he was doing for me. He grabbed my forearm and roughly shoved me away. I bolted out the door, feeling wretched and remorseful.

I was trembling as I ran back to my studio. I was nineteen years old and untouched by any man. The rumors around the *atelier* were that he had frequently taken advantage of models, thinking like many artists that he was entitled to his seigneurial rights (*droit de cuissage*). But that wouldn't work with me. I've always been very stubborn and never yielded to anyone who wanted to exploit me, no matter what the price. But I had tremendous respect for Rodin as an artist, and he was the only sculptor I wanted to work with. If there was anyone else of his caliber in the art world, I didn't know him. Also, I suspected that my future as a sculptor depended on Rodin for contacts and commissions. I didn't like him being angry with me and I didn't want to lose him as a colleague and a teacher. And last but not least, there were my own feelings of excitement at the thought of being seduced by him, which I tried to push away but couldn't. I tried to talk myself out of him. "Who needs this problem?" I said to myself. "I've been satisfied with fantasies about great artists all my life. Things don't have to change." I almost believed it.

Then something happened which forced me to examine my relationship with Rodin. In his review of the Salon exhibition where I showed the bust of my sister Louise, Paul Leroy praised my work in general, but upset me with his comment about me and Rodin. He said, "It is essential that the young artist be Mademoiselle Claudel herself, and not a mere reflection." *(L'Art.* Vol 11 (Paris 1886, p. 67). Leroy obviously was referring to a lack of originality and the influence of Rodin on my work. But the portrait of Louise did *not* suffer from a lack of originality! The stupid man didn't see that it was the model, not the sculpture, that was commonplace. Louise did not have an ounce of imagination in her, and the bust portrayed her just as she was. I gritted my teeth and thought that if Leroy ever came near me he would be lucky if I didn't spit on him.

Not long afterward Maurice Guillemot reproached me for having copied Rodin's *Celle qui fuit la belle heaullmière, (The Helmut-maker's Wife).* I indignantly replied that unlike many artists I do not have to imitate anybody, that "I get ideas from inside myself. I don't need to copy *anybody*, as there are too many statues I want to sculpt rather than too few." I began to think I would have to leave Rodin to protect myself from such unfounded slander. My friend Jessie invited me to visit her home in Nottingham with her for a few weeks. I decided to go. It would get me away from Rodin, and give me time to decide what to do. Jessie and I left Paris at the end of May, 1886. I did not plan to return until mid-September.

We stayed at Wootton House, her parents' beautiful mansion in Peterborough that the dapper, dignified Sidney Lipscomb had built for his family a few years after making a fortune on the London Coal Exchange. Their home looked like a seventeenth century country house built in Cotswold stone. It was surrounded by a magnificent walled garden, which abounded with the nodding yellow heads of daffodils, while roses graced the walls of the house itself. Umbrellas and tables were dotted around the garden and used well into the evening, where we enjoyed many a take-away meal and a quiet glass of wine (or two). I liked both Monsieur and Madame Lipscomb right away, and was pleased to be accepted so warmly. To my surprise, I learned that she had been a barmaid in a Grantham railway hotel, where Monsieur Lipscomb had met her while he was traveling on business as a colliery agent. As I always said, yes, dreams do come true, if we dream them very hard and earnestly, and never, never give them up. At least for some lucky people.

I'm afraid I gave Rodin a difficult time. He wrote to me several times a day, but I refused to answer his letters. Of course the harder you are to get, the more a person will pursue you. Rodin became frantic. He wrote letters to Jessie begging for news of me and asking her to give them to me. Jessie was our go-between, and although she didn't say so, I knew she didn't like it one bit. She was a plain-looking woman, and Rodin never was interested in her sexually. I'm sure she loved Rodin too, and was jealous that he loved only me. But unlike Maman, Louise, and practically every other woman I knew, Jessie seemed to get enough from my friendship to keep her envy of me hidden, for a while, anyway.

Rodin kept writing to me, but I never answered. Nevertheless, I was up early every morning waiting for the postman to bring me another one of his letters. I guess I was mean to him, like Maman was to me. I couldn't help it. I was scared to have him be so important to me. On the other hand, I didn't want to renounce forever the possibility of being loved by him. I had daydreamed about having a lover like him since I could remember, and I worried that another might never come along. After all, I was lame. What man in his right mind could love a cripple? I was ashamed to take my clothes off in front of him, and so long as I kept them on, I could fool myself that he didn't notice my limp.

I even had a recurring fantasy that I asked him about it. I'm walking with Rodin in a magnificent garden as the rays of the luminous moon outline our faces. The stars are bright in the sky, and the wind is whispering through the treetops. We are holding hands.

Me: "Monsieur Rodin, did you—uh—notice that I have a limp when I walk?"

Rodin: "A limp? What limp? You don't have a limp. If you did, I certainly would have noticed. You merely have a Byronic gait." Then he would take me in his arms and say, "Even if you had a limp, I would love you just the same. You are my own perfect love." We would begin to kiss and I would forget all about my limp. And I would be cured forever.

But fantasy or not, somewhere inside of me I knew that as long as I could keep him confused and uncertain, I didn't have to find out the truth about myself, that I was just a crippled country girl with a talent for sculpting. I know I tormented him, but given the dilemma I was in there was nothing else I could do.

One night I had a nightmare that terrified me. I dreamed I was in a child-size buggy drawn by a huge horse. The animal bolted and dragged the cart up the side of a steep mountain until he approached the cliff of an abyss. He raced faster and faster as he neared the edge and was about to gallop off the precipice when I woke up screaming. The dream seemed so real that I wondered if Monsieur Lipscomb had such a large horse.

Then an unexpected turn of mind almost pushed me over the cliff. I was flooded with fantasies in all their dazzling details about what I wanted Rodin to do to me and what I wanted to do to him, and yearned more and more for our bodies to meet in the sweet embrace of love. The reveries took me over completely and continued night and day. For the first time in my life, I was unable to work. I was supposed to arrange for an exhibit of my work in England, but I couldn't concentrate. Thank goodness Jessie did it for me. I just sat in the Lipscomb's beautiful garden and daydreamed. Nor could I eat or sleep, and the pounds dropped off me like melting ice on a summer's day. Jessie's parents worried that I was sick.

The climax occurred with another dream I had shortly after the first one. I dreamed Rodin was making love to me. It moved me to such ecstasy that *I knew I would go ahead.* But I couldn't enjoy the sensation very long before I began to shiver. I was petrified that if we made love, I would disappear altogether. Being with him would become central in my life and would replace what was most important to me with what was most important to him, and there would be no more Camille Claudel. I would become his appendage at work, and be known, if at all, as his pupil and lover. All my creations would get lost in his. When he didn't deliberately take them over and say that he had done them, he might forget that they were my work and sell them as his own. I had sculpted all of his hands and his feet since I came to his studio, remember, and nobody even knew they were my work. Then I had an even greater fear, for my life itself. A great love is central to a person's being. What if I had him and then lost him? I didn't see how anyone could survive that kind of loss. For me, anyhow, losing a lover would mean insanity or death. There was no solution. I would die either from being taken over by him or disintegrate from losing him. Either way I couldn't win.

I learned that he was in as bad a shape as I was. An assistant at the *atelier* wrote me that Rodin was pale and wan, with deep circles under his eyes, that he too had lost weight, and was wandering around the streets all night long. He wrote pathetic letters to Jessie every day, begging her to get me to come see him. "Where were you last night?" he wrote. "You said you would come to the café and bring our dear young lady with you. I'm afraid we love her so much that we let her move us around like a checker." She showed me the letter, and I forbade her to answer it.

Nevertheless, part of me didn't trust him, as he recognized in this letter: "Camille, my beloved, why are you so suspicious of me? Why won't you acknowledge that I love you?" I suspected he was desperate that he couldn't have his way with me, and that as soon as I gave in, he would tire of me and drop me. And I was even more scared that he just wanted me around so he could copy my ideas. Although he complained that I didn't believe he loved me, he didn't believe I loved him, either. Even after we became involved sexually, it took him a long time to accept that I really loved him. It's apparent in the bust of him I sculpted around that time. His favorite portrait of himself, which earned a prize when it was exhibited a few years later at the 1892 Salon (and about time, too, that a woman won a Salon prize!) shows what he really felt about me. He looks sad, so sad—like the wary and skeptical peasant he was. He sank deep inside himself because he was so suspicious of everyone. The bust seems to be saying, "What are you trying to put over on me? Do you think I can make you successful? You say you love me, but I know you don't." It's very painful to be mistrusted, so I know how he felt.

Rodin got more and more frantic, until I received a letter which sounded as if it were written by one of the lunatics in this asylum. He said I was absolutely ruthless and had him so confused he could barely manage to get out of bed. He had spent the last night wandering all over town daydreaming about me. He wished he were dead, or could escape to some foreign country where he wouldn't have to be reminded of me at every turn, but no such place existed, as memories of me would haunt him wherever he might be. He begged and cajoled me to have sympathy for him, like a condemned prisoner pleading for his life. He cannot work, he cannot eat, he cannot sleep, he cannot laugh, he cannot sing, on the days he does not see me. Nothing interests him but me. "Please please please agree to see me every day," he pleaded, "as only you can cure my terminal illness." Then, like a true madman, he shifted his tone and said how happy he is to know me, that I've given meaning to his dreary life. And, would you believe, after that pathetic tale of woe he thanked me for his happiness!

He wrote like a lovesick boy demonstrating his neediness, not a potent man who was sure of himself. I was not impressed. In fact I was slightly amused that this man old enough to be my father was pleading with a mere girl. He insisted. He cried. He beseeched. He repeated how needy he was, as if by dwelling on it he could force me to love him. He reminded me of the seventeenth century poem by Sir John Suckling I read in Papa's library, *Why so Pale and Wan?*[8]

Why so pale and wan, fond lover?
Prithee, why so pale?
Will, when looking well can't move her,

looking ill prevail?
Prithee, why so pale?
Why so dull and mute, young sinner?
Prithee, why so mute?
Will, when speaking well can't win her,
Saying nothing do't?
Prithee, why so mute?
Quit, quit for shame This will not move;
This cannot take her.
If of herself she will not love,
The devil take he!

I'm afraid I wasn't very sympathetic. I felt that it was either him or me. Rodin, who was invited by a former student and friend of his to visit his home in London, followed us to England. Of course I was suspicious that Rodin had engineered the "invitation." Then Jessie invited him to visit us at Wootton House, an invitation he quickly accepted.

I was not at all happy about Rodin's visit, as I still hadn't made up my mind what to do about him, and decided I would punish Jessie for not consulting me before inviting him. She had a lovely voice and had just learned to sing some Scottish ballads, and was serenading us with them. I thought she couldn't bear that he loved me, and was trying to steal the spotlight. Rodin was sitting there enjoying the songs when I was filled with a rage so strong I lost all sense of judgment. I stood up and shouted, "Stop that, Jessie, I can't stand it another minute!" Jessie was shocked and stopped singing. There was an agonizing silence for a few moments. Then we all began to talk at once, trying to cover over the gaffe. The evening was ruined, of course. Rodin told Jessie that he knew it was wrong, "but our dear Camille is a very strong-willed lady."

The situation was driving me out of my mind. I decided to have it out with Rodin, whatever the consequences. I stopped him in the hall, as we were leaving the salon.

"Listen here, Monsieur Rodin," I said sternly. "I'm angry that you followed me to Jessie's house. I told you I needed time to think over our relationship."

Flushing like a scolded child, he answered, "No, dear one, I am sorry you are angry with me, but you are wrong. I did not follow you. My former student just happened to invite me at the same time that you were visiting."

He hesitantly laid his hand upon my shoulder. I roughly shook it off. "I don't believe you, Monsieur Rodin! Let me be! I will see you in the *atelier* when we get back to Paris."

"All right, sweet one," he said, panting like a dog begging for a bit of food at the dinner table. "I won't bother you again until we return."

But he didn't keep his word, of course, and kept deluging Jessie with letters imploring her to arrange a meeting with me.

I got away from Rodin again by going with Jessie to visit our studio partner, Amy Singer, at North Hill Cottage, her family home in the lovely town of Frome, which was built on the banks of the river in Somerset. Amy and I were never close friends, but I enjoyed meeting her family, especially her father, John Webb Singer. I was impressed that practically her whole family were involved in some form of art. Monsieur Singer, a professional clock-maker, was a wonderful man. He encouraged his children to be artists, helping his two sons to became fine silversmiths and his daughter Amy a sculptor. (Isn't it interesting how many of us women artists had supportive fathers? Me, Jessie, and Amy. That makes three, just in our little *atelier*. It does make one wonder whether it's the daughters or the fathers we should revere.) To my delight, Monsieur Singer was the founder of the Frome Art School, where young artists of the town could receive an excellent education in art, the Frome Art Metal works, and the local statue foundry. He carefully showed me through the foundry and taught me a great deal about metal casting, which I was to use years later when I supervised the work on my *L 'Age Mûr* sculpture. My stay in Frome was a nice hiatus in *l'affaire Rodin*, but it was soon over and I had to return to my dilemma.

My mother didn't make my decision any easier. She felt that only a "loose woman" would have sex with a man outside of marriage. (Sometimes I think she wasn't so sure about sex inside of marriage, either.) The only possibility of getting into her good graces was to marry Rodin and become a respectable housewife. It was hard for me to abandon the hope that she and Louise would accept me as a decent human being. It was not that I loved them so much, but their opinion of me sank deep down inside of me and taunted me where I needed my confidence the most. I still believed that if only Maman would love me, I could love myself, too.

After my affair with Rodin was *a fait accompli*, I had her invite Rodin and Rose, his paramour, to dinner. Maman never forgave me for "tricking" her into the invitation. She was furious that she had been "naive" enough to fall for the "trick" and invite the great man and his concubine, Madame Rodin, to sit right under her nose, when I was living with him as his mistress. For a change, she held back an insult to me, saying that she didn't dare say the words that came to her mind. She didn't have to. I knew what she was thinking. It *was* kind of funny to have my lover sitting right there under her nose, and her not suspecting it one bit, but I certainly paid dearly for my few moments of fun. She and Louise harangued me about it for the rest of their lives. I became a *persona non grata* in Villeneuve. My mother felt disgraced and shut her door against me. Louise, happy to find any reason to rationalize her hatred, looked upon me with renewed contempt. Paul had recently become a devout Catholic, and naturally was of no help. Only Papa was there with his devotion and a little money once in a while. Mostly, I paid no attention to Maman's hateful remarks, as I had decided when I was very young that if I let her get to me all the time, I'd never be able to think of anything else. But one nasty crack she flung at me about Rodin hurt me badly. She shrieked, "You're just 'the other woman' in his life, and ruining his relationship with his wife!" *I* was not "the other woman." *Rose* was. *I* was the one Rodin really loved.

One reason I could pull the wool over the eyes of my parents was that Rodin was so much older than I that people never dreamed we might be lovers. Jessie and her friends, who of course knew about the romance, teased me that Rodin was so old, they called him *Grandpère* behind his back. "And have you seen *Grandpère* today?" They'd laughingly sing. I didn't pay any attention to them, but went right on with my sculpting. The age difference didn't bother me at all. After all, I had a father who was eighteen years older than my mother, and I never heard anyone mention that he was too old for her.

*I*n 1886, Jessie introduced me to an English friend of hers who was visiting Paris, a Miss Florence Jeans. She was to become a dear friend, and I would experience with her the most beautiful and the least conflicted relationship of my life. She came to the *atelier* to visit Jessie, and stayed to give me a few English lessons. I always love anyone who has something to teach me, so our relationship started off in a promising way. When she invited me to visit her at her family home on the Isle of Wight, I was delighted to accept, although my parents were astonished that a French girl like me would not be afraid to undertake such a long and laborious trip alone. I took lots of paper and charcoal with me to draw as many sketches as I could of the sea.

At Portsmouth I took a ferry, where I exuberantly stood at the front of the ship and rode up and down with the waves. I didn't want to miss a moment of the trip or an ounce of the delicious sea spray. I was the only one on board who didn't get seasick. The ferry took me to Shanklin on the Isle of Wight, where Florence stood waiting for me at the dock, her hair loosened and blown about by the wind. When I saw her, I took off my hat and waved it wildly. When she merrily waved back I knew right away that my stay would be one of the best months of my life. The Jeans lived in a charming little house at the foot of a cliff, right by the sea, which was a perfect setting for my mood. The delicious air on the Isle of Wight filled me with pleasure. It's exceptionally fresh and sweet smelling, and I imagine that everyone who comes to visit leaves a stronger and healthier person. That certainly was true for me, where I felt better than I ever had in my life. The weather was fine, and there were really good views over the English Channel. Florence said that on a clear day, you can see all the way to France. I guess the day we went there was not all that clear. The island is famous for fossils of dinosaur bones, which I excitedly studied and sketched, so I could understand how the huge lumbering creatures balanced themselves. Florence sat there watching me, smiling indulgently at my childlike pleasure. Then we went to Shanklin Chine, one of her favorite spots on the island. There's a garden of exotic plants in a ravine leading to the beach, which ends with a majestic forty-foot waterfall. It made me marvel at the beauties of Nature, and to wonder what possible importance my little sculptures could have, compared to them.

We visited Queen Victoria's home at Osborne House, which is full of portraits of the Queen. I must admit that one of the things that impressed me the most about the place was how much the Queen in her portraits resembled Maman. We learned that Queen Victoria and Prince Albert had bought Osborne House and its thousand acres about twenty-two years ago. The home, which is really a castle, was a wonderful retreat for the royal couple. They loved the Isle of Wight, which was far away from the pressures of court life at Buckingham Palace and Windsor Castle. After Albert died in 1862, (two years before I was born) the Queen continued to find the home a refuge. I don't know if I could do that. I think it would hurt me too much to be alone in places my loved one and I had enjoyed together.

I was happy to explore Carisbrooke Castle, which I proudly interpreted to Florence through the eyes of Rodin, who taught me so much about architecture. I pointed out that the oldest part is a Norman *motte* and bailey—a stone shell built on a mound, with a curtain wall round a courtyard. There's also a well, with a tread wheel worked by donkeys, and a gatehouse, with twin drum towers. A fortification which was built in the 1590s as a defense against a threatened Spanish invasion encloses the castle. With its long straight walls and arrowhead bastions, it was designed for use with cannons. Florence said that I helped her see the castle in a whole new light, although she had been there many times before. I couldn't help thinking of Rodin all the time we were there, and of how much he would have enjoyed seeing it. Not that I missed him all that much, as by this time I was quite attached to Florence.

We had a lot of fun in Shanklin in the evenings. Jessie, her fiancé William Elborne, and Paul and two friends of his came over to the island before I left, and we had a great time playing games. One of them was answering questions. If you refused to answer, you gained points, and the one with the most points was the loser. I answered all of mine, mostly in a carefree, jaunty manner which really didn't say very much. Paul asked, "Of all the artists in the world, past and present, which one do you think is the best?" Without missing a beat, I answered, "Me!" Jessie wanted to know who my favorite fictional character was, and I said, "Lady Macbeth." That was only half a joke. When she asked me why I chose her, I said that I was ambitious like the Lady, and there was little I wouldn't do to get what I wanted. When William asked what my favorite occupation was, I said, "Doing nothing." I was really clowning around with that one. How would I know? I was never doing nothing!

Somebody questioned me about my favorite historical figure, and I said, "They're all obnoxious." Everybody laughed as though I had said the wittiest thing in the world. Paul's friend, who was making eyes at me, grilled me on my favorite food and drink. I surprised him by answering, "Love and wine." I think I scared him away. And when I was asked what shortcoming I had the most tolerance for, I answered, "I have all the tolerance in the world for my own shortcomings, and none at all for those in other people." Then Florence asked what were my favorite qualities in a woman, and was alarmed when I answered, 'To know how to infuriate your husband!' I don't think that was what she wanted to hear. So I'll tell you now, dear Florence, my favorite qualities in a woman were those I saw personified in you. And Florence, you were the loser! You wouldn't answer my question of what your favorite fantasy was.

We watched the most magnificent sunsets, one from a jetty in Yarmouth and one looking towards Tennyson's Monument on Tennyson Downs. But best of all was the morning we dragged ourselves out of bed at 5 a.m. to watch the sunrise from a pier in Shanklin. The moment the sun rose above the horizon and lit up the world with its magnificent rays we silently turned to each other and hugged. I loved it when you said, "See where the rays of the sun are pouring through that open space in the clouds? That's the voice of God coming down to us from the heavens." My eyes filled with tears at the splendor of the tableau and the rare joy of being with a friend I loved. Of the few close friends I've had in my lifetime, I cared for Florence the most. The quality of love an adolescent girl feels for an older friend is extremely intense. I've always loved Paul and was to come to love Rodin passionately and deeply. But the time Florence and I spent together was a time apart, a dream come true for a maturing young woman who really had no mother to guide her. Somehow, I was able to tell Florence things I couldn't tell Rodin, Jessie, or even Paul. Perhaps it's because she listened so intently to every word I said, as if no more interesting person had ever lived, and was so accepting of all my faults. I think if I had said, "Florence, I want to kill my mother." she would have answered, "she must have done plenty to deserve it." Then too, I've always loved my teachers. She was teaching me English and I worked hard to learn it for her, although I must say my progress was not spectacular.

When I got home, I missed Florence terribly, and couldn't believe I wouldn't see her or the ocean and the magnificent scenery of Shanklin anymore. I thought I saw her in the bedroom, on the beach, in town, everywhere I went, and found it hard to accept that it was only figments of my imagination. Life was boring and empty without her. I cried like a baby all the way from Shanklin to Southampton, and was afraid to think about her any more lest I start bawling again. My brother mocked me and said he was going to cry too, because he had fallen in love with the Jeans' fat kitchen maid and wanted to marry her. He wasn't very funny.

We left Florence in Shanklin at four-thirty and had to wait five disagreeable hours in Southampton for the boat. I was happy to fall asleep to help pass the time. The ocean was very rough, and it took us eleven hours to cross the Channel instead of the usual nine. To my delight, the soaring waves didn't bother me, and neither Paul nor I got seasick at all. I slept well all night, except when William Elborne, Jessie's beau, threw up. When I arrived at Le Havre, I was disgruntled to learn that the train for Paris had already left, and we were obliged to wait seven more hours for the next one. To make matters worse, I'd forgotten to register my luggage, and when we got to Paris, no one could find it. I didn't know if it ever would show up, which upset me dreadfully, as all my sketches of the Island of Wight were in it. It was especially troubling because the trunk didn't close firmly, and William had tied it up with twine. It was still half open, and anyone could have reached inside and stolen the drawings. Fortunately, the trunk showed up, and all my sketches were intact. Of course, I worried then that nobody thought them good enough to steal. The trip ended with a good tongue-lashing from my brother about my carelessness. Just what I needed to complete the exhausting day. I really didn't want to be home, and longed to be with Florence at Shanklin, where we could take magical walks at night under the moon and watch the luminescent black boats leave winding troughs through the sea.

To hold on to the summer, when I got home I wrote down many of the wonderful memories I had of my stay in Shanklin and sent it to Florence.

"Do you remember, dear Florence," I wrote, "the luminous night you couldn't sleep and woke me at three in the morning to go swimming under the stars? We swam in perfect accord through the clear cold ocean. When we came out we dropped onto the damp sand and remained silent in a wild mixture of happiness and sadness. I ran for miles against the stormy wind, and returned to find you appearing in the distance, profiled against the sky. Then we walked for hours, our heads bent against the wind, our steps in perfect rhythm with every crash of the surf. The night walks by the sea were the most beautiful of all, accompanied by the celestial orchestra of the sea and the night, as the waves smashed against the jetty and the wind swished through the air. We traced the pattern of silvery moonbeams on the water, and memorized the cliffs and the sea. Then I tried to memorize your face, so I could keep it with me always.

"Remember the night you said you had only ashes left, and trusted me with the bitterest parts of your life? You asked me never to tell anyone what you had told me. I promised I would keep faith with you, and never reveal what you said to anyone. And I won't.

"But the memory I treasure the most is the day I gave you my sketch of you inscribed, "In memory of a smile, a sigh—and a tear." You put your head on my shoulder and said, 'Who'd ever have thought it would be like this?' It was then I knew the friendship wasn't one-sided and you cared for me as much as I did you. You embraced me then, both of us in tears, and your dear smell of lavender and rose petals enclosed us both. I felt loved and protected, as I never had before in my life. And weren't we lucky that day to find not one but two four-leaf clovers gleaming in the sunshine? I will keep mine forever.

"Remember right before I left when we were sitting in our bedroom and I said, 'Florence, I'm scared! I'm afraid our friendship won't be the same when we're not together.' You took my hands in yours and said, 'How could we ever forget one another? Even when we're miles apart for years, I'm sure we would only have to look at each other to know things will always be the same.' Because I loved you, I believed you…

"Thanks for our beautiful summer, my dear friend, the loveliest of my life.

Camille

We enjoyed writing to each other for several years, although in the beginning it took some prodding to get her to answer my letters, and then later the same was true of me. As such things go, Florence married and had children, and I became more and more preoccupied with my work, and we gradually grew further and further apart. In 1887 I wrote her seven times, in 1888 four letters, and in 1889 only three. After that we didn't communicate with each other for four years.

In 1893, I was overjoyed to receive an invitation from Florence to come visit her and her new family in Shanklin. Remembering the joy I'd experienced in her company, I accepted the offer with pleasure. But as the wise man said, you never stand in the same river twice. My stay was pleasant enough, but the magic was gone from our relationship, like a played-out love affair. I sculpted the bust of her husband, Monsieur Back, but we really didn't care for each other. I didn't like the bust very much, either. It has a grouchy expression, just like his. He and the children and I fought all the time for Florence's attention. Walking on the beach with a couple is quite different from walking alone with your dearest friend. Unlike my visit seven years before, I was happy to leave, and suspect Florence was just as pleased to see me go. This time I didn't cry at all. Florence must have felt the same way about my visit as I did, for we never contacted each other again. When I got home I burnt up all her letters that I hadn't destroyed before, to get rid of embarrassing material. Why does the bubble always burst? Why can't I maintain my love for anyone permanently? Is there something everybody but me knows about keeping a relationship going? How do other people manage to stay close, or are they just faking it, like Maman and Papa? It's sad but true that "Man proposes and God disposes." Only Paul do I continue to love, no matter what he does or says.

*S*peaking of Paul, it's strange that he suddenly became so devout. When he was eighteen years old, during Vespers on Christmas Day at the Cathedral de Notre-Dame, he suddenly had a vision. In it, a voice from on high said, "God exists." This religious revelation became the motivating force of Paul's world and the power behind his creativity. He saw God as the producer and director of the drama of the universe, who selected mankind to play the leading role in His production. Every play, poem, or letter that Paul wrote after that reflected his newly-discovered philosophy, as did all his actions. I was not too happy about his conversion, as it took us farther and farther apart.

Unfortunately for our relationship, I was not the least bit interested in Catholicism at the time, as I knew it would move me away from the path of freedom of thought, feeling, and action that I wanted to follow. The Catholic Church is very beautiful and soothing, and I envied Paul, who partakes of its gifts so often. And I'm sure, too, that the religion helps many people with more limited horizons than mine to follow the straight and narrow. But I could not in good faith be a Catholic, because the religion claims to be infallible and the ultimate authority on just about everything, and relentlessly enforces a discipline I did not believe in or want. Come to think of it, the Catholic Church is exactly like Maman. Odd that she was not a practicing Catholic. You'd think she would love the religion. But I suppose she never would have accepted any authority but her own, not even God's. Paul and I sought unsuccessfully for a while to convert each other. But like the horse that's brought to water but can't be forced to drink, the attempts to influence each other's religious beliefs didn't work, and we soon learned to leave the question of the existence of God out of our communications.

It's funny about brothers and sisters. Rodin had a sister, Maria, with whom he was every bit as close as I was to Paul. Three years older than Auguste, she looked after and took care of him. The two looked almost like twins, with the same piercing gaze, deep blue eyes, long nose, large mouth, and protruding chin. Jean Rodin, their father, constantly grumbled that he refused to have an artist for a son, saying "They're shiftless, worthless bums I would not have in my house!" (Sounds familiar, doesn't it.) Despite his opposition, Maria's quiet insistence and the extra money she was earning enabled Auguste to enter the 'Little School," The School of the Decorative Arts. Feeling that he wasn't learning anything, Auguste urged his parents to allow him to change to the Beaux-Arts School, known as the "Great School," but his father wouldn't hear of it. Maria came to his rescue once more, and managed to meet the famous sculptor Hippolyte Maidron, who had created a statue in Luxembourg Gardens. Somehow she convinced him to look at her brother's work. Maidron was awestruck by the boy's drawings, and told *pére* Rodin that his son was a genius and would become one of the greatest artists in France. Still unconvinced, the boy's father reluctantly gave in, and allowed Auguste to compete for a place at the "Great School." Rodin took the entrance examination three times, and failed each time. Although this was the first of a lifetime of rejections by conventional sculptors, Rodin later felt it was for the best, and many of the better French sculptors agreed with him. According to one of his colleagues, Jules Dalou, "Rodin was fortunate enough to be turned down by the "Great School."

Maria had a quiet depth of soul that sustained her brother in his times of need. Throughout the long years of weariness and poverty, Rodin turned to his sister for his only comfort. She had the gift of being totally present for her brother whenever he needed her, and that quality of absolute support and love could always bring him out of his despair. He kept her portrait by his bedside all his life.

Like Maria, I've always been a person who threw myself with all my heart into whatever I was doing. For both of us, the moment was forever. It's no coincidence that she and I served the same function for Rodin.

Rodin had a close friend, a painter named Arthur Barnouvin, who frequently came to visit the Rodins. Auguste was thrilled to watch Maria and his friend fall in love. Barnouvin began to join the family on their Sunday outings through the parks and groves along the Seine, and the whole family, even the grumpy father, was delighted at the thought of a betrothal. As a gift to the family, Barnouvin began to paint the portraits of brother and sister. While doing so, he might have decided that Maria was not pretty enough for his taste, too disturbed a person, or even more likely, that she reminded him too much of Rodin for him to stay comfortably involved with her. Whatever the reason, Barnouvin stopped visiting the family and married another woman. Maria, who had fallen deeply in love with him, was mortally wounded. Auguste threatened to find the painter and beat him up, but Maria refused to allow it. The good woman said that Barnouvin was simply a light-hearted artist who had loved her, laughed with her, and left her, and that he couldn't help being a shallow person.

In despair, Maria joined a convent and prepared to serve a two-year novitiate as Sister Saint-Euthyme. She never finished her term. About half a year into it, she fell ill of peritonitis and came home at age twenty-four to die. I can understand that well. I do not think she died of peritonitis at all, even if she had the symptoms. What really killed her was a broken heart. Such a calamity would kill me, too, and for all practical purposes, did.

Auguste was devastated, and wanted to die along with her. At her funeral he found a bit of consolation in putting a locket with their two portraits in her coffin. For months he walked in sorrow through Paris, his unfocused eyes glazed in misery. His family and friends feared for his sanity, and that he would take his own life. In desperation, his devout mother turned to the parish priest around the corner for advice. He recommended that Auguste join the monastery of the Fathers of the Holy Sacrament, a new religious institution on the rue du Fauberg Saint-Jacques. With no desires of his own and unable to work, Rodin decided to follow in his sister's footsteps and turn to the Church. As Maria had done, he prepared to undertake a two year novitiate, to be followed with an oath which would make him a monk of the Holy Order. Fortunately, Father Pierre-Julien Eymard, the wise founder and Father Superior of the Order, intuited Rodin's true vocation. As the Holy Father watched the gifted youth passionately work on figures of the saints and holy ornaments for the monastery, he understood that Rodin was unsuited for the Church and that it was necessary for him to return to his God-given calling. With the tact of a great priest, Father Eymard asked Rodin to sculpt his bust, so it could remain after his death in the monastery.

Although Rodin was only twenty-two when he molded it, the finished bust was one of his greatest works, and he was able to leave the solace of his beloved priest and the monastery to return to the artistic world. Rodin kept a cast of the bust in his studio ever after.

In the attempt to master his grief, Rodin sculpted a statue called *Brother and Sister,* which speaks of the great love he and Maria had for each other. A nude adolescent girl is clasping her baby brother on her lap and tenaciously hugging him to her body. A blissful, loving expression lights up her face. All the tenderness Maria felt for little Auguste, as I did for *le petit Paul,* is carved into her face and figure, while the little fellow is cleaving onto the sister he undoubtedly considered his own private person. As if I had any question about it, Rodin told me that the touching statue was a memorial to Maria.

It's uncanny how closely the relationship between Paul and me paralleled theirs. It seems our lives as siblings prepared us for each other. In spite of my youth, I was like an older sister to Rodin, and he behaved like my younger brother, no matter what our real ages were. Like Maria, I was said to tyrannize him, just as I did Paul. Maria and I both valued our independence and were headstrong and stubborn about reaching our goals. Like me, she was always giving him advice. She was his conscience, his muse, his advisor, his comforter. As was I. She supported him against their father, worked to help pay for his lessons, and believed in his genius when no one else did. Like his sister, I looked after Rodin, and made sure he took care of himself and got the acclaim he deserved. I often had to pacify him, as when the citizens of Calais kept hounding him about finishing *The Burghers of Calais,* the group statue they had commissioned in 1884. It's true that the sculpture took until 1895 for him to erect, but to his credit, he would not be rushed, and insisted that creativity runs on its own timetable. When ignorant critics belittled his sculptures, I alone was able to reassure him that he was the greatest sculptor in Europe and that the critics knew nothing about art. I told him that standards of art will change, that what critics revere today they will turn up their noses at next week, and that his art will help to create that change. Besides, I would say, there's always tomorrow and the start of a newborn day. He believed me because he knew I was honest and direct, and never, never lied. At the peak of our passion, he rarely made a move about anything important to him without consulting me.

Rodin had a quality of utter simplicity and goodness that made you give him anything he wanted. He had the soul of a beautiful child. It still makes me smile that I sometimes called this aging man more than twice my age *"Mon petit garçon."* My body also reminded Rodin of Maria, in that we had the same long legs, slim hips, and rosy breasts. When she went to visit her aunt Annette Hilldiger, Rodin asked Maria to write every day. "A sister who is far away is loved twice as much," he wrote her. "A faraway lover, too," he might have added. He never recovered from Maria's death. As long as I knew him he cried every time he mentioned her. Nor did he ever really get over his love for me. I suspect that when he found me, he rediscovered his sister, and that when he lost me, he lost Maria all over again.

Sometimes I wonder how Rodin healed enough from his grief to go on living. If I had lost Paul at age twenty-one, I think I would have died along with him. There's something about such a loss at that age which would have made survival impossible for me. Young adulthood is the time when we're setting our course for the future and preparing for the long journey ahead. We choose careers, get married, have children. That's when our philosophy of life solidifies. Losing the one you love most at that stage of life means that all is lost forever and there's no hope for the future. I could never have let myself be even as successful as I was, with Paul in the grave. I would have been too filled with guilt that I survived and he did not. It would have made the knowledge of my own mortality too real to tolerate. Such an excruciating loss brings home with a terrible force the lines from Swinburne's poem, *The Garden of Proserpine*, "…that no man lives forever/ that even the weariest river/ winds somewhere home to sea."[9] Yes, if Paul had died when I was twenty-one, there would have been no reason to go on living. I most certainly would have killed myself.

*I*n 1888 while I was still ruminating about Rodin, I met a nice young composer named Claude Debussy at the home of his friend, Robert Godet, who regularly invited both Debussy and me to his house. He was a dark young man with two large pointed lumps on each side of his forehead.

I was twenty-four years old and Claude twenty-six. I was frightened at the intensity of my feelings for Rodin, and wanted to see if I could dilute my love for him by becoming involved with another man. It helped that Rodin hated Debussy's music, and I hoped that my interest in him would arouse Rodin to a jealous frenzy. When Robert introduced me to this short, thickset man with an undulating gait, I thought, "Uh-uh, I don't think so!" Then Claude told Godet that he was immediately attracted to me, because he sensed that I had an extraordinary gift of intimacy that came from a place deep inside me. What woman could resist such flattery, especially at a time when I was particularly distressed about Rodin?

Debussy was a young, unmarried man only two years older than me, and I thought, "I'll bet this one would marry me!" His youth was a welcome change at first, for much as I loved Rodin, something in me had hungered for a casual playmate and the touch of a youthful skin. Debussy was a quiet, uncommunicative man, who never talked about himself, except for an unpleasant habit of grumbling about the weather, inconveniences, the fact that he had no money, the food, and anything else that happened to displease him. He had few friends, and most of the friendships he had didn't last; they either spiraled down to nothingness or disintegrated into disdain.

Claude was even particular about who he talked to. When he was introduced to someone new, he would keep a straight face until he decided whether it was worth his while to bother to know the person, so I was flattered that he was interested in me. He disliked parties altogether, and said that making small talk over the hor-d'oeuvres was his idea of forced labor. He even resented greeting people in the street, so he usually didn't. (I don't like to either, but I usually try to say hello anyway. At least I did when I lived with real people, and not these miserable caricatures of human beings who wouldn't know if I said hello or not.) Many people disliked him. Even his godfather Achille-Antoine Arosa, said that he couldn't stand Claude's "distant manner" and referred to him as a lout and a libertine. He was a person who was always bored, and I guess I was one of the few people who didn't bore him. He said I livened him up.

We had fun together, and I enjoyed his delicious sense of humor. One day when we were walking along the river holding hands, he said with a straight face, "Why is music the only art identified with religion? How come angels play the harp but never paint or sculpt?" We both laughed until our stomachs hurt, as I did with Paul when we were little. Claude was a wonderful mimic, and did devastating imitations of actors, singers, and politicians. He also had a gift for the colorful turn of a phrase. He once said to me that "compared to mine, the life of a convict is one of frivolity and extravagance." I knew what he meant. Once when he told me about music he had written and dropped for a dissonant trumpet, he said, "I am skeptical about the extraordinary." I loved that he named a wastepaper basket "the graveyard of worthless dreams." He was very playful, *un grand enfant*, one of those people who never grow up. I'm not a musician, but I think his impishness showed in his music, as in *Golliwog's Cakewalk*, which always makes me smile. When he chose, Claude could be the life of the party.

He liked my simplicity and lack of guile. It's true that I speak what's on my mind, so you always know where you stand with me, but I must say that not everybody agrees with him. Life would be much simpler if they did. In my opinion, you might as well speak the truth, because people always know what you mean anyhow. Perhaps Claude's natural reserve was why he preferred improvising music to talking. "Music is made for what cannot be expressed in words," he said. I sat motionless while he settled himself at the piano for hours and played whatever came into his head. One time, he played so long that his hands were frozen stiff. I put my arm around him and said as I walked him to the fireplace, "I have no words, Monsieur Debussy." He was very moved, and said that he had never had a more priceless compliment. We always talked about art and music, and helped each other grow.

Claude had a tremendous influence on several of my works. I'm practically tone deaf, and thought I hated music until I met Claude. I don't anymore. He taught me whatever I know about it, so I can imagine what it's like to play as he does, perhaps as I feel when sculpting. Claude inspired me to model one of my greatest successes, *La Valse (The Waltz)* in which a man and a woman lovingly surrender to the whirling rhythm of the music. Just as Rodin and I were one with our art and our love, so the waltzing couple become part of the music and each other. I was particularly pleased with this statue, because the spiraling movement of the dancers allows the work to be viewed equally well from all sides.

I particularly wanted a commission from the State for *La Valse* so I could sculpt it in marble. To me, a statue is not complete until it is carved in marble, which is different from all other materials used in sculpting. It captures the light and makes the figures seem to glow from within. It gives an ethereal luminous quality, approaching that of religious ecstasy. In my opinion, marble statues capture live human beings at their most beautiful. I petitioned the Minister of Fine Arts for a commission, but my request was denied. When the group[10] was finished, I wrote him again requesting a marble commission, and included the fact that several major artists, including Rodin, had found it excellent. The Minister responded by sending Inspector Dayot to investigate my claim. Unfortunately, Monsieur Dayot was as prejudiced against women artists as other men of the times. He reported to the Minister of Fine Arts that although the details of the group were magnificently carried out, the sculpture could not be considered for a commission. According to him, the sex organs of the dancers were too close to each other's bodies and were emphasized by their complete nudity. He gave me a choice of forgetting about the commission or changing the objectionable details. I wanted the commission (and the marble) badly, so I changed the details.

What twisted morality we French have! It's all right to sculpt a man in the nude, but woe to any sculptor, particularly if she's a female, who dares to portray a naked woman! I spent the summer working on draperies which would hide the terrible sin of nudity without disguising the motion of the dancers. I fooled the officials by following the letter if not the spirit of their laws. I draped the woman in such a manner that her body is displayed as much as if she were naked, in a robe that swirls around her legs to follow the movement of the dance. If anything, the addition of the gauzy draperies makes the sculpture more, not less erotic. I laughed when Jules Renard said in my *atelier* that "The couple looked as if they were about to lie down and finish the dance by making love."

Although *La Valse* received many complimentary reviews, Léon

Daudet gave it what is perhaps the loveliest critique of all, which almost made all my sacrifices seem worthwhile. He wrote in *Germinal* that although the beautiful naked bodies clasped in each other's arms are imprisoned in stone, they give the impression that they are whirling about furiously. A dress or gauzy robe curls around them and forms spirals in the air which trace their movement, as one can deduce the path of a comet by observing its tail or recognize courageous cavalries by the particles of dust that surround them. To my great pleasure, Daudet wrote that "Only a great artist like Camille Claudel could make the invisible visible, as the bodies of the waltzers speak to us and transport us in their mobile shroud. The *chef-d'oeuvre*[11] carries us away from our boredom with life and this dismal planet up through space in a dance of love and hope. We turn as the world turns," he continues in words that I love, "and our waltz follows that of the atoms, for we ourselves are merely pitiful atoms, little bits of dust in the tempest. But until some catastrophe detaches us from life, let us merge with the hurricane and turn and pivot until our headlong spiral blends into that of the universe."

Despite the acclaim *La Valse* received, and my agreeing to clothe the figures, the sculpture had dared to enter an arena forbidden to women, that of the erotic. In the philosophy of the day, "good" women experienced no sexual feelings. Therefore, either I was not a good woman or I was rendering an untruth. According to the state, neither alternative deserves to be immortalized in marble. My request was put on hold and I never received my commission. Nevertheless, the raves of the critics enabled me to make several copies in reduced size, one of which found its home on top of Claude Debussy's piano.

Because of what Claude taught me about music I also was able to sculpt *The Blind Old Musician* and one of my favorite statues, *The Siren* or *The Joy of the Flute*, a young woman who's so consumed by her flute playing that she's lost all sense of time and outer space. Her eyes look deep into a hidden world, as she fights to reveal it in her art. With body arched, she reaches aloft with the music. Her head is lifted high, as if she would send the sounds to the very heavens. Her robe floats upward like angel wings. Every part of her naked body is fueled with sensation. She sits quivering in creation, as her sensual lips and gently loving fingers make love to the music. I wish I could play the flute like *The Siren*, which is why I gave her my face.

In return for his musical tutoring, I helped Claude develop his visual sense. If I'm not mistaken, it shows in the music he wrote after we met, like his exquisite *Clair de la Lune*. He told me he worked differently after meeting me, and that I taught him to look at pictures the way he listened to music.

Sometimes I wish I were a musician like Claude instead of a sculptor. I did make one aborted attempt at playing the violin when I was about seven or eight years old. Some church people sent an orchestra for young children to the Sunday School, and the rector invited Papa to bring Louise and me to their concert. I had never heard classical music before. The violinist played a short piece and I was enchanted. I went home to Papa and said, "I need a violin, Papa. I must have a violin!" He signed me up at the church for some free lessons. There were fifteen kids in the class, and the rector lent some of us violins. Unfortunately, I was busy drawing the music teacher and was hung up on his moustache, when I should have been paying more attention to what he was saying. I'm afraid that when I practiced I didn't sound much like the violinist in church. Papa left the house when I began to play. He was ecstatic when I decided to stop. He was right; my violin career was short lived. It was another story with Louise. Papa was pleased when she took piano lessons at the church. I'll have to admit that I was jealous, because I was always the one whose artistic gifts he was most proud of. But her musical "career"didn't last very long, either. Louise gradually gave up her music, which left Papa badly disappointed. And I, of course, gloated about it.

Speaking of my lack of musical talent, a funny incident happened when a fellow musician gave Claude some free tickets at the Opera House for *Cavalleria Rusticana*. I found myself enjoying it, especially one aria that enchanted me, that I kept humming. Claude heard me droning on and on and began laughing.

I said, "What's so funny?"

He answered, "Do you know what you're singing?"

I said, "No, what is it?"

He said, "You're celebrating Christ's arising from the dead. 'We will sing of the Lord now victorious…Let us sing of the Christ ever glorious; He is risen, in glory, to reign. Praise the Lord!' Some atheist you are!"

"Well, it *is* beautiful," I said. Then we both burst out laughing.

Claude and I had a lot in common artistically. Each of us was largely self-taught (he never went to a formal school at all until he entered the Conservatoire in 1872, where his unwillingness to follow directions gained him a reputation as an outcast and pariah) and believed that the source of all good art is within us. "If we just wait to hear the inward voice," he said, "creativity will always come." He listened to his inner music, as I did my inner visions, and followed only what was essential. We shared the belief that one must not hurry creative work, as the unconscious cannot be rushed. Both of us were atheists. Although he had no use for religious dogma, he kept the faith with his music, as I did with my art.

We shared many opinions on artists, as well. Neither one of us cared much for the Impressionists, but we adored Degas, admired Clouet, and spent many sensational hours pouring over the works of Katsushika Hokusai. I was deeply moved by *The Great Wave* and similar paintings, which may have inspired me years later to sculpt *La Vague*. But it was his fantastic fifteen volume *Hokusai Mangwa*, in which he sketched animals, plants, scenery, historical and supernatural figures, and demons and monsters like *Le Gèyn*, that utterly absorbed us for months. They were the stuff my dreams were made of for many months thereafter. His exquisite landscapes and bird and flower prints did not keep abominable critics from massacring him, however, and calling him vulgar, childish, and under-developed. When I saw what they did to Hokusai, I didn't feel so bad about some of the "critiques" I've gotten.

I can't continue without saying a few more words about Hokusai, because his philosophy that the older one gets the more creative one becomes, puts my life to shame. He said that none of the work he did before the age of fifty was any good, and that he didn't even count anything as a work of art that he had painted before he was seventy years old. He said it was only when he reached the age of seventy-three that he began to understand the structure of human bodies and the functioning of animals and plants. By the time he was eighty-six, Hokusai believed he would have made great progress, and by ninety will have approached the meaning of truth and the quintessence of art. When he got to be one hundred, every line and brush stroke of his would come alive. "Oh God, grant me but ten more years," Hokusai prayed, "and I will become a great artist." Perhaps it was Hokusai's will to grow that accounted in part for the fact that he lived and worked to the age of eighty-nine. Just think what I could have created, if I had shared his philosophy of the extraordinary flowering of genius in old age! I could have been the greatest sculptor who ever lived. I wish I'd had his will to grow.

Debussy and I each, in our art, were absorbed with matters of childhood and with death. We were alike in other ways, too. We both were poor and had little money to waste. We agreed that although the arts are not lucrative professions they are divine ones, and despite our poverty we considered ourselves fortunate to be part of them. Our time together was spent taking long walks by the river, hiking in the hills, and browsing through the mysterious world of Bailley's Bookshop. We spent hours there reciting Edgar Allen Poe's poetry to each other. My favorite was "Annabel Lee" who "loved with a love that was more than a love," which is the way I love, too. And once in a while, when we had enough money, we paid a visit to Le Chat Noir, where we had a drink or two or sometimes more. I agree with Aeschylus, who said, "Bronze is the mirror of the form; wine, of the heart."

Then too, we each had a physical defect. I walk with a slight limp. Claude, who had been a fat boy at ten, was still short and chunky as an adult, and never got over being awkward and clumsy. That made two of us. We must have been quite a pair, walking down the street together!

We both experienced problems with our mothers. Madame Debussy didn't like children, and remained apart from them as much as possible. She even shipped off two of them to her sister-in-law to raise. Unlike his siblings, she taught Claude at home until he was ten years old. Although he had been singled out by her for this "honor," he didn't much appreciate it. According to him, his mother wanted him with her all the time and was a noose around his neck. I don't believe it. I think she probably kept him at home because she understood her son and knew that he would be a misfit and a trouble-maker at school. She was a very harsh disciplinarian, who, unlike my mother, often slapped her children. (Thank God for small favors!)

Although we had much in common, we had one major difference which contributed to our break-up. I was a hard worker, and spent all my free time trying to achieve the perfect sculpture. Claude, on the other hand, didn't like to work hard, and passed many days sitting in a chair and daydreaming. In the beginning, when our relationship was new and exciting, he was the only one I allowed to tear me away from my *atelier*. But as time passed, my excitement about knowing him diminished and the obsession with work pulled me back into it. Many was the time Claude wanted to be with me and I wanted only to sculpt, which left him unhappy and angry. I also didn't like his "wandering eye," and that telling the truth was not a matter of great importance to him. I questioned his morality in other respects too, like keeping his word only when he felt like it. But most important, he was in love with me and wanted more than I could give him. The "romance" wasn't working for me, for despite all my attempts to forget Rodin, I loved him, not Debussy. So although I'm glad I knew him, in the end I left him. I felt bad about hurting him, but as the Bible says, the spirit moves as it will, and no one can consciously direct it. Nor has anyone yet discovered how to resuscitate a dead friendship. Years later, I was told that my statue of *La Valse* remained on top of Claude's mantelpiece all his life.

While I was in England, Rodin dealt with his *angst* by molding a magnificent marble statue of me called *The Danaid*. I had posed for some sketches before we went to London, thinking it was for another sculpture, and was taken by surprise with the magnificent *Danaid*. The name is from an ancient Greek myth about murder and love. Bellus I, who inherited the kingdom of Egypt, had many children, among them Danaus I and Aegyptus I. The two brothers quarreled about the division of the kingdom. It just so happened that Danaus had fifty daughters and Aegyptus fifty sons. The sons demanded to be wedded to the daughters of Danaus, all of whom were very beautiful. Danaus objected to the marriages, but was afraid to refuse his powerful brother. Instead, he allowed his daughters to marry the sons, but secretly gave each young woman a sharp knife. "On your wedding night," he told them, "kill your husbands with these knives so that you can escape from these undesirable marriages." All the brides except Hypermnestra obeyed their father's command. As a punishment for the murders, the remaining forty-nine Danaids were sentenced in hell for eternity to fill up a leaking jar with water carried in a sieve.

Rodin dedicated *The Danaid* to me. I still don't know whether he saw me as one of the forty-nine Danaids who killed their husbands or as Hypermnestra, the only one who didn't commit murder and lived happily ever after with her bridegroom. Or maybe he saw me as both.

I thought *The Danaid* was the loveliest sculpture I'd ever seen. I loved the beautiful curve of its body that made me want to stroke it, its purity, its whiteness as if it were sculpted in the moonlight. I was deeply moved that he had dedicated the exquisite work to me. But pulled as I was to be loved by him, my fear and doubts persisted and I still hadn't made up my mind if I wanted to be his lover. Then a strange thing happened which solved my dilemma, so that no thought was necessary.

It was dusk when I came upon him in the *atelier*. He was standing silently at the window, leaning onto it with his back against the sky. In the twilight his face had a strange, quiet beauty, an almost luminescent quality. It glistened like the stars.

> In the grey-white light
> of waiting day
> When the sun's twin sister to the moon
> I saw him,
> Saw him with his back
> against the sky

The falling of light was flawless that evening. The sun was just setting, and over his shoulder a full moon sparkled, casting its dazzling light upon his figure. His body was aligned between the two silvery bodies, the sun and the moon.

Against God and nature
Sky and man
Twixt the miracles of sun and moon
Twixt and of the silver twins—
Facing me.

I looked at the scene in wonder and thought, tonight there are three heavenly bodies framed by the sky, just like in my poem. How could I have known then that a window of the future had opened up for me? I must be clairvoyant. It was as if he, too, knew I was coming, and was waiting for me that night.

The universe had provided the answer to my dilemma. If I had any remaining doubts of what I wanted to do, my poem-come-to-life removed them. I threw myself at his feet, clasped my arms around his legs, and cried out, "Thank you! Thank you, for squaring yourself against the stars, and facing me! I love you, Rodin. I love you! I love you! I love you!"

He lifted me up and held me close, and began to gently kiss my eyes, my ears, my nose, my lips. His fingers traced my body lightly at first, as if he didn't dare to touch me with all his force. Then gradually, under the moonlight, his courage returned and he began to take off each piece of my clothing, tenderly kissing each newly exposed bit of skin. When I stood there naked before him, he lifted me up on the model's stand and slowly turned me around so he could see every aspect of my body. He devoured me with his hungry eyes, checking out every inch. Rodin ordinarily was not a great talker, but sex seemed to loosen his tongue and he loved to murmur in my ear as we were making love. He spoke in poetry all the while, like "You are my Aphrodite, my Love Goddess. How beautiful you are, so beautiful you make me want to die! My lovely Goddess, you shimmer like white marble in the moonlight. You are my faith, my hope, my living dream."

When he had drunk his fill of looking at me, he lifted me down from the model's stand with his powerful arms and retraced his visual path with his gentle, skillful, sensitive fingers. He kept gently stroking my face, my neck, my breasts, my hips, my buttocks, my legs and my feet with those huge marvelous hands until I couldn't stand it anymore. Then he began to kiss my entire body. I don't believe there was a single inch he missed. All this time, I was not allowed to do anything but lie there passively and enjoy his administrations. But by the time he had enough looking, stroking, and kissing, I was frantic with desire and ready to yield completely to any wish he might have for himself. No wonder so many women loved him! He seemed to take as much delight in satisfying me as in his own pleasure. As in his work, he felt no pressure of time. He always said, "Nature follows its own clock." We finished when we finished, whatever the hour might be. Rodin was a man who knew no sexual positions. One never knew what form his lovemaking would take. But however his actions might differ from time to time, the pleasure he gave me was always pure heaven.

Somehow I gradually was able to overlook Maman's morality and to ignore my fear of closeness enough to risk the loss of the me in me and submerge myself in Rodin. And why not, since he was what I had wanted since I was five years old? My childhood dream of being carried off by a "great artist" had come to pass and I never was happier or more productive in my life. For a while, a little while, Rodin and I were able to stop yearning and to immerse ourselves in each other and our work.

For they were the same thing; our work was our love and our love was our work. There was no difference between love time and work time, so easily did one flow into the other. He would come over to check out a pose I was modeling for him. Since he couldn't see well, he would have to touch my body from head to foot. Naturally, he began to caress me. Our ecstasy was carried to the sculpture he was working on, so that the fingers that embraced me became the fingers that enveloped the statue. Over and over he moved from me to the sculpture, and back from the sculpture to me. The smells of our bodies hovered over the embracing couple and I swear remain there still. And as he savagely kissed my bruised lips, the secretions of love melted into the clay of *The Kiss*.

One after another masterpiece poured out of our union, so that it's often difficult to tell which of us had done the sculpting. We used the same model and the same pose for his statues of *Galatée* and *Cybèle* and mine of *Jeune fille à la gerbe* (Young girl with a sheath), and they look as if they were created by the same person. I'm sure that some of the pieces signed by him were sculpted by me and a few of the works credited to me were created by him. Or maybe by both of us together. I worked as much on *The Gates of Hell* as he did, and would be hard-pressed to say where his contributions ended and mine began. What I had been afraid of had actually happened, he really had taken over my work and I no longer cared which of us got the fame and the money. It was as if we were one person. His work or mine, his fame or mine, what difference did it make?

One night we were sleeping together and our arms and legs were intertwined so that I couldn't tell which limbs were his and which were mine. It scared me not to know which arms belonged to me and which legs to him, so I started to move away. Then I sleepily thought, "What does it matter whose arms and legs they are? Who cares if I'm Camille Rodin and/or he is Auguste Claudel? It's all the same to me." We slept the whole night in that position without moving once. When I woke up we were still entwined. It was very gentle and very lovely.

The next night I dreamed I was encased in a statue of Rodin's. I think it was *La Pensée (The Thought)*, but in the dream I was completely engulfed by the marble. I struggled to breath, but couldn't. I woke up screaming.

Years of passion, years of joy passed like dandelions blown away in the wind. Sometimes I couldn't believe that I really had *my artist,* and was scared that I would wake up and find it was just another fantasy. Nothing can carry a person to the crest of rapture like having childhood dreams come true. It adds a special kind of euphoria to ordinary mundane happiness. Everybody should have their deepest desires fulfilled at least once. Then whatever happens afterwards, they can say "I'm glad that I was born." I feel sorry for people who haven't experienced what should be the crescendo of life. How can they ever feel complete? It's like endlessly plodding up a mountain and never reaching the summit. Even though I paid dearly for its consummation, in my better moments I gloat that my sweetest dreams came true. I dreamed them very hard and passionately, and never never gave them up. That's what brought them about. And then they also became real in my work, for dreams are the stuff genius is made of.

There were many other changes in my life around this time. One started in 1887 with the only fight Jessie and I ever had, which led to the end of our friendship. It seems I've never been able to get along permanently with anyone without quarreling.

One day, after Jessie and I had lived and worked together for three years, she came up to me and said with downcast eyes, "Camille, I have to talk to you."

I was frightened, because Jessie had never confronted me like that before, so I decided to bluff my way through whatever was bothering her. I answered casually, "What's on your mind, Jessie?"

She looked me straight in the eyes. "I think I pay too big a share of the rent for the *atelier*. You know I've always paid more than you towards it. My father's been cutting down on my allowance. He says it's time he began to make some money on his investment, as he can't afford to send me so much money anymore. So, Camille, I would like a large decrease in the amount you charge me for rent."

I was outraged, and demanded, "How come all of a sudden you're paying too much for rent? You never said anything about it before! Maybe you *have* been paying more than your share, but you volunteered to do it."

Jessie looked down at her feet. I added, "And Jessie, while we're settling matters between us, you should know that I don't appreciate that you stole those young British students away from me, and have been giving them lessons behind my back!"

Jessie looked at me as if she had no idea of what I was talking about, but I think that was just a ruse to get me off the track.

I continued, "I also think I deserve to pay less than the others, as I don't have as much money. Anyway, shouldn't the three of you be paying extra for working with a more advanced student?"

Jessie looked even more befuddled and still didn't answer. I took advantage of her momentary lapse to say firmly, "If you want to stay in the *atelier* you'll have to keep on paying the same amount!"

To my great surprise, gentle Jessie straightened up and answered in a bold voice, "Well then, Camille, I'm leaving France! It's just too hard being a woman sculptor. In my whole career, I've had only one small exhibition in London. You get many more exhibitions than I."

I thought, "If you were a better sculptor, you'd be invited to exhibit more."

She continued, "You've been selling a few of your sculptures, and even Rodin likes your work better than mine."

"Of course he does," I thought. "He knows what good art is."

"As for me making any sales, forget it!" she said. "Nobody ever buys my sculptures except my father. I keep trying and trying and doing my best work and have nothing to show for it." Suddenly I realized that the situation was serious and had stopped being a laughing matter.

"I'm going home to marry William," she went on. "At least he appreciates me, and I know that with him I'm Number One."

And so I lost my good friend. I'd thought at first she was just threatening me, and must admit I was shocked when timid Jessie finally took a stand and went back to England. Nevertheless, I was furious with her, and thought she was unreasonable to change the rules all of a sudden when things had been working so well. I punched the air and vowed never to talk to her again. And we didn't for half a century, until she came to see me in the asylum.

Looking back on it from my vantage point of fifty extra years, I believe what really caused the rupture between us is this: I think Jessie fell out of love with me when I told her to stop singing in front of Rodin at her home in Peterborough, and she decided then and there that she'd been giving me altogether too much and getting too little in return. In my experience, people fall out of love just like that, and are never able to return to the earlier state of mind. Pouf! That's how it happens. One moment you're in love and the next minute you're not. Nobody knows what sets off such a transformation. It may be a little thing like the singing incident, or it could be some sudden insight into the loved-one's character that completely changes one's concept of the relationship. Ask me. I know. After the "romance" was over, everything Jessie had agreeably put up with in the relationship, my lording it over her, picking the best spot in the *atelier*, selecting the models, giving them poses, etc., etc., etc., began to boil inside of her, and she carried her grudge onto the matter of the rent money. For instance, it was clear to me that she'd been upset for a long time that Rodin used her as a liaison between himself and me, but she never told me she didn't want to do it anymore. I might have listened to an ultimatum. It's too bad when people can't say what they mean. I was angry about the relationship the two of them had and felt betrayed by Jessie. She wrote Rodin all the time with news about me, although I specifically asked her not to. He was very appreciative, even though I wasn't, and made her a present of a lovely statue he had sculpted of two children. He never gave me one of his statues until I threatened to leave him.

I realize too that William Elborne, Jessie's childhood friend and longtime fiancé, was a very nice man who was devoted to Jessie and made her a fine husband. Actually, she was marrying the whole family. She'd been an only child and enjoyed being part of a large clan, as William was one of eight children. She told me she found in his brothers and sisters the siblings she'd always wanted. But it's sad she had to give up her art, never to work seriously at it again, even though she diddled around on and off with busts of her children.

The other girls in our *atelier* soon followed suit, and also went home disheartened. Aside from a few years more that Emily grappled with her art in England, they too renounced sculpting. In a way, I don't blame them. What a miserable life it was for women in the arts! We were given no support from the art world, little from the critics or galleries, and had practically no sales at all. Most of the time, we may as well have not bothered. The results would be the same if we'd stayed home and whittled sticks. Maybe Jessie was smart to leave it all for a man. As for me, I didn't mind giving up the *atelier*, because I was planning to live and work with Rodin in a house he was renting for us.

In 1894, I had some wonderful news about Paul. His first book, *La Tête d'Or* (Golden Head), was published, and he was only twenty-six years old. (He was doing better than his big sister!) How right he was when he was six and said he wanted to do "thinking work" when he grew up! That's exactly what he has done with his life. He shyly dropped the book off for me to read. I was reminded of the time when he was a little boy and shamefacedly handed me a flower and then ran away.

I held the book in my arms for a long time before opening it, trying to make the moment last as long as possible. I kept looking at the title printed in gold on the cover. What a magnificent book! *La Tête d'Or.* What a beautiful name! It sounded to me like a sculpture. How I would have loved to mold a sculpture in pure gold, a sculpture of Paul! Only gold would be suitable for a man of his genius. His descriptions of Villeneuve took me back to the beloved memories we share. I got so lost in the book I forgot it was written by my brother. How I miss the enchanted shapes of *Le Geyn*, the comforting wisdom of *le Géant*, and the mysterious stillness of the Grotto! How thrilling to have it all brought back to me! And the presbytery where Paul was born, the humble Gothic church, the chiming of the church bells, the lovely linden trees bordering every road, even the large wicker fireman which was a signboard to the hardware store, and Saint George, the staunch patron of Villeneuve-sur-Fère slaying the dragon, one of the first sculptures I ever saw and loved. Reading Paul's book was as good as going home.

I hurriedly turned the pages to see if I could find myself in it. When I came upon the princess, the symbol of joy and beauty, there was no question in my mind that she was me. I understood right away that my brother was saying he needed me to help him in his fight against sin. Sexuality is an evil force for Paul which he must resist at every turn. His terrible conflict is reflected in that of the hero, Simon Agnel, called Golden Head because of his shining hair. Glowing like the sun, the princess offers him grace. A soul to whom God grants sanctifying grace receives not merely a gift from God, but God Himself. He's bequeathed a new life, a new nature, as if an old and decrepit man were suddenly to become young and vigorous again. Anyone in possession of sanctifying grace is free from mortal sin. Such grace does not cure us of the weakness of the flesh, but merely strengthens our will so that the war against sin becomes easier. Simon tries to conquer the earth along with his own sensuality, but unfortunately is defeated in battle and dies. As Golden Head needed the Princess to grant him a state of Grace, so Paul needed me to be a saintly, non-sexual person. Then he, like the sanctified me, would be freed from sin.

Why was his need to overcome his emotions so strong? What fear of sex kept him a virgin until the age of thirty-five when, at the advice of his priest, he married? I alone in all the world knew the answers to those questions. Paul adored me as a child and loved me above all others. He was terrified of his incestuous feelings for me. I *know* he had them, as I for him. But they never scared me. Paul was a delightful, vibrant, handsome boy, and anybody would have found him attractive.

I will let you in on a secret about the great poet, Paul Claudel. His sexual problems began when we were children. When we were in bed together, we played around with each other, as children will do. With his vibrant curiosity, he passionately explored the openings of my body, as I satisfied my curiosity about his. As I remember, I bled a bit, but thought nothing of it except that perhaps I had gotten scratched in his probing. Did he always feel guilty about that? He is so overrun with guilt about everything else that I wouldn't be surprised. In contrast, I never felt guilty about our sexual investigations at all. I thought they were fun, and remember them with a smile. My body remembers, too, and has always taken pleasure in similar activities. I'm even grateful to Paul. My erotic experiences with him were delightful, and laid the groundwork for the passionate romps with my spiritual brother, Rodin. Even now, the image of the little Paul intensely burrowing beneath the covers to explore my body awakens me from the stupor of my endless days. I only regret that our youthful fumbling caused Paul so much difficulty in later years. I'm sure he was talking about me when his heroine Lala says in *The City*, "I am the tenderness of what is; as well as the regret of what is not."

It's gratifying that Paul felt I offered him grace in *La Tête d'Or* (me, the atheist!) although by the end of the play the princess has fallen out of grace and is crucified, so she turned out to be like me after all. Was the book my brother's premonition of my fate? What a ferocious man is my Paul! His book is permeated with violence and cruelty. Characters are brutally ripped apart, torn, burned, and bruised in their blood rituals, ruled by blinding forces. Tenderness and love as such are as unknown to Golden Head as they are to Paul. No wonder he needs the restraining forces of fanatic Catholicism, lest he, like Simon, destroy himself and everyone about him.

I see evidence of our youthful explorations in all of Paul's work. *Break of Noon* like his other writing dramatizes the hero's struggle between good and evil. Mesa, who resembles Paul, is madly in love with Ysé, a married woman. The character of Ysé, a memorable *femme fatal*, happens to be patterned after Rosalie Vetch, a married woman with four children who Paul was madly in love with for many years and probably never got over. He fell in love with her on a boat to China, where she absolutely bewitched him with her beauty and intelligence. Fortunately or unfortunately, as the case may be, Rosalie fell in love with another man on the return trip and left both her husband and Paul to live with her new lover in Belgium. It's strange that none of the million scholars and critics who write about Paul have picked up on the fact that *Rosalie is my middle name*. That's me, Camille Rosalie Claudel.

I think Paul was in love with me when he was little and only got over it enough to transfer his passion to another Rosalie, who seduced him into temptation. Paul believes that morally and physically there's only one woman for each man on earth and only one man for every woman. Only he thinks that for him that woman is Rosalie, while I think it's me. Another man in the play compares Ysé to a "high bred mare," and says it would amuse him "to mount her back. She runs like a nude horse…breaking everything, breaking herself." Ysé sets off a terrible conflict in Mesa, in that he passionately desires her but feels she comes between him and God. He tells her that, like a starving man who can't hold back his tears at the smell of food, he can't bear to be in her presence and not possess her. Although he wants her fiercely and urgently, when they do consummate the relationship he falls apart. His core is destroyed, as his wish to sacrifice himself to God becomes weak and ineffectual. He compares himself to a shattered and crushed "broken egg." Much as he lusts for Ysé he is not able to devote himself to her completely, as his tyrannical conscience perpetually chokes off his desires. Dissatisfied, she says she never possessed him completely. Unable to forgive him for withholding his soul, she abandons him. But Paul, the mega-devout Catholic, cannot allow anyone (in or out of his books) who yields to sexual desire to get away unscathed. He has Ysé return to expiate her sins and seek atonement. She has learned from Mesa that there's more to life than carnal passion: Her conscience has been awakened and she feels ashamed. "This is the Break of Noon," she says. "And I am here, ready to be liberated." Poor Ysé! Poor Paul!

When I read his play, *The Tidings Brought to Mary*, I realized that our early sexual grappling had an even more catastrophic effect on Paul than I knew. He had woven our sexual encounters into the story of Pierre de Craon, an architect eager to continue his work on the building of the Cathedral of St. Justitia at Rheims, in which he is intensely absorbed. But he strays from his rigid path when he falls in love with Violaine *(viol* in Latin means to violate or rape), a beautiful, luscious, young, and hitherto untouched maiden, who's the image of exquisite beauty. Pierre desperately yearns for her soft body and the sensuality of her blossoming womanhood. Unable to control himself, he attempts to take her by force and in so doing cuts her on the arm with his knife, symbolically deflowering her. Pierre said later, that Violaine had been the first woman he had known in the Biblical sense. The devil had taken hold of him, Pierre explained, and before he knew it had forced him to take advantage of her. As a result, he was inundated with guilt.

A year later, he's struck down with leprosy. When Pierre de Craon saw the first signs of the illness on his body he felt duly punished for his misdeeds, and believed that God had anointed him with the illness so that he would follow his destiny for the glory of the Church. From that moment on, he stayed far away from Violaine, who was promised to another. His sickness poisoned both his mind and body. He loathed himself and was submerged in guilt for what he had done. In a moment of weakness he blamed Violaine for his leprosy, saying it was her fault he was ill, as her beauty had tempted him beyond the ability of a mere man to control himself. "O my beautiful one," he said, "no mortal man could look at you without loving you."

According to my brother's beliefs, sexuality is a great sin which can only be purged by remorse, pain, and punishment. In practically all of Paul's plays, love is thwarted and ends unhappily. Even married couples should not love each other too much, he told me, as that detracts from their love of God. The redeemed Violaine speaks of the danger absolute love for another human being has for the soul who seeks God. "It was too beautiful and we should have been too happy," she says. Fortunately, I

116

was able to resist Paul's philosophy for many delightful years.

I did not like *Violaine*. I did not like that a leper seduced her. I did not like that she was shamed and deserted by her own mother, who chased her away. I did not like the hatred between the sisters which led to murder. It's too much like my own story. *La Jeune Fille Violaine* is a hard and bitter play. Like Paul.

In *The Satin Slipper*, Rodigue, the Paul-like character, is madly in love with Prouhèze, of the deep deep blue eyes, of such deep blue they are almost black (like-you-know-whose). Prouhèze, like Ysé, is a married woman. Rodigue cannot allow himself to defile the sacrament; therefore their passion must be repressed. Love must be replaced with shame and punished, as "Punishment heals the sinful soul." When the would-be lovers meet, they stand far apart and do not allow themselves to touch, for were they even to brush hands they would become vulnerable to mortal desire. Cutting the bonds to other human beings is the lifetime goal of all of Paul's characters, even though Rodigue is bleak with sorrow and despair. Prouhèze has disavowed her love for him, which enables her to detach herself from all earthly ties. According to Paul, to renounce what one loves most is the evidence of true sacrifice, to know torture and humiliation is to make oneself worthy of God. Because of his philosophy, I've relinquished all that I loved most on earth. I hope he is satisfied.

Despite his harsh view of life, my little brother is a genius. He writes as well as Rodin sculpts. It makes me sad that Paul became a diplomat. How wrong, wrong, wrong! A person with such great gifts should devote his entire life to writing.

*I*n contrast to Paul, Rodin was a great believer in the joys of passionate love and to my knowledge never felt a moment's guilt about taking his pleasures where he found them. Late in 1888, he rented us La Folie Neufbourg, the ideal setting for our love affair. It was a sprawling, semi-derelict eighteenth century château in the middle of a large unkempt garden at 68 Boulevard d'Italie in Paris. Hedges, once meticulously clipped to border the gardens, straggled along in unearthly shapes of their own choosing. A circle of willows grew like an enveloping fence and surrounded the house. An orchard of fruit trees which was fit for a king had been neglected for a decade and no longer bore a crop. The once-graveled paths were overgrown with low trailing herbs, until there was no longer any trace of a passageway. La Folie Neufbourg, with its doors and windows nailed shut, its lush grasses and abandoned rooms, was a romantic setting very much to Rodin's taste. It was our home, our studio, our honeymoon.

We both fell madly in love with the house and the facade, in which six columns supported the terrace. Best of all were the recesses in the wall, in which statues of Pomona, Flora, and other goddesses rested. It was an idyllic retreat for our passion, like the retreat Queen Victoria and Prince Albert found at Osborne House on the Isle of Wight.

Georges Sand and Alfred de Musset had lived in La Folie Neufbourg together many years before. There had been a huge age difference between them, too, only in their case she was much older than he. It didn't seem to bother them any more than it did Rodin and me. I'm sure the vibes of the happy lovers came up to us through the floors and added to our joy. I felt so good about being in the house where they had lived that I refused to think about how their romance ended. Indeed, thoughts of their mighty passion inspired Rodin and me to similar heights. Hidden by the overgrown hedges and the trees so densely packed that no sunlight could shine through the leaves, we spent many naked hours rollicking among La Folie's beds of wild flowers, where our lovemaking was as untamed and lustful as the garden itself. Rodin immortalized our love in *The Eternal Idol,* a caress in clay. We were together all night and all day, when we ate and when we slept, when we worked and when we played. He couldn't bear for us to be apart for a moment and even followed me into the outhouse.

I didn't allow Maman and Louise's disapproval to take away one iota of pleasure in our lovemaking. I couldn't have chosen a better lover to introduce me to the rhapsody of sex. Not that I'd had much experience, but I can't imagine a more generous lover than Auguste Rodin. There was nothing he wouldn't do to please me. In the act of love, we were as one person. No sooner had I thought of something I would like, a place I wanted touched, a moment I needed a kiss, something I wanted to try, he sensed it without words and gratified me. When I reached a climax, followed by another, and another and yet another, I was filled with a glow starting in my heart and radiating all over my body which lasted all through the night. In my humble opinion, a woman who hasn't been made love to by a sculptor hasn't been made love to at all.

When I felt secure in his love, for fleeting moments I could even understand and forgive his many alliances with other women. There was a quality about Rodin that I never have seen in anyone else. He had a aura of goodness and purity as in his love making that made you give him anything he wanted. He had the soul of a naive child, as if he were innocent at his core. An unexpected compliment would make him blush, although he was also capable of a sudden outburst of rage over a trifle like a misplaced hammer, that vanished as quickly as a storm on a summer's day. He was truly a lover, in the best sense of the word. He gave himself to the world with such generosity, such genuine desire, such devotion and intensity that every living creature opened up to him. True love is impossible to resist, and everyone who came near him, men, women, children, or animals, fell in love with him. That's how he was, and it opened him up to falling in love with many women and having his feelings reciprocated. In my better moments, at least at the height of our passion, I understood that was simply his character and it didn't mean he loved me any the less. Unfortunately, my better moments became fewer and fewer as our romance progressed.

His love gave me the confidence to become a society lady. Unlike my parents and their inhibited friends, artists considered Rodin's *amoureuse* a respectable woman. I accompanied him to the homes of the Daudets, the Concourts, the Ménard-Dorians, Octave Mirbeau, Robert Goder and their like, where I was by far the junior member of the group. They affectionately called me "the little Claudel" and raved about how beautiful and witty I was. The women mothered me and the men looked at me with tender indulgence. They didn't even seem to notice my limp. It was the only time in my life I felt loved by a whole group of people. They gushed about my looks, my sculpture, and even the originality of my clothes, like the colorful *canzou* embroidered with large Japanese flowers that I discovered in an oriental novelty shop. That was the beginning of my love for Japanese art, which was to become an important influence on my work.

One afternoon Rodin took me to visit Renoir in Cannes. It was a colorful April day, with the sky looking as if Renoir himself had painted it, and the gentle wind making music through the trees. I was thrilled to meet the great artist, who gallantly escorted us around his *atelier*. Thrilled, that is, until he showed us into his study, where I was distressed to see his pet canary cooped up in a cage. It makes me angry when living creatures are locked up in a prison. It's not fair to deprive them of their birthright, of the clouds and the rain and the smell of the trees and the flowers. They have as much right to be there as we do. So when Renoir and Rodin became absorbed in each other and forgot about me, I yanked open the shutters, grabbed the bird, and tossed it out the window. I swear he tipped his beak to me and flew up up up into the glorious blue until he disappeared forever. I didn't even mind that I was never invited to visit Renoir again. I wonder if I had a premonition that some day I, too, would be a caged bird. But I'm not as fortunate as the canary. No counterpart of Camille Claudel ever came along to rescue me.

In 1888, my sister Louise married Ferdinand de Massary. I liked him a lot, and sculpted a bust of him in which he looks intelligent, thoughtful, and kind. (I wonder what he saw in her?) He was a good husband all his short life, which was more than she merited. What a terrible sister she has been to me! Not once did she sympathize with my terrible lot, or come to visit me in the hospital. If asked why not she would say that I got what I deserved. Fate is not always fair. Louise had Maman as a child and then she had a good husband. I wasn't even invited to the wedding. Not that I expected to be, as I was *persona non grata* with her and Maman. But it will always ache that my little sister doesn't like me, even though I never liked her either.

Not only were Rodin and I ecstatic in our love, but things also began to go better for me in my career. In 1887, I showed my bronze of *Young Roman* at the Salon des Artistes Français. In 1888 I exhibited *Sakountala* and in 1889 *Charles Lhermitte as a Child*, both at the Salon. Then in 1892, I had my first really important exhibition, in which I showed the *Bust of Auguste Rodin*. It received excellent reviews. I was delighted to have finished the bust, as it took years to complete. He was a terrible model who was always squirming, and could never be still long enough for me to capture his likeness. When he was supposed to pose for me in the model's chair, he would sit there for perhaps five minutes, then jump up, stretch his legs, walk around the *atelier*, return to the chair to relax for a few moments, and then abruptly leap up again to check out a statue he was working on. (He reminded me of Paul, whom I had to drag home from under the bridge where he was hiding, so I could finish his portrait.) Because of Rodin's fidgeting, my work on the bust had to be abandoned and started over many times. Once it got so dried up that it began to fall apart, and was only saved for posterity because I happened to have made a mold of the original. Finally I was able to finish the sculpture, and have it cast in bronze (at Rodin's expense). People loved it, even Rodin who said it was the best portrait of him that was ever sculpted and the "finest head sculpted by any artist since Donatello." I was happy that all the critics except Paul Leroi praised it.

Monsieur Leroi objected to the bust because he said it was an imitation of Rodin. Can you believe it? How can anyone do a portrait that has no trace of the sitter in it? How can Rodin be an imitation of Rodin? Leroi doesn't know it, but his criticism was the highest praise he could have given me. It's because my sculpture is the essence of Rodin that Leroi thinks it's an imitation. If I had it to do over again I would sculpt it exactly the same way, Leroi be damned.

It's a funny thing about my sculptures. They seem to have a mind of their own. Sometimes I have a clear idea of how I want a piece to turn out, how it should look, and what it should say about the personality of the model. But much as I fight it, something inside me takes over and sculpts it just the way it wants to. It doesn't listen to me at all. Of course "the something inside me" always turns out to be right. You'd think I would have learned. Take the statue of Rodin, for instance. When I sculpted it, we were madly in love and I wanted to make him kind, loving, and honest. But in the finished work he looks wary, untrustworthy, and suspicious. Which is just the way he turned out to be. Who was it who said, "The heart knows things the mind will never know?" Apparently so do my fingers and so does my heart. But more about that later.

I showed the bust at a new Salon called the Société Nationale des Beaux-Arts. There'd been a split in the Salon that year because a special international committee, which was formed to oversee the works of art at the Universal Exhibition, refused to recognize fine artists like Jules Dalou, and in their place rewarded only newcomers and foreigners. Rodin and I protested the new Salon policy by walking out of the Société National des Beaux-Arts. To our satisfaction, the board of directors of the new Champ de Mars decided to bestow neither medals nor awards. I prefer it that way. I think people should admire a work of art and buy it because they like it, not because it got a medal. From then on, Rodin and I showed only at the Champ de Mars. That we did the right thing was evident later on at the 1892 exhibition, when I was chosen to be part of their jury. I hoped the honor would bring equality to other women artists, as well as to me.

I was beginning to get recognition as a sculptor at last. Gustave Geffroy began to write regular articles about my work in *La Vie artistique*. Morhardt's long article about me appeared in the *Mercure de France*, in which he wrote, "Unlike most artists, she pays no attention to the commotion that arises around her, but thinks only of her work. Regardless of little income and a shocking lack of commissions for so gifted an artist, she perseveres! Camille Claudel is a hero!"

I appreciate very much that Morhardt understood my work was independent of the voices around me. Not many people do. I never liked harsh criticism, especially when it was unfair, but it never stopped me from working. Criticism is criticism and work is work, and they are two different things. People died, I lost a commission, my feelings were hurt, but still I plowed ahead. Each sculpture seemed to exist on its own, unconnected with my mood or whether I thought the work was good or bad. If I was cold or hungry or had to answer the call of nature, my personal needs got lost in the compulsion to go on with my vision. (Speaking of food, I never really cooked for myself anyway, and usually just chomped away on bread and cheese, which I held in one hand while continuing sculpting with the other. Somehow, the idea of wasting all that time and attention on a supper that would soon disappear struck me as frittering away my life.) If anything, brutal criticism made me work harder, to prove to the critics and Maman that they were wrong about me. Even after the abortion, which I will talk about later, I sculpted *La Petite Châtelaine,* and the decade after I broke up with Rodin, I created *La Sakauntala* and *L'Age Mûr,* my *chef-d'oeuvre.* I believe these three sculptures are my best works, as each one dramatizes a unique moment in my life history. If I were a teacher, I would tell my students that the finest works of art illustrate the climax of a narrative.

It helped, too, that many critics raved about my creations. At least one journalist, Gabrielle Reval, called me the greatest sculptor in the country. I was even invited to serve as a judge to select entries for the exhibitions of the Société des Beaux-Arts. Funny, I was unhappy when my career didn't go well, and furious when my sculptures got bad reviews. You'd think I would've been in seventh heaven when I met with success in my professional life. But when I received wonderful reviews, they somehow left me unmoved. It's as if my heart went cold and said, "You're just getting the reception you deserve and should've been having all along."

One kind of criticism, however, never failed to leave me in a rage. Comments such as "The statue is pretty good, considering that it was done by a woman" were frequently interspersed in otherwise fine reviews, as if a woman were an inferior, abnormal kind of being if she showed any talent at all. Even my friend Mirbeau, who greatly admired my work, wrote that my sculptures went far beyond what one could expect from the hands of a woman. Robert Godet, who thought enough of me to invite me to his home and introduce me to Claude Debussy, said that I was the only woman genius in the history of sculpture. Paul Leroi wrote that although *La Sakountala* was the most extraordinary exhibit of the year, it was especially astonishing because it had been sculpted by a woman. What are we, idiots or something? How can such thinking permeate the minds of otherwise intelligent men? Worst of all was the comment by Edmond de Goncourt that if we had performed autopsies on prominent women like Georges Sand, we would have discovered that they had genitalia more like those of men than normal women! How can women live with such insults and stay quiet? Isn't it because most of us have been brought up with such convictions and agree with them? It's outrageous that most "normal" men think that way and nobody in power does anything about it! I was fortunate indeed that my dear father believed I was as gifted as any man. He was way ahead of his times. Otherwise, I probably would believe along with that imbecile Goncourt that I was just "little Claudel."

I never could have loved a man with such an attitude. That's something I always admired about Rodin. Unlike other men, he never discriminated between male and female artists, and took Jessie and me into his *atelier* when other artists hired only men. I still am grateful for that, despite his later about-face. When all was well between us, I enjoyed his lack of prejudice, and my rage at the reviewers took a back seat.

A trip we took to Touraine in 1890 was the closest to ecstasy I've ever known. It was a time apart, a time out of life, a time like a dream. It reminded me of nothing so much as the excursion to the ocean with Papa when I was five years old. Lignière is a charming little village in the Loire Valley about two hundred kilometres southwest of Paris, twenty kilometres from the city of Tours and six kilometres from Azay-le-Rideau. Rodin was fascinated with the architecture of old churches and cathedrals and particularly wanted to visit Lignière because there's a magnificent church in it that dates from the twelfth and thirteenth centuries. He examined it for hours and drew many sketches. We both loved the vault of the choir painted with frescoes (especially the one representing the Temptation of Adam and Eve in the Garden of Eden) and the unusual apse, vaulted like an oven. Directly over the organ is a nice bust of Canon Brisacier, who was also a sculptor and carved in marble the statue of Our Lady of Lourdes situated at the entrance to the great chapel. I was enthralled by the Stone Towers, where it's said that Joan of Arc stopped, because I intended to sculpt a statue of her some day (and came closest to it with *Le Petite Châtelaine*, which also is known as *Jeanne enfant*). Lignière is larger than Villeneuve, but looks a lot like it. I even found an ivy-covered house that's much like our family home in Villeneuve. Rodin sang and whistled as we walked through the lovely little town. People turned to look at us as we passed. Holding hands, we joyously strolled through the woods, learning sculpture from the trees, as we studied the lines that formed their grace and balance. And like happy children, we joked and giggled as we observed the cloud formations.

"That girl over there with her head sticking up above all the others—that can only be you!" he said.

"And the man sitting astride the beautiful young lady with the untidy hair, guess who that one looks like?" I countered.

He answered with a rowdy "Haw!" And quickly assumed the position of the man in the clouds. When we finally broke apart, I looked again and was saddened for a moment to see that our cloud people had disintegrated. Rodin comforted me with a kiss. "That's all right," he said. "There'll always be more."

"Would that life were like the clouds!"

"I'll sculpt them for you," he said, "so bring back that smile on your face." When he got home, he immortalized our cloud lovers in marble and named the statue *Sin*.

Oh those wines, where lush vineyards and fruit trees grow! The best we ever tasted. Each savory sip left us craving another. On a hillside radiant with the dark purple of ripe grapes, Rodin and I ran hand in hand under the trees. We stopped and kissed at every tree, with lips that dribbled with wine. I was overcome with the same musical, drunken laugh I'd laughed on that day by the sea so long ago, only this time it was Rodin who laughed with me. For a little while he was all mine, and I had the love I'd dreamed of for so long. Life was absolutely perfect, a fantasy come true. I was afraid to go to sleep at night, for fear I'd awaken, as so many times before, to find it had all been a dream.

To add to my happiness, it looked as if I was going to get my first commission, a bust of the Republic, to be placed in front of the fountain in the town square of Villeneuve. I was particularly pleased because the invitation came from my own town. The city council was planning a centennial to honor the birth of the Republic, and Etienne Moreau-Nélaton, a historian from Fère, thought there would be no better way to pay tribute to the Republic than to commission Fère's "favorite child," me, to sculpt the bust of a woman to represent it. Unfortunately, the city council of the conventional little town was shocked at the idea of commissioning a woman to undertake so important a project and turned it down. Except for my anger at the discrimination against women artists which I never could get used to, I didn't mind very much. I was young, and thought there'd be plenty of other commissions in the future. Besides, I had the greatest sculptor in Paris to tell me between kisses how stupid the council was.

*T*he only real thorn in the rosebush was Rose Beuret, the peasant woman and seamstress Rodin had lived with without benefit of marriage since he was twenty-four and she was eighteen. I knew Rodin loved me, for no one could fake how his face lit up every time he saw me. He couldn't keep his hands off me for years and years, and it took only an inviting look from me to fire him up for hours. But much as he wanted me, adored me, devoured me, he insisted on hanging on to his Rose. I often brooded about why he stayed with this stupid country bumpkin who could barely read and write, who my friend Mirbeau called "the little washerwoman." Did she take care of him like Maria did? Was it some sense of misplaced loyalty, that she'd stuck out the lean years with him and therefore he wouldn't desert her when things got better? Apparently, she was devoted to Rodin, had supported him with her dressmaking through many years of appalling poverty, and nursed his senile father until he died. Originally his model, she posed for some of his finest early work, like *Bouquet of Life, Young Mother, The Action of Grace,* the destroyed *Bacchante, Rose Beuret, Mignon, La Défense,* and *Bellona.* From his sculptures of her, I can see she'd been a beautiful woman, with somewhat masculine features, large eyes the color of a bronze statue, and abundant brown hair. Nevertheless she looked like an old hag when I met her, who reminded me of nothing so much as my statue *Clotho.*

Although she and Rodin had a son, Auguste Beuret (to whom Rodin wouldn't even give his last name) it was clear to everyone that Rodin was first in her heart. She washed his clothes, took care of his home, cooked his favorite cabbage soup every night, and looked after his studio when he was away. She kept his clay moist to protect it from drying up, and saw to it that his marbles and plasters were safely stored away. With a woman like Rose to coddle him, Rodin had no need of a maid.

Did he remain with her because Maria had died a few months after she was rejected by her lover, and Rodin was determined never to abandon a woman and cause a similar tragedy? (Too bad he forgot about Maria's misfortune, when it came to his rejecting me.) Or was he ashamed of me because of my physical deformity? Surely a man who sculpted such perfect figures must have been aware of my defect. I didn't know. I only knew I loved him and wanted him with me all the time. Despite my understanding of the way he gave love to everyone, it got increasingly harder to share him with his decrepit old lady, who he always went home to at night.

After I ranted for hours and then cried in his arms, Rodin agreed we should spend more time together. In 1887 we discovered the delightful Château d'Islette in Azay-le-Rideau, not far from the town of Lignières, where we had experienced so many rapturous moments. It felt just right from the moment we stumbled on it, and we went there as often as we could. I stayed for the summer, and Rodin would join me on weekends. The Château became a refuge for our passion for years, so that we were not always under Rose's nose. He told her he needed to be in the area to search out features like Balzac's, on which he could model his statue of the great writer. The plump old landlady of the Château, Madame Courcelles, liked me very much and bustled around me to try to make me comfortable. She was a romantic old soul who was enchanted with our love affair and looked forward to Rodin's visits as much as I did. She didn't seem to care whether we were married or not, and I found her natural acceptance of our love very healing, in contrast to the scalding reactions of my mother and sister.

It was very beautiful at L'Islette. But I missed Rodin dreadfully. Every morning I strolled around the garden and kept thinking of how much he would love it. Then I sauntered into the park and kept sniffing the newly-mowed wheat, hay, and oats, which smelled so luscious I chewed on a snippet of hay. I ate my meals in the middle room that Rodin loved, where you could see both sides of the garden from my table. Madame Courcelles asked about Rodin all the time, and said he could always eat in the middle room when he was here, since he enjoyed it so much. She also said he could have any room he wanted to work in and she'd make sure it was available when he needed it. The old lady couldn't do enough for him. I think she was in love with him. In fact, I think she was in love with the two of us, and imagined herself in my shoes, the lover of the great Rodin.

That place could have been Paradise, if only Rodin had kept his promises to me.

Madame Courcelles said I could bathe in the river. She thought it was quite safe, as her daughter and the maid bathed there all the time. I told Rodin that if he had no objections, I'd go with them, and then I wouldn't have to take hot baths in Azay. Down at the river, I basked in the water and glowed like the rays of the sun that warmed my skin. I lay there with closed eyes, drinking in the delicious smell of the fresh air and the drooping chestnut trees. I daydreamed of Rodin as I floated and wished he were there to share it with me. With tongue in cheek, I decided to write and ask him to buy me a little two-piece bathing costume of dark blue with white piping in a medium size at the Louvre. That way, I told him, I'd have a bit of him with me to share my watery bliss. When he brought it to me the next weekend, I threw myself in his arms and said I would keep it forever. It's the last bathing costume I ever owned.

At night when he wasn't there, I went to bed naked so I'd feel like he was with me, but the next morning it wasn't the same at all.

Ah, Rodin, my lover, my artist, I'd have been in Paradise if only you'd been true to me!

When he was not there at night, I reverted to my childhood fantasies of being held by him until I fell asleep. But even though I was naked it wasn't much good. After you've tasted real food, imaginary meals don't fill up your stomach very well. Once when he "forgot" to come see me, probably because Rose insisted he stay home, I was so furious I took my wax *maquettes* and banged them against the wall. There they lay, decapitated and forlorn, looking ever so much like the dolls I destroyed when I was a child and angry with Maman.

My greatest pain was that he wasn't faithful to me. In his opinion, he was doing nothing wrong, but only did "what a man does." He felt that a married artist has to be ultraconservative in his work in order to feed his family and he was unwilling to jeopardize his art. He used to say that a man has to sacrifice himself for a wife, while women sacrifice themselves for their children. He refused to get caught in the marriage trap. Good for him, but where did that leave me?

I'm afraid my understanding of his love for all beings (including other women) was short lived. It wasn't bad enough that he had Rose, but he had to make love to practically every other woman he saw. I was getting more and more upset and jealous, not only of his other lovers, but because he now had a new student, Mademoiselle Paulette, whom I was afraid he would like better than me. My sister took my mother away from me. Can you blame me for being a jealous person? By this time I knew how badly Rodin wanted me, so I asked him to compose a contract that would put in writing what I wanted from him or I'd have to end the relationship. He said he loved only me and would be happy to oblige. This is what he came up with:

Contract between Auguste Rodin and Camille Claudel

1. As of today, October 12, 1886, I will accept no students other than Mademoiselle Camille Claudel. In particular, I no longer will visit Mlle Paulette, nor teach her to sculpt. Thus no rival talent to Mademoiselle Claudel could possibly surface, although it is highly unlikely that I would ever come upon an artist as talented as she.

2. I will protect Mademoiselle Claudel from unscrupulous thievery of her art by any artist, including me.

3. I will share my friends with her, particularly those who are influential in the art or journalistic worlds.

4. I will try to the best of my ability to have her work placed advantageously at the exhibition and to see that she gets publicity in the newspapers.

5. I joyfully offer the young lady a marble statuette of her choice, should she so desire.

6. I promise to commission Cariat to photograph her in both day and evening clothing, particularly in the outfit she wore at the academy.

7. When the exhibition closes in May, she will travel with me to Italy, where we will live together for a least six months. Should I receive my Chilean commission, we will go to Chile together instead of Italy. No other models will accompany us.

8. At the end of the Chile visit, we will be married.

9. Until then, I promise that there will be no other women in my life. Should I break my word on this pledge and have intimate relations with any other female, this contract will be null and void.

10. In return for these promises, Mademoiselle Claudel guarantees that she will remain in Paris until May and accommodate me at her studio once a week until that time.

Auguste Rodin

Camille Claudel

That suited me just fine, and I was delighted to accept the proposal and to sign my name under his. The contract was very successful in keeping Rodin away from other women—for the period of one week. Rodin was as quick to break promises as he was to make them.

I wanted to marry Rodin, to ensure that I would have him forever, as well as for his own sake. For Rodin, with all his genius, remained a peasant. He still lived with Rose in a provincial atmosphere. He didn't know how to dress, to dine, to speak of intellectual matters. I tried to tell him that I, as the daughter of a family which had been educated for generations, could teach him the ways of culture and scholarly life; that the salons would then be open to him, and his work would grow richer and more meaningful. He could have all that, if only he'd marry me. He could have that and I could have him.

So I would often say, "Marry me, Rodin!" He'd answer with a vague "Harumph…next month…harumph…next year…harumph…when such and such an exhibition is over." But the months passed and the years passed and the exhibition was over, and still we did not get married.

In 1892, I finally realized he was lying, and did not intend to marry me at all. This time my need was so urgent I no longer could control myself. I went to his studio where he was working on the head of Balzac, to demand one more time that he marry me.

I said, "Marry me, Rodin."

He said, "After Lent."

"But Rodin," I cried, "this time is different. After Lent is too late."

He fondled Balzac's ear. "Why is Lent too late?"

"I'm pregnant," I blurted out.

He dropped his tools. "Pregnant? That can't be! How did it happen? Did you do it on purpose?" What he did next left me short of breath. He emptied out all the money he had in his pockets, slapped it on the work table, and said coldly, "We'll get rid of it. I don't want another child. I have one bastard, that's enough."

Then I knew for sure what I had hoped never to know, that Rodin really didn't love me and would never marry me. With a leaden thud in my chest, I realized there was absolutely no way I could raise a baby alone, with no money, a family who would throw me out into the streets, and no friends to help take care of me and my child. In my despair I had no choice but to let Rodin arrange an abortion, in a dirty little (so-called) doctor's office in the slums of Paris. I covered my head, put a huge scarf over my coat, and stole into the filthy alleyway without another thought. What happened after we opened the battered door is a gap in my mind, as if someone had taken a pair of scissors and cut my head out of a photograph. I survived the horror only by blacking it out, and know nothing of what was done to me and my poor child. I only know that it was the beginning of the tragedy of the rest of my life.

The Breakup

1893–1901

The first thing I did before the bleeding even stopped was to go to my *atelier* and begin work on *La Petite Châtelaine*. I thought it would relieve my torment if I could replace my creation of a living child with one of marble. Sweet little Madeleine Boyer, granddaughter of Mme Courcelles, posed for me. She sat for the statue sixty-two times. *La Petite Châtelaine*, like her model, is pure and innocent as a newborn kitten. She looks up with widened eyes, so stunned she hasn't taken in yet what she sees. She has a faint, mysterious smile, but underneath is a profound sadness, as if she's thinking, "I'm seeing what I don't want to see; I'm learning what I don't want to know." The sculpture has caught her in that split second when she's about to lose her innocence. Only six years old, and already life is a grave disappointment. So is mine, little one, so is mine. Let us mourn together.

Although there are many clay and bronze adaptations of this

sculpture, I like the one I personally carved in marble the best. In sculpting, as in life, different materials make for different results. Bronze is for eternity. Marble brings out *La Petite Châtelaine's* purity (the purity I had brought to Rodin) as no other material can.

Out of spite, because I was two days late in paying them, the technicians ruined months of an earlier work. I didn't want to take any chances with *La Petite Châtelaine* because I loved it, so I chiseled the marble myself. Besides saving money, I enjoyed being a technician almost as much as a sculptor. I relished picking up the hammer and chisel and cutting deep deep into the stone, and all of a sudden seeing a living being appear. It gave me a feeling of power and strength I haven't felt since. Even Rodin didn't know how to carve directly into marble. He hired *practiciens* to do it for him. In fact, no sculptor since Michaelangelo has known how to cut his own marble. I felt as he did when he wrote "Just as by cutting away, O Lady, one extracts/ From the hard Alpine-stone,/ A living figure which alone/ Grows the more, the more the stone diminishes."

La Petite Châtelaine is the closest to perfection I ever reached. I sculpted four variations of it. The first was shown at the 1895 Salon, and was entitled *Jeanne enfant* (The Child Joan of Arc). The version I did the next year is a particular favorite of mine, for technical reasons: her hair is sculpted in braids. This is a very complicated and delicate feat to attempt, and is very frustrating, because the strands constantly break off in the modeling. With the price of marble so high and the amount of money in my purse so low, such a project required great courage to undertake. My work on the back of the woman's head in *Le Psaume (the Psalm)* is equally complex, but somehow it didn't make me love her the way I do *La Petite Châtelaine*. Frankly, I don't know of many sculptors who could do such intricate work. I made the figure hollow to allow the light to play upon her features, which gives her an ethereal aura. Indeed, she does look like Saint Joan!

Incidentally, isn't it interesting that in the portrait of me taken by César when I was twenty, the one published in all the articles about me, no one ever noticed how much my posture in it is like that of *La Petite Châtelaine?* It's just as well. My enemies would have had a field day.

Since everyone who saw the statue loved it, I decided to apply for a commission from the Ministry of Fine Arts. Surprise. The state turned down my offer. I was fortunate in that Baron Rothschild bought the bronze, and Morhardt acquired the plaster for the Société Populaire des Beaux-Arts.

Speaking of Morhardt, when he saw the sculpture, he said that I had become a worthy rival of Rodin's. According to him, our work was quite different. Rodin avoided sudden clashes, and showed a gradual progression between shadow and light. My sculptures, on the other hand, were full of intense dramatic contrasts, with no transitions between shadow and light. Rather like the difference between Rodin's and my personalities, isn't it? Morhardt told me that Rodin said *La Petite Châtelaine* inspired him to compete with me. I *knew* it, and was relieved to have my intuition confirmed. Everybody always told me I was crazy when I said he was jealous of me. They should be so crazy. Although I was pleased to be recognized at last as "a worthy rival of Rodin," I'm not sure Morhardt did me a service. His comments marked the beginning of Rodin's persecution of me, and were to change the entire course of my life.

*T*hat summer I went by myself to the Château d'Islette and paid my own expenses. It was sad to walk alone in the beautiful garden where Rodin and I had strolled together so many times. Although everything was mowed, as in previous summers, the hay, wheat, and oats didn't smell as good anymore. They were just hay, wheat, and oats. When I took a piece of hay in my mouth, it was bitter, and I quickly spat it out. I couldn't bear to eat at the table in the conservatory that Rodin had loved so much, where you could see both sides of the garden, so I had my meals in the smaller room off to the side. More often than not, my head hung limp over my food. I think Mme Courcelles was as unhappy about the breakup as I was. She cried when I came into the dining room alone for the first time. She held me against her soft round bosom and I cried, too. I felt a vast and bottomless emptiness at the Château, and in contrast to former years, couldn't wait to go home. I needed to collect my things to take back to Paris. Since I had to pay three hundred francs to Mme Courcelles, and sixty to the movers, I only had twenty francs left and couldn't afford to pay them to bring back all my possessions. I left many of them with Mme Courcelles, and arranged with her to return the following summer to pick up the rest. I took only one sculpture, a bronze, and my linens, drawings, and books with me. Unfortunately, I couldn't bear to return to pick up my things. For all I know, they're there still. I was light-headed as I climbed into the carriage. As the horse and cart clattered down the road, I turned around and watched the Château d'Islette grow smaller and smaller in the distance.

My funds at this time were at their lowest ever. It would be inaccurate to say I had *no* money: As I owed large sums to the landlord, the butcher, the baker, the wine seller, the *fondeur,* etc., etc., I should say that I had a *negative* amount of money. One day, when my friend, the critic Henry Asselin, came to pose for me (because his services came for free), I said to him, "Henry, if you're planing to visit me tomorrow, please come at lunchtime. You bring the lunch. Otherwise we'll pass out from hunger." We both thought that was very funny. I don't think so now.

Completely strapped for eating money, to say nothing of food for my cats, I again contacted the Ministry of Fine Arts to ask them to buy *La Petite Châtelaine.* Once again they turned me down. Turned down that beautiful little girl whose eyes reveal her soul! What is wrong with people? Can't they tell the difference between truth and beauty and the gawky cupids that adorn so many living rooms? How different my life would have been had the world valued me as they did my male counterparts and treated me as my talent deserved! Fortunately for my grumbling stomach, my friend Morhardt came to my rescue again and purchased another clay model of *La Petite Châtelaine* for himself.

Luckily, I had a few patrons who were interested in my work, including my friends Robert Godet, Johany Peytel, Léon Lhermitte, and Maurice Fenaille, the famous collector and patron of the arts. But my favorite benefactor was La Comtesse Arthur de Maigret, who was an enthusiastic collector of my sculptures and kept me in funds for years. At various times, she bought the marble version of *La Sakountala,* and a plaster of *Persée et le Gorgon,* which she ordered in marble to decorate her Parisian mansion. Then she commissioned me to do busts of her arrogant son, Le

Comte Christian de Maigret whom I wasn't too fond of, and her darling daughter-in-law, Marie d'Anterrouche, La Comtesse Christian de Maigret, whom I loved sculpting. We laughed and giggled together like girlfriends. I believe I caught on the face of her bust the delightful exuberance she exuded. La Comtesse Arthur de Maigret ordered the busts of the young couple in 1899 to commemorate their marriage.

It's funny how clearly my feelings about the models came through in the sculptures. I enjoyed working on the bust of the young countess, but couldn't wait until I finished the one of the count. It wasn't the kind of portrait that welled up from the core of my being, but I was glad to do it for La Comtesse. I still like the statue of her daughter-in-law much better of the two. It didn't seem to affect the way they were received, however. Critics preferred the one of him. But what do they know of the ways of the heart?

The next year, La Comtesse ordered a bust of herself. Madame de Maigret was a great and noble lady, the epitome of elegance. She carried herself with the dignity and poise of a queen. I would have treated her like royalty even if she hadn't been a countess. For reasons unknown to me, she seemed to take a liking to me and my sculptures, although the customary reserve of her class kept her from demonstrating it. But despite her efforts at constraint, the warmth she felt shone from her eyes and the special little half-smile that played around her lips whenever she saw me. I believe I captured that smile in the bust, but the glow in her eyes is more visible in a pastel drawing I did of her a few years later. I liked the garland effect of the drapery and lace I carved around her bare shoulders in the sculpture, and the ornate hairstyle that was truly befitting a queen. I couldn't help loving the woman. If I'd been able to pick the mother of my dreams, I think it would've been La Comtesse.

But true to the pattern of all the relationships of my life, this one didn't last either. The bust of her was the last commission she gave me. My mother, who delighted in replacing me with my sister Louise, got to Madame de Maigret and told her falsehoods that turned her against me. Maman was jealous because she knew how much I admired the countess. As a result of her schemes, I lost the affections of that good lady, the only buyer I still had. I missed not only the commissions she gave me and the money they brought in, but the encouragement and admiration of that lovely woman.

Nevertheless, by 1899 I had earned enough money from Madame Maigret's commissions to enable me to move into two rooms at 19 Quai Bourbon on the Ile St. Louis. The apartment was in a much lovelier location than the Boulevard d'Italie where I'd lived before, which was losing the rural atmosphere I'd enjoyed. The former seventeenth century mansion on the Quai was divided up into small, inexpensive apartments for people in my financial circumstances, or perhaps it would be nearer correct to say for those people who lacked any financial circumstances at all.

My new *atelier* was on the ground floor with windows that faced the river, and I stood there many an hour with Tabasco #7 under my arm following the great barges gliding down the lovely waterway. The river brought me the only beauty left in my narrowed life, as I watched the magnificent sunrises unfurl each morning before I began my work. I used to tell myself that if I were given the choice of owning a Rembrandt or being able to see the sunrises over the Seine, I would easily pick the sunrises. And yes, I even thought of Jessie sometimes and our vow to remember each other when we saw a river. I'm glad I could enjoy the magnificent views, as they, like every other pleasure in life, would not be given to me indefinitely. When I selected the *atelier* on the Quai Bourbon, little did I know that it would be my last home.

In my new *atelier* I sculpted two small statues which were different from any of my other work. They were similar to each other in that in both a woman is warming herself before a fire. In the first sculpture, *Rêve au coin du feu (Dream in front of a fireplace)*, a pure and innocent young woman sits alone daydreaming, and hoping that her dream will come true. In the second one, *La Profounde Pensée (The Profound Thought)*, the woman, who now looks older, is kneeling in utter despair in front of the fire. She no longer sees any possibility that her dreams will become real. The plaster of *le Rêve au coin du feu*, which originally had been ordered by the Comtesse de Maigret, was shown at the Exposition Universale of 1900, and Blos cast sixty-five copies in bronze, more than of any other of my sculptures. The sculptures were done two years apart. It would be easy for anyone comparing the two pieces to see that my feelings for Rodin had changed radically.

Rodin must have had some pangs of conscience about what he did to me, as he sculpted *La Convalescent (The Convalescent)*, a portrait of me sunk in misery and despair, and *L'Adieu (The Goodbye)*, in which an imploring, weeping Camille claps her hands over her mouth as if to keep from screaming. He got it exactly right. I wish he were as reliable a lover as he is a sculptor.

Since I first became Rodin's lover, I thought he surely would marry me, if not today, then tomorrow. If not tomorrow, then some day soon. That was how I was able to live with the situation. Despite my defiance of the values of my family, something deep inside of me cried out to be "respectable." Marrying Rodin was the only way I knew to assuage the hatred my mother and sister had for me and to live within the morality of my beloved Christian brother. But when I told Rodin in the Château L'Islette that I was pregnant he woke me up to the truth, that he was a liar and a cheat. With pounding heart I realized he'd never give me what I needed, and that he'd never help me be accepted by Maman and Paul as a decent human being. It was the great disappointment of my life and I didn't know if I could live with it.

Not that it helped to assuage my pain, but I understood very well why Rodin insisted that I have an abortion. Rodin already had a son, the young Auguste, with Rose Beuret. The boy looked very much like his father and even had some of his artistic ability. But his gifts all came to naught. Rodin was a terrible father and wouldn't even allow his son to take the name of Rodin. By being abusive and rejecting he turned Auguste into a human wreck, a psychopath and a drunk. His crude, abominable manners, his nose picking, his uninhibited bodily noises, disgusted me. It was embarrassing to have him around, and I was relieved when he left the art class I had invited him to join in my *atelier* with the English girls. According to Rodin, even the boy's mother couldn't stand him. I can empathize with her on that, if nothing else. It's just as well that Rodin didn't have any more children, certainly not with me. I couldn't have borne it if he'd ruined our love child as he did young Auguste. I've no doubt he would have. Rodin was utterly incapable of being a father. He believed that art is purely sexual pleasure derived from the force of love, and that with every work of art the artist creates he defeats the instinct to reproduce himself. Rodin refused to care for Auguste or to have another child because he directed the full intensity of his power to love into his sculptures. That's the way he wanted to live and that's what he did. It made him a great sculptor but a deplorable father.

One day as I was walking alongside the Cathedral of Notre-Dame crying, a mangy old orange cat came and rubbed itself against my feet. It was as if it was saying, "Don't be sad. I'm here with you." I picked it up and rubbed it against my cheek until it purred. To my surprise, I saw that the cat had wiped away my tears. It made me laugh, and I realized that I felt a little less sad. I thought, if one cat makes me feel good, shouldn't many cats make me feel that much better? I will bring Tabasco a brother. I tucked the cat under my coat and took it home. Ever since then, whenever I saw a stray cat, I brought it to my *atelier*. Cats are loving, cats are good. They're better than having children, because they don't require much money or care. They never disappoint you. They never grow up and leave you. They never betray you for another woman. They never promise more that they deliver. If one gets lost you can always get another. Would that I had loved a cat instead of Rodin.

Despite everything, I couldn't give up my old habit of fantasying my wishes come true. This time I did it through working on the statue of *Sakuntala*, (also called *Vertumne et Pomone*) the story of another woman who was loved but wronged. I'd been wanting to sculpt her life story since Rodin and I stayed at La Folie Neufbourg and made love beneath the statue of Pomona. As the cliché goes, when it rains it pours. I had a terrible time trying to create the sculpture, as my male model ran away to Italy and stayed there. That meant I had to start all over again with another model and make many time-consuming and expensive changes. It was a big disappointment to me, as the model was the man I'd used for *Giganti* and was so enamored of. Fortunately, Jasmine, the female model, didn't give me any trouble. (Thank God for small favors.)

I worked twelve hours a day, from seven in the morning to seven at night and was so exhausted when I finished that I went straight home and collapsed in bed. To make matters worse, I had come down with a miserable cold that went on endlessly, and sculpted *Sakuntala*'s hair between coughs and sneezes. Nevertheless, with tearing eyes, a hoarse throat, and hacking convulsions, I worked on and found just enough breath to finish the sculpture. The idea for the statue was taken from an old Indian fable recorded by the fifth century Sanskrit poet Kalidasa that I'd read in Papa's library when I was a child. I always was fascinated by myths and knew from very early on that they would provide me with an ever-flowing fountain of images to dramatize in sculptures. I believe that every work of art should tell a tale. I was particularly mesmerized by the legend of Sakountala, as if I sensed it would become the story of my life.

While out hunting one day, Prince Dushyanta came upon the maiden Sakountala and fell in love with her. He had to return to his palace, but left her his ring as a pledge that he would come back to her. While Sakountala awaited the reappearance of the Prince, she lived with a hermit, who was visited by the sage Durvasas. But she was so preoccupied with thoughts of her lover that she neglected to show the guru the respect he was entitled to. The old man was so furious with her he avenged himself by casting a spell on the Prince so that he would forget Sakountala and only recognize her when he saw the ring. In the meantime, Sakountala secretly bore the Prince a child. Then she went to the palace to seek her love and tell him of her joy. But the Prince did not know her. Since the ring had mysteriously vanished, she was unable to show it to him and prove she was his true love. Fortunately, a fisherman found the ring in the belly of a fish and brought it to the Prince. This woke him from the cruel spell and he went off to search for Sakountala. He found her in the forest where she lived, acknowledged their child as his son, and took her back to the palace as his queen. Would that my story had continued like Sakountala's, and that my "prince" had returned to me, acknowledged our child as his own, and taken me back to the "palace" as his queen! The sculpture depicts the loving couple at the precise moment when he recognizes Sakountala, and kneels before her to re-pledge his love. How happy they were! How happy I would have been, if only dreams came true. I wish!

I had an intimate problem working on Sakountala that I never told anyone. In fact, I'm wary of writing it down now. Someone who reads it might blackmail me. (Although there isn't very much they could blackmail me for, I must admit.) As I worked on the statues and had to run my fingers over the beautiful sculpted bodies of the lovers for hours, I became highly aroused. When Rodin wasn't around there was nobody to satisfy me. Nothing I could do myself worked. Sometimes my need was so strong I was in actual pain. There was no solution except to wait until it went away. It often took hours, and I was lucky if I could get any sleep at all before it was time to go back to work. Then, of course, the same thing would happen all over again. In my statue, Sakountala has all but collapsed, and like me needs the vibrant, passionate Prince to rescue her. You can see from the sculpture the emotional shape she (and I) was in and what we needed to heal us.

Many important critics raved about the finished statue. André Michel found the study passionate and chaste at the same time, and wrote that it gave him a feeling of restrained rapture. Paul Leroi, who had made me angry by saying that I imitated Rodin in the bust I did of him, sang a different song about *Sakuntala*. He said it was the most unusual exhibit of the year, and particularly remarkable in that so extraordinary a work had been sculpted by so young a woman. His remarks were so moving that I forgave him for *Rodin*. I guess I won't spit on him after all!

But certain critics, on the other hand, seemed to be looking for proof of Rodin's influence on me. They kept comparing *Sakuntala* to *The Kiss*, which made my brother Paul furious. He said that my work was inestimably superior to Rodin's. He angrily wrote that Rodin's statue reeked of vulgarity, while mine was the essence of spirituality. The man in *The Kiss* is about to take possession of the woman in a lewd and carnal manner, Paul wrote, while in my statue the man is so exalted by the woman's sanctified flesh that he barely dares to touch her. I'm glad he liked my work and considered it spiritual, but that didn't stop him from setting off a series of events that got me thrown out of my parents' home.

Someone in Paul's circle of artists, writers, and musicians apparently had been to L'Islette and seen Rodin and me there together. When the busybody asked Mme Courcelles about it, the old gossip was delighted to tell him the exciting news. (I wouldn't go back to L'Islette now if they paid me in gold!) The artist then repeated to Paul the rumor he'd been told about the nature of my liaison with Rodin. At first Paul refused to believe it. "Not my sister, you monkey-brained tattletale!" he shrieked at the meddler. "Take that back or I swear I'll kill you!" But when the artist gave more and more details of our affair, Paul was forced to remove the blinders from his eyes and face the fact that his beloved sister was a sexual being. He took the knowledge very hard and was so upset that you'd think he had discovered his wife was unfaithful to him. Our sex play as children clearly had allowed Paul to consider me his own private person, and he became intensely jealous of Rodin. I found out later that he didn't eat or sleep for weeks, and was so filled with rage that it poured out of him wherever he went. He lost so much weight that even our parents couldn't miss seeing that something was terribly wrong, and badgered him until he told them what he'd learned.

You can imagine what effect Paul's report had on Maman. One day when I was visiting, she burst into my room in the middle of the night where, exhausted from weeks of hard work I'd just fallen asleep, and began to shake me vigorously.

"Get up, you miserable harlot!" she screamed, shaking me all the while. "Wake up and get out of my home and never come back here again! Get out immediately! I won't stay in the same house with you!" I was in the deep sleep of utter exhaustion, and must have thought I was in the middle of a nightmare, so I curled up in my quilt and went back to sleep. With surprising strength, Maman yanked the covers off me and pulled me by my bad leg off the bed and threw me on the floor. I screamed, "Stop it, Maman! Stop! Stop! You're hurting my bad leg. How *can* I leave now? I can't get to my *atelier* at this hour."

Her foot poised to stamp on my hip, she answered, "I don't care where you go or what you do, just get out of here before I do something I will regret! You are no longer my daughter!"

Papa, who was in the house at the time, was awakened by the ruckus, and rushed up the steps and into the room just in time to keep her leg from thumping down on me.

"What're you doing, Louise-Athenaise?" His voice boomed out through the house.

"I'm throwing your filthy strumpet of a daughter out of my house! She's Rodin's whore, and I will not allow her to soil my home."

142

"Come on, Louise, stop that!" he shouted, while pulling Maman away and helping me to stand up. "I don't believe what you're saying. What makes you think it's true?"

"Your dear son told me."

He froze. Then he turned to me. "Is that right, Camille? Are you really Rodin's lover?"

"Yes, Papa, I'm afraid it is." He gasped and turned purple, then pale, but it soon became clear who came first in his life.

"I'm so sorry, Camille," he said, as tears washed down his face. "But you will have to get dressed and leave the house right away. It belongs to your mother and there's no way she can live with you now. I'll take you home." He put his hand in his pocket and drew out one hundred francs, which he put in my hand. "Take this, Camille. It'll help you feel better."

Maman ran down the stairs, screaming and yelling all the way. Papa took me in his arms and said, "She'll get over it in a little while. You'll see. It's just that she's in shock." But he was wrong. She never did get over it. And I was to pay the penalty for the rest of my life.

In 1895, I had begun a series of studies of the head of *Hamadryade,* which was also called *Young Girl of the Water Lilies* and *Ophélie.* I sculpted at least ten versions. The marble rendition was exhibited at the Salon in 1898, but I wasn't happy with it. I wasn't able to get it right until it was cast in bronze many years later. Like the other myths whose stories I sculpted, I'd been fascinated by the Hamadryades since I was a little girl.

In Greek mythology, Hamadryades were lovely spirits or nymphs who looked after the forests and woodlands. These nymphs were the guardians of oak trees. Each Hamadryad came into being with her own tree, in which she lived. Her job was to preserve its life and protect it from the onslaught of woodcutters, to watch over her tree and share its fate. The Hamadryads were jubilant when rain quenched the tree's thirst and mournful each autumn when it shed its leaves. The very existence of the wood nymphs was dependent on the state of the trees they inhabited, as they could survive only so long as their personal trees remained alive. Like a vine that entwines itself around a tree and can be nourished only by it, when the tree died the life of the Hamadryad perished along with it. If the

143

tree's fatal injury was caused by a mortal, the gods would be sure to punish him for the deed. The Dryads also would penalize an irresponsible human being who stupidly or cruelly abused the trees.

To the early Greeks, Hamadryads were holy and revered as the life force of the oak tree. The very name Dryad is derived from the Greek "drus," which connotes an oak tree. It's interesting that Dryad also means Oak Daughter. My father was an oak tree. Even when I was little and first read the myth I liked to think of myself as a Hamadryad, an Oak Daughter who protected my father from the onslaughts of Maman. That accounts for the name of *Ophélie* that I gave the statue, Ophelia, the girl who loved her father above all others. When Papa died, I, too, perished. That was the last of my sculpting, my ability to love, my interest in the world. Like the Hamadryades who died along with their trees, for all ostensible purposes the death of my father was the end of my life, too. But I'm getting ahead of my story.

In the legend, Sakountala, or Pomona, was a Hamadryad who lived in the forest. The Prince was her tree, and it took the rapprochement between them to revive her, for she was dying without him. Rodin was my tree for a while, and when the relationship died, a large piece of me faded away. But unlike Sakountala, he did not rescue me. In fact I have to reevaluate our entire relationship. I used to think he loved me, but now I realize he was deceiving me all along and passing my work off as his own all the time we worked together. He really didn't love me at all but was simply spying on me to get ideas for his work.

Water lilies also have a deep allegorical meaning, which is why *Young Girl of the Water Lilies* is one of the names I gave the sculpture. To the ancient Egyptians the blue water lily was a symbol of sexuality, and bowls of water lilies implied fertility and rebirth. Sexuality was considered a form of creativity in Egypt, and the lily, a flower of creation, became linked to thoughts of fertility and sexuality. I suppose I was saying that even if I aborted my child, *Hamadryade* was a fertile woman who would become pregnant again, were she to lose her baby. A vain wish, if referring to me! She looks joyful in the sculpture, as if she'd just found out she was pregnant. In case anyone wonders, the foliage in her hair represents the tree she lived in.

The flower was also used at funerals as a symbol of rebirth. For example, the gold coffins of kings frequently were lined with the petals of blue water lilies. The Egyptians believed that their souls would come to life again "like the reopening of a lily," that the departed soul, like a water lily, shut down at dusk and reopened with the rising sun. I suspect they're still waiting for the resurrection of their kings.

The Book of the Dead has a spell which transforms a corpse into one of these flowers. Paul and I used to practice it when we were children so we'd be ready when our time came. Atheist that I am, a vain little wish keeps sneaking into my head that some day I'll be reborn into the life I've been denied here on earth. Maybe I should grow some blue water lilies. But despite my miserable life this time round, I suppose one can say that both *Sakountala* and *Hamdryade* are sculptures of hope and optimism.

My dear brother Paul, who is supposed to be my best friend, thought it inevitable that the relationship between Rodin and me would break up eventually, because I'm "quick to get furious and have a vicious sense of humor that no one can take for long." I didn't take his words seriously. I thought it was just what Paul wished to happen because he was so jealous of Rodin. He also said I was unable to provide the sense of security the great man experienced with his old peasant lady, who loved housekeeping, cooked and cleaned for him, and made sure that his tools were laid out where he needed them and the linens were always damp on the unfinished clay. (I must say Paul had a point there. Can you picture me cooking and cleaning for a genius, while my sculptures turned to dust?) Paul also felt that two geniuses of similar power but different ideals could not possibly share the same *atelier* and clientele indefinitely. I don't agree. Whose side is Paul on, anyhow? His temper isn't so easy to take, either. He only manages to get along with his wife because he leaves town all the time. And why were we two geniuses able to get along so well before I got pregnant? Contrary to my brilliant brother's thinking, I'm certain that if Rodin had married me, we'd have ridden out my rages and penchant for mockery. I'd have discovered my own ways to make him feel as secure as he did with Rose.

Despairing as I was, I didn't absorb the full horror of the abortion until 1893 when I created *Clotho*, my statue of an ancient woman caught in a

145

death struggle. In Greek, Clotho means both spider and fate. Both are fitting titles for this work. Shriveled and grotesque, she is entangled in the skeins of the lives she is weaving, like a spider trapped in its own web. Her flesh is hanging, her breasts have slipped, her bones droop downward, as the strangling spider web of death drags her ever closer to the grave. Her left arm accepts the rope as trustingly as a child holds onto its father's hand. But the expression on her face is not that of a child; it's of a woman ecstatically surrendering to the only lover left to her, Death. The sculpture catches Clotho as she is dancing her last dance, fluttering her last flutter before she drops to the ground in a passionate embrace with Death.

Clotho was the name of one of the three sister Fates, the one who presides over birth and lays down at that instant what the child's lot in life will be. Like the spider that spins its web, Clotho spins out men's destinies like thread. I look over my life and ask which Fate could possibly have presided over my birth. Surely for me the fairy godmother of Birth was the fairy godmother of Death. She's been hanging around me since the moment I was born. Too bad she didn't finish the job then, when instead of the gift of a loving mother and a perfect body, the Fates dealt me Maman and a defective hip.

But there's a deadlier reason I called the statue *Clotho*. I'd barely survived the greatest catastrophe of my life, the abortion of Rodin's child. The Fate who presides over birth, indeed! In place of the Goddess of Birth, my poor baby's entrance into the world was overseen by the Goddess of Death. In fact, my child never made an entrance at all. For her, the Fate of Birth and the Fate of Death were rolled up into one. That's why I ironically called the statue *Clotho*.

The Fates are often confused with The Furies, female spirits of justice and vengeance, who stood for righteousness within the order of the universe. They were persecutors of men and women who broke "natural laws," particularly those who murdered a fellow human being. I broke the law, "Thou shalt not kill." Could it be it was preordained at my birth I would one day kill my own child and my life of Hell was plotted by the Furies in revenge? Paul, who believes that vengeance is ultimately evoked for all sins, might agree. The effect of the Furies on their victims was madness, hence their Latin name from *furor*. If my incarceration in a lunatic asylum is their vengeance for my crime, surely being locked up for so many years is just retribution. Haven't I been punished enough, O Ladies of Fury? Can I please leave and go home now? Please?

I'm not surprised that beauty and death are linked together in my mind. It's just another of the gruesome legacies left to me by Maman. She was only three years old when her own mother died of unknown causes, just one month after the birth of Maman's brother. Then, when she was twenty-three, her infant Henri died at the age of fifteen days, only sixteen months before my own birth. The year she was twenty-six brought the birth of my sister Louise and the death of Maman's younger brother, who drowned in the river Marne in what was probably a suicide. It's certainly understandable that birth and death were intertwined in Maman's mind. It's also understandable that she saw me as the Child of Death. Understandable yes, but understanding a fact didn't prevent it from ruining my life.

Then in 1896, as if to complete the conception of my baby in the typical family tradition, my brother-in-law, Ferdinand de Massary, the only one in the family who was decent to me outside of Papa and Paul, passed away. Naturally, I wasn't told about it or invited to the funeral. When I found out, I was desolate, as he and I had always liked each other. That, of course, had given Louise one more reason to hate me. It'd been nice to have a supporter in their home to temper her fury at me, and I always fancied that some day he would influence Louise to change her mind. After he died I lost all hope that the unmitigated fire of her jealousy of me would burn itself out. When I heard about Ferdinand's death, I punished myself by taking my wax *maquettes* and hurling them into the fire. The flames reared up as if to say, "Burn! Burn! Burn away the agony that's strangling Camille's soul!" They made an awesome blaze, and I toasted my freezing hands over it. That's what I do when I hear bad news, I destroy. If I don't burn up my sculptures, I take my mallet and pound a statue to dust. It gives me a good feeling to know I've paid for my crimes.

My brother Paul made the painful situation far worse. Because I needed his consolation and there was no one else to give it to me, I made the terrible mistake of telling him about the abortion. I should have known better! Paul's as religious and conservative a Catholic as ever lived.

His major objective in life is to strangle the man of flesh inside himself he considers evil and debasing so the Godly side of his nature can take over. I see his dilemma clearly reflected in all his plays. For example, the character of Simon Agnel in *La Tête d'Or* is torn between sensuality and the need to be saintly and fleshless. Paul, like Simon, lived in two worlds, and was unhappy in both, because whichever state he was in he longed for the other. Simon yearned to be a saint but it was the sinner in him that won out. To achieve the godliness he idolized he had to destroy the sexual force in himself. Simon did so by leaving the woman he loved and with whom he lived. Despite his great love, he traveled far away from her to escape the passionate ties that imprisoned him. To do so he had to kill, to tear up, rip out, to smash the relationship so that the other parts of his nature could flourish. He did so cruelly, viciously, and irrevocably, as did my brother, in order to become Paul Claudel.

"Paul," I said to him shortly after he had given me *La Tête d'Or*, "I have to tell you something I did that I know you will abhor."

He looked up from his book of Rambeau's poetry. "What's that, Cam? Have you spent the money on wine again that I gave you to pay your rent?"

"No, Paul. I wish it were as minor a transgression as that."

"Well, what have you gone and done now?" His eyes were twinkling.

"I'm serious, Paul. I've done something that's nearly destroyed me, and it's making me suffer as I never have before."

He slammed his book shut.

"I've had an abortion."

He jumped to his feet. "What's that you said? Is that your crazy idea of a joke? Well, is it? You're not answering! I can't believe it! How could a sister of mine do such a thing? To kill a child, an immortal soul, what a horrendous thing to do! How shameful! How terrible! How can you live with yourself with such a crime on your conscience? You'll rot in Hell for that. The good Lord will never forgive you!"

My tears did not soften him. I fell on my knees before him and took his hands in mine as I said through my sobs, "Love me, Paul! Please! Understand me! Forgive me."

He shook loose my grasping fingers. "It's not important whether I forgive you or not. Your eternal life is what matters. You must punish yourself for your terrible deed. You must destroy all you care about and spend the rest of your life atoning for your sin. Then maybe—maybe— our Lord will forgive you." He stood up abruptly and started walking to the door.

"Paul! Paul!" I screamed after him. "Don't do this to me. Have you forgotten how much we've meant to each other?" He looked at me with disdain and kept on walking. "Oh God," I wept, "how will I ever face tomorrow?" Paul slammed the door shut and left the house without even turning around. I didn't see him again for five years.

I tried to forget his harsh words, but they permeated my soul. In *Cinq grandes Odes (Five Great Lyric Poems)* , he wrote, "May he who hears my voice/ Return home troubled and heavy." His wish certainly came true with me. Because I loved him so much his voice became part of my self lore. Like an echo of Paul, I've never ceased to chastize myself for what I did. There's nothing worse than a Catholic conscience in an atheist. There's no priest to confess to, to give absolution from one's sins. "You're a terrible person, you murdered your baby, you must be punished," reverberated in my brain.

People ask how I could stay in the asylum so long in relative quiet. For thirty years I've said to myself, "This is what you deserve for killing your child." I knew I had to punish myself, for Paul said so. I gave up what I love best, my sculpting, in penitence. I gave up my work, my love, my life. Surely no sinner can be more repentant. The asylum is the worst Hell any person can think of. Sometimes I'm glad I'm here, because if I'm punished enough on earth, perhaps the everlasting fires of Hell will go on burning without me. Only Paul could have released me from this scourge. If he had taken me out of the asylum, I would have felt forgiven. Or even if he had taken me in his arms and said, "I will always love you, no matter what you do," I would have felt redeemed. But he didn't, and I wasn't, so I've stayed where I was, in penitence.

Paul is a genius. Paul is a success. Paul is a man of God, so he knows about such things. I on the other hand am but a poor failed sculptor. Who am I to think I know anything important? Yet sometimes in the agony of the endless nights, I'm flooded with the knowledge that I've never recovered from Paul's brutality. Then I think perhaps he's getting back at me for how cruelly I treated him when we were children. At those moments I want to ask him if he really believes that God is merciful and good. If so, then why does He let me rot away in this ungodly asylum?

There's another torment a harsh and ruthless God has bequeathed to me. Every time the nuns take me into town to run an errand, we're sure to pass some child or other. Be it an infant in a carriage, or an older child, I never fail to think, "That's the age my baby would have been, had she lived" or "That one is older—or younger—than my child would be if she were alive." Will I ever stop grieving for my unborn infant? Is there no end to my punishment? At such moments, I even feel sympathy for Maman, who never stopped crying whenever she thought of Henri.

Just when I needed Paul the most, the state dealt me another terrible blow. When Paul decided he wanted a career as a diplomat, Rodin wrote a highly complimentary letter to the State about Paul. My brilliant brother was appointed Vice-Consul to New York and then Consul Suppliant to Boston. I was afraid he would be gone forever, and I didn't know how I could get through the years without him. Even a day was intolerable. He'd been my only confidant from the time I was seven years old, and I needed his forgiveness above all else. He was away for fifteen years. except for three brief vacations in 1895, 1900, and the summer of 1905, when I destroyed all the work I had done that year. Imagine, I saw my beloved brother only three times in fifteen years, for no sooner had he returned to Paris and Villeneuve than he was appointed Consul to Shanghai, and a year later, to Foutchéou. He didn't return to France for five more years, and then only for a short while. Not that I wasn't proud of him, especially much later in 1922 when he was appointed an Ambassador, but his distinguished career as a diplomat meant that I had lost my brother as well as Rodin, along with all hope of forgiveness.

When Paul came back from Boston for four months in 1895, I decided to give a little party to celebrate his return. Besides Paul, I invited Maman and a few of Paul's friends, including the playwright Jules Renard. I don't know why I invited him, as he's the most miserable person I ever met, including the lunatics in this asylum. He was always humiliating people with what he considered his wit. I really tried to fix up my *atelier* for my guests. I pushed the armoire against the wall, and hung lanterns by their strings from the crossbeams. I also stuck candles on the iron points of my chandelier, which I thought was very original and clever of me. But of course Renard made fun of the *atelier*, calling it the devil's haunt.

He ruined my party with his sarcasm. He had the nerve to say to me, "Why is your face so heavily powdered, Mademoiselle Claudel? It makes you look dead, and only comes alive through your eyes and mouth." Was he trying to be funny? I still don't understand what he meant. I thought I looked quite nice in a dress I'd made from red velvet curtains, which highlighted the whitened look of my skin that powder gives. Although I never learned how to dress, and know I'm awkward when it comes to women's arts, I never accept bullying and gave it right back to him. I said, "You scare me, Monsieur Renard. You make dreadful fun of everyone. Please don't insult me in one of your books." Neither Paul nor Maman escaped his sharp tongue. "Madame Claudel," he said to Maman, "you answer everything anyone says, but you speak so softly I can't hear a word you are saying." So much for honoring the older generation. Nor did Paul, who supposedly was Renard's good friend, evade his pointed remarks. He said, "Paul, I admire your genius as a playwright, but you irritate me with your stiff affectations and dogmatic thinking. (I'm with you there, Monsieur Renard!) Why don't you ever show any feeling in your voice? It reminds me of recorded speech on a machine. I don't trust your emotions. either. Whether you love or hate something, your feelings are as primitive as those of a child. And yet you would have us believe that you enjoy art more than Victor Hugo or Lamartine!" As if he hadn't been malicious enough, Renard raised the edge of his hand to the side his mouth and said behind it, "Paul has been furious all evening, with his head buried in a plate and his hands and legs shaking from anger under the table." Renard pointed his chin in my direction to imply that Paul was in a rage at me, but I think it's more likely that his wrath was caused by Monsieur Renard's "humor."

Why did Paul put up with that man? Was he used to being abused, because of what I did to him when we were little? Was it because he believes in suffering as a pathway to God? If so, he certainly picked the right friend. Renard may be a famous playwright but he's a dreadful person. Surprisingly, the two men remained friends for five years, probably because Paul was away all the time. Then, oddly enough, it was Renard who ended the friendship. He said that Paul's rigidity and intolerance about the Dreyfus affair made it impossible to keep him as a friend.

My party, of course, was a complete failure, and I determined never to give another, at least with people like Jules Renard as guests. And I didn't. Whenever I had a little windfall and wanted to celebrate, I called in the bums who slept in the courtyard to rejoice with me. They were thrilled to be fed champagne and hors d'oeuvres, and there wasn't a single criticism of me in the entire bunch.

*T*hings got worse and worse between Rodin and me, until the tension was so bad I couldn't move without hurting. In 1892 I decided to find out once and for all whether he loved his old lady more than he did me. Early one summer morning I got a ride in a milk cart to Rodin's estate at Meudon-Val-Fleury, the quiet little town where he lived on a hill high above the Seine. I sniffed the heavenly iris blossoms and enjoyed the dazzling beauty of the country sky as I walked through the double row of chestnut trees that led to his home. I went around the low barrier of hedges to the left for the main entrance on the east side of the villa, which overlooked a magnificent view of the valley. From there I could see the three stone steps that led up to the wooden entrance of the square old house with a high pointed roof. I thought Rodin and his paramour surely would enter or exit through that door if I waited long enough, and concealed myself between two large rose bushes that were nearby. At first the great chestnut trees cast their shade upon me, and it was fairly comfortable. But as the hot sun rose overhead, my sweat began to gush like a horse trough. What was worse, my body began to itch all over, and every time I tried to scratch I was stuck by the thorns of the rose bushes. Soon my feet in their heavy clogs began to throb, especially the shorter leg, as I shifted from one foot to the other. I only wanted to go home, toss off my clothes, and grab a drink of water. Nevertheless, I had come for a reason—to find out which of us Rodin loved more—and I was determined to stick it out despite my physical misery.

Somehow, Rose saw me as I wriggled around, or perhaps the rising sun threw my shadow towards their window as the hours passed. She rushed out into the garden brandishing a shovel, and started to beat me up with it. Rose was a strong lady, old peasant that she was, but I was younger and able to duck most of the blows. With wild hair streaked with white flying behind her, dressed in somber black with scarves flapping in the wind, she flew at me, shrieking like some strange legendary creature from Rodin's *Gates of Hell.* Battering me with the shovel, she screamed, "You think you are the first one, Missy? No! There have been hundreds of others, and he always leaves them to come back to me. Mark my words, he'll leave you, too! Listen to me, girl. We didn't have two crusts of bread and were living in a stable. I went out to work as a seamstress to keep us from starving. I kept his statues wet while he was out gallivanting around with other women. I put up with his abuse because I always knew he would return to me. Do you think he can forget all that?" Here the old lady misjudged one of her blows. She swung the shovel at me one last time, and hit the air. The momentum of the shovel swung her around and pulled her down to the ground. As she fell, she shrieked, "Rodin! Rodin! Your whore is killing me! Come and take her away!" Rodin came running out, yelling, "Rose! My Rose! Are you hurt? Are you all right?" He cradled her in his arms, as he murmured, "Oh Rose, are you hurt? How's your heart? You shouldn't have come out. Come, let me take you inside."

Then he said, "I'm sorry, Camille, but she has a bad heart. I have to take her inside." And he escorted her into the house. I was shocked. Although he had "rescued" me, I was outraged and humiliated that he'd stayed with her and not me. I sat there in the dirt beside the roses until nightfall, sobbing and rubbing my bruises, hoping Rodin would come back to comfort me. But of course he didn't. I'd found the answer to my question. I now knew which one of us Rodin loved more. It reminded me of when I was a child and Maman and Papa would go into their bedroom and lock the door.

I remember standing outside their door when I was five years old. What were they doing in there that they needed to lock me out? I knocked on the door. No one answered. I knocked again, louder. "Go away, Camille," my father said not unkindly. I tried to peek through the keyhole, and saw something that looked like a camel under the bedclothes. A camel? Under the bedclothes? I knew that couldn't be, so I figured I must be wrong. Then I put my ear to the keyhole. First I heard strange cries like a savage animal from what must have been Papa. There were no sounds at all from Maman. Then I heard thumping noises. Whatever was going on in there? What was Maman doing to Papa? Was she beating him? I was terrified, humiliated, and excited, and tried not to throw up or wet my pants. My dear Papa, my own person! What was he doing in the bedroom with that woman? Why wasn't he doing it with me? If they couldn't let me be part of it, at least they could let me watch. I knew that things would never be the same again. I lay down outside the door on a little rag rug and cried and wet my pants. The urine seeped through the rug. Years later the stain was still there. When Maman came out I thought she'd be furious with me, but for once she said nothing and just walked away.

When I finally left Rodin's garden and went home, I was possessed by an enormous rage, the like of which I had never experienced before. It was as if a huge fire flamed up inside me and filled every available space from the tips of my fingers to the bottoms of my feet, throughout my chest and into my head, where it blazed even behind my eyes so I could hardly see. It was so mighty a feeling I couldn't contain it, and could get a bit of relief only by fantasizing that I kicked Rodin, sliced him into bits with his sharpest sculpting knife, took his favorite mallet and pounded him to death. The fires blazed away inside of me until I couldn't bear it any longer and blacked out.

For years I'd wavered back and forth about leaving Rodin, not wanting to give up the last shred of hope that somehow, some day, he would come back to me as the man of my dreams. This time was different. When I regained consciousness, it was with the clear understanding that I'd been fooling myself, that my love affair with Rodin was over and I *never* would be restored to the good graces of my dear brother. As the knowledge penetrated to the bottom of my soul, unnatural sounds like the shrieks of a wounded bird erupted from the darkness inside me. I got dizzy and passed out again on the floor.

When I awoke what I presumed to be several hours later, a miracle had happened. My love for Rodin and the pain it brought about had disappeared, never to return. Instead of a god who could do no wrong, he was just a funny little old man who was out for his own pleasure and nobody else's. Strangely enough, I hated him for that with a monstrous passion as powerful as my former love. I didn't understand why my love had changed to hate, but I was so relieved that I didn't care.

Feeling the way I did, it was not difficult to move out of Rodin's studio. He stood there watching as I packed my things, mopping away with a massive hand the tears that cascaded down his cheeks. But my heart was hardened and I paid him no mind. I swept out the door without even saying good-bye.

At this time, Rodin and his Rose were living in an ancient house at 23 rue des Grands-Augustins, near the Seine. According to Eugène Blot, my friend and gallery owner, a neighbor said she walked by the house one day and saw that a moving cart had stopped in front of their door. Rodin himself was overseeing the placement of some furniture and many of his sculptures onto the cart. They were moving to the country to Meudon. The neighbor said that Rodin looked dreadful, that he was suffering from neuralgia and couldn't sleep. She said he suddenly looked old, that his skin was pasty and veined with dark patches and his eyes were bloodshot and red. He no longer smiled and his features were tight. He spoke of serious problems. His shoulders automatically jerked forward as if he were trying to throw off his worries. If we hadn't already broken up, his move to the country would have done it, as it was positive proof that he didn't intend to leave his bizarre old lady.

Rodin and I saw each other from time to time after I left, but the relationship continued to deteriorate. One day I said to myself, "Why should I meet with that old goat? He only wants to steal my work. He won't be satisfied until he gets it all." Monsieur Morhardt was planning to visit me the next Monday to see my new statue, and Rodin wanted to accompany him. He said he wanted to see how I was, but I'm sure he just wanted to spy on me to get an idea for his next sculpture. I wrote Morhardt a letter to ask him to do everything possible to keep Rodin from coming with him. I told him that I don't like to show unfinished pieces and there's no reason why people shouldn't wait until the work is completed before seeing them. I said that if he could get the idea through

Rodin's thick head that I do not want to see him ever again, I would deeply appreciate it. He certainly knows people are saying he's the real creator of my sculptures, so why add oil to the fire? He did terrible things to me. He stole all my work and sold it under his name for a tremendous profit. As soon as I finished a statue, he snuck into my *atelier* and smuggled it away. He forced me to quit the National Salon because of the spiteful things he did to me. He paid a mold maker to destroy several finished pieces in my *atelier*. He insulted me by making postcards of my portrait despite my asking him not to and selling them for a lot of money. He was scared that when he died, I would be given the respect as an artist that was given to him in his lifetime. He couldn't bear the thought and wanted to clutch at me after his death as he did during his life. I knew I'd be followed all my life by this vengeful monster.

Fortunately, Morhardt honored my request. Apparently he got through to Rodin, who listened to me for a change and did not try to contact me for two years.

*E*ven though Paul's rejection of me stung deeply, I loved him enough to reconcile with him, at least on the surface. The memory of our last meeting lay on my heart like a lump of lead until the end of my life, but I couldn't renounce him any more than I could myself. Paul was my oldest friend and sometimes I think he's engraved in my bones. Gradually, he began to drop in on my *atelier* as if nothing had happened between us. The first time he came I was so happy to see him I threw myself into his arms. A tear rolled down his cheeks; I didn't know if it was his or mine. I pulled up a chair and the very same moment he shouted, "What are you sculpting?" I yelled, "What are you writing?" We laughed uproariously like old times and our words gushed out like a dam that has burst its barriers. Then we started to write to each other again, never mentioning the horrible affair of the abortion.

After I left Rodin, my entire social life revolved around Paul and his friends. They filled the empty space left by the circle of artists Rodin and I had socialized with, and I looked forward with pleasure to our meetings.

In 1893, to my dismay, Paul was temporarily appointed to a diplomatic post in Boston and departed for the United States. Naturally, his friends weren't interested in seeing me without Paul. I was desperately lonely for him and soon was reduced to talking to myself, or chatting up the concierge so I wouldn't forget what a human voice sounded like.

I filled what little time I could take from my sculpting to walk the working class neighborhood of the Boulevard d'Italie, where I got many ideas for new sculptures. There I saw the old blind musician, little girls playing in the streets, and workers strolling home for dinner. Then I went home and modeled small terra cotta images of what I'd seen, which were both lovely and unique. My goal at this time was to work as differently from Rodin as possible so it would be harder for him to copy from me. Since he did nudes I put clothes on my people. Where he worked large I worked small. Where he concentrated on naked women I worked on completely original subjects. Where he stole from others my ideas came only from inside my head. I sculpted so many figures I didn't know what to do with them, so I stuck them away in a drawer. That's where they stayed until I got so furious with Rodin I couldn't bear it and chopped them to bits. I wish I hadn't destroyed them all, as I think no other artist has sculpted anything like them.

Now and then I received a letter from the great master himself, pleading to visit me. He wrote he had come to see me many times but the concierge would never let him in. Good! I'll have to give him a tip. Rodin said he banged on the door over and over again until he was forced to go away in despair.

"Why wouldn't you open the door for me?" he wrote. "You must know how much I love you and how painful it is for me to bear your hatred. Do you realize how agonizing it is to have a person one loves hate one as you do me? The pain cramps up my stomach from the moment I wake until I go to sleep. I push Rose away in the nighttime because she isn't you. I turn to one woman after another to make me feel better, but not a one makes the pain go away.

"Why do you hate me so much? Is it because I didn't marry you? I thought my love would be enough for you. We worked side by side and created our finest work together. We made sweet and passionate love, as I have with no other woman, before or since. Why did our love have to stop? Why do you continue to reject me? I've done all for your career that you will allow me to do, but you still have nothing to do with me. You leave me confused, bewildered, and despondent. Won't you reconsider and at least answer this letter? Your hatred is my despair.

Avec amour,

Ton Auguste"

I ripped up the letter right after I read it and threw the pieces up into the air. Then I laughed gayly with the only pleasure I ever experienced in the living death he abandoned me to. "Good," I said to Tabasco #7. "Now he knows a little of what I've gone through!"

Apparently things weren't going well with Rodin either. I know because my dear friend and gallery owner Eugène Blot told me about it. Here's the conversation we had:

Blot: I met Rodin in the street the other day and he looked ghastly. I asked him where he was going and he answered that he was wandering around looking for you. He said he does that all the time, as he finds it difficult to work. It's as if he suddenly got old. He said he can't sleep, and was in pain from neuralgia night and day. He has red eyes and never smiles anymore. He's in mourning for you, Camille.

Me: (smiling) Isn't that just too bad.

Blot: Can't you at least write him a note, so he'll feel a little better?"

Me: Eugène, you don't get the point. I don't want him to feel better. Why should I, when he's done such terrible things to me?"

Blot: I don't see that at all, Camille. Even though you've broken up, he keeps trying to help you with your career. He gets you exhibitions, tries to find you commissions, and even manages to find patrons to buy your sculptures once in a while. I wish he would help me with my gallery the way he does you! I wish *anybody* would help me with my gallery the way he does you. Whenever a person brings up your name, he tells them what a wonderful sculptor you are. He tries to get museums to buy your sculptures. And he keeps on paying the rent at 113 Boulevard d'Italie.

Me: I let him do that because he owes me a huge amount of money from the profit he makes selling my sculptures as his own.

Blot: Camille, I don't know where your head is!

Me: Well, sometimes he does a few nice things for me. He asked Henry Roujon at the Ministère des Beaux-Arts to see that the state gives me the block of marble I needed for my *Sakountala*. Unfortunately, they turned me down again, saying that marble was reserved for the exclusive use of commissioned works. Maybe it was for the best, because I'd hate to owe that monster anything. I still don't understand him. He did the most abominable things to me, like having the *mouleur* blow up my statues. And then he does something nice, like trying to get the marble for me. It's awful, being catapulted back and forth from one set of feelings to another. I'd be better off if he was always vile.

Blot: (Shakes his head and walks off.)

Then I got another letter from Rodin saying only, "I love you. My heart is broken. Don't do this to me. You are destroying me. Your Auguste."

I was sick of his whining. I held up the letter, raised a sharp sculpting knife as high in the air as Perseus hoisted the head of Medusa, and with one mighty downward motion slashed the letter in two. Then I stuck the dismembered slices of paper into an envelope and sent it back to Rodin. Blot told me later that on the day Rodin received the letter, he arrived at Marx's house in a state of shock, submerged in grief, and weeping piteously as he explained that I had severed all connections with him. Good! It served him right. Why didn't he worry about his broken heart when I needed him?

Although I hated to say so to Eugène, I can't deny that Rodin did a few good things for me. When a banquet was scheduled for January, 1895 in celebration of Puvis de Chavannes' seventieth birthday, Rodin, the president of the organizing committee, said he believed women should attend and he wanted to invite talented women such as Camille Claudel to the ceremony. Morhardt, the secretary of the committee, said he didn't even dare to bring it up for a vote at a meeting. The members would be horrified and say that it would make us the laughing stock of all Paris. I was very upset when Morhardt told me this story. *The laughing stock?* What's with these men? Don't they understand anything? Don't they know that women are as human as they are, and that men have no right to deny us our birthrights? I would like to take away all *their* rights and show them how it feels! Some day they will be put in jail for fostering such inequalities. I only wish it were now.

Although the committee didn't follow through on the request, Rodin and Morhardt saw to it that my *Clotho* was donated to the Musée du Luxenburg in Puvis' honor. Rodin started the subscription to raise the money to purchase the statue with a thousand franc contribution, which enabled me to carve the marble version of *Clotho*. With the remaining funds, Morhardt bought the plaster copy of *La Petite Chatelâine*. Even though the money I earned from these sales saved me from starvation for a while, I must admit I had mixed feelings about accepting it. I vastly preferred to be paid by any other source. Rodin just does these things to confuse me. He's impossible! Why doesn't he just leave me alone?

Another piece of good luck for Camille this year, for a change. An assistant of Rodin introduced me to a patron, Monsier G. Lenseigne from Châteauroux, who worked out a plan with me in which *Sakountala* would go to the museum at Châteauroux, where it was installed in a place of honor in the main hall. Unfortunately, the piece was trashed by an anonymous critic, who wrote among other things that the statue was "a catastrophic accident" and "depravity in plaster." Imagine that dimwit calling the beautiful *Sakountala* that I planned and worked on for five years an "accident!"

Even worse was the vicious reaction of some of the villagers of Châteauroux. The ignoramuses joked about the beautiful Hindu legend, with snide comments about its sexual implications. They said my work was unfinished, out of proportion, and that it was impossible to tell which figure was the female and which one the male. That really bothered me, as I've always thought it very important to keep peoples' sexual identity straight and I went to a lot of trouble to differentiate the two bodies.

Many women began to ride bicycles in those days and to wear trousers like a man. I never rode a bicycle. Even if I could have afforded one, I was lucky at the end of a twelve hour work day if I could even stand up. More important, I've always seen myself as a woman, as my sex has given me more pleasure than anything else in my life. I liked being female and saw no reason to dress like a woman pretending to be a man. I always wanted to wear female clothes and not look like some hermaphrodite. Even if it might have been more comfortable to wear trousers while sculpting than the voluminous skirts real women wear, I had no wish to don men's pants. What sex would I have looked like if I had? If those idiots couldn't tell the difference between a naked man and a naked woman, what would they have said if they'd seen me wearing pants? I can only imagine. Somebody even wanted to hide the sculpture behind a curtain, to keep the public from seeing naked figures. Can you believe those filthy minds that find lewdness where others see beauty? How perverted can you get? I tried not to let it hurt, but it did—badly. I wanted to take my ax and destroy the statue. If it had been in my *atelier*, I would have.

Apparently, I didn't have to destroy the sculpture. The museum did it for me. To add to other indignities the statue (and I) suffered, in the process of moving the group upstairs to the second floor (where ostensibly not as many people would see it) one foot was broken off. Over the protests of the officials, it stayed in the main gallery. To the best of my knowledge, the broken foot has never been repaired and lies there covered in dust to the present day.

A few of my friends found the treatment of *Sakountala* as obnoxious as I did. Gustave Geffroy, the well-known critic, answered the ridiculous critique by writing in *Le Journal* that visitors to the Salon remembered *Sakountala* as a sculpture in perfect scientific proportion, and were proud to defend it throughout France.

At the time, I considered Morhardt one of my good friends. After he bought the plaster copy of *La Petite Chatelâine*, he introduced me to one of my few good clients, Maurice Fenaille, who bought several of my works. Fenaille was an editor of *Le Temps* and connected to some of the most influential people in the art world, so I was very happy to be in his good graces. Morhardt also was the organizer of another exhibition in Geneva to celebrate Puvis de Chavannes, and invited me to contribute a plaster of *Les Causeuses* to the exhibition. I did so, and was grateful to have it purchased by the Geneva Museum.

Later in 1895, I accidently bumped into Rodin at an art opening. Since I suspected that he may have been behind Morhardt's recent efforts on

ALMA H. BOND

my behalf, I tried my best to appear warm and gracious. Rodin was delighted and wrote me a letter about how thrilled he was to have me seem so friendly. He said he'd paid for his sins. At least he admitted that he'd committed sins against me. That's more than he ever did before. He also offered to introduce me to the President of the Republic. I was not interested in meeting the President of the Republic or any other politician. I thanked Rodin and turned down his offer. I answered that I could not attend the meeting as I had nothing appropriate to wear for such an auspicious occasion. I added that I also had to finish the marble version of the little women, which I was sculpting for the Norwegan artist, Fritz Thaulow.

The "little women" were my statue of *Les Causeuses*, which I was trying hard to finish for the 1896 Salon. Unfortunately, I was unable to complete it on time. It's very difficult to work on marble and onyx. Then I worked very hard to have it ready for the next Salon exhibition. Thaulow didn't get his sculpture until 1898, and it never made it to the Salon. Nevertheless, those critics like Jeanniot who saw the sculpture raved about it, saying it was haunting and beautifully realized. I don't believe a man could have sculpted that piece. I much prefer to see a sculpture of a woman sculpted by a woman. It seems to me we see more profoundly into the female soul and nurture some secret men will never understand. *The Gossips* was different from any of my other work. It was gentle and delicate, and so small it could be held in the palm of one's hand, as though the whole sculpture were a secret to be hidden away from the cold-hearted world.

The idea for *Les Causeuses* came to me as I was sitting in a railway compartment on my way to visit Villeneuve. Four ladies shared the compartment with me and kept blathering away about their "friends." They reminded me so much of Mme Mohardt and her cronies I was inspired to sculpt *The Gossips*. It turned out to be one of my best sculptures yet, one of the most original ever created by anyone. Four women are leaning into each other and yapping with malicious delight, talking about someone as the women on the train were doing, the way people are always casting aspersions on me. You can see the pleasure in the eyes of the young woman in the marble model, as she bites deeper into the juicy scandal she's spewing out. The others lean in with intense curiosity, as if there's nothing more exciting than to besmirch (my) character. The bronze version reminds me of Maman's sewing circle and the person they are defaming is me. But I got even with them. I took all their clothes off. For those suppressed ladies, there's nothing worse I could have done to them (even if they don't know about it).

When I was forty-one years old, I did another rendition of the statue I like better, because the idea of the gossips is less personal and miles away from Maman and her buddies. This time, the gossips, four maturing young women with fresh, perfect bodies, are much more beautiful. I would guess they're gossiping about men. I like the statue so much it was almost worth being gossiped about to get the idea.

Eugène Blot said in his catalog he cast fifty copies of *Les Causeuses* in bronze, but I think he lied about the number to make his gallery (and me) look good. He probably only cast twenty-five. I love Eugène. What a good friend he has been to me, probably the best I ever had. It was typical of him that he had one cast in bronze for his personal collection. My friend Philippe Berthelot bought the original plaster model, the one which was shown at the Champ de Mars in 1895 to great acclaim, and Sotheby's acquired one of the bronze versions in London. Models in marble were purchased by Fritz Thaulow and one without a screen for Pontrémoli, the famous architect.

Despite this temporary flare-up of sales, however, I still was not able to support myself. I sculpted other variants of the sculpture in plaster, bronze, and even one in green onyx, an exquisitely difficult material to work with. Some were made with a screen and some without. My favorite is the one with a green onyx screen, in which the figures are cast in bronze. The whole sculpture is only about two feet wide (forty-five centimeters high and forty-two-and-a-fifth centimeters long). Nobody can say this work is anything like Rodin's. And he certainly couldn't copy it because he never could carve in onyx.

I exhibited two sculptures at the 1897 Salon, *The Bust of Madame D*, which I myself cut directly into the marble, and *La Vague (The Wave)* which I later sculpted in onyx and bronze. In it three women are holding hands in the ocean, as a huge wave hovers above them and threatens to overwhelm them. The piece is somewhat like *Les Causeuses*, as both sculptures are small and delicate and illustrate a group of deeply involved women. I believe *La Vague* was inspired by Hokusai, the great Japanese artist. To my relief, Morhardt bought the plaster of the sculpture. That was the last time I had any satisfactory dealings with him, for I soon discovered he was not the friend he pretended to be.

All of a sudden, I was becoming known and many journalists wanted to write about me. An article which particularly pleased me appeared in 1896 in the *Revue encyclopédique Larousse*, which said I was a contemporary woman who was not afraid to be successful in the arts. The author was not named. He must have been afraid of the attacks that would follow the publication of the article. Otherwise, why would he want it published anonymously?

The last direct communication between Rodin and me was in 1897. When he began the sketches of his statue of *Balzac*, we were at the apex of our love and I had contributed many ideas for the work. He used to whisper in my ear, "You are my muse, my inspiration, my great love. How did I ever sculpt without you?" He apparently felt that gave him the right to consult with me about the statue even after we were estranged. When it was finished, Rodin wrote to ask me to drop by and give him my opinion about it. I thought I would for old time's sake, and because even though he steals my work, he's still the greatest male sculptor in France.

I stopped into his *atelier* to look at the Balzac when I knew Rodin was in Rome receiving one of his numerous awards (probably one that should have been given to me), so I wouldn't have to see him personally. Then even though I hated him, I knew I had to be fair about his work. I left him a note which said the Balzac is a truly great work of art, much better than his sketches had prepared me for. I told him I particularly liked the contrast between Balzac's head and the draperies and I thought the loose sleeves were wonderfully creative and a clever demonstration of Balzac's hotheaded rebelliousness. I wondered how he got that effect and asked if he had ripped the sleeves. (I never did find out.) I also wrote I thought the work was very exciting and better than any other artist of our times could do.

I continued with what was probably the real reason for my letter. "I would also like to ask your help about a problem that is causing me much *angst*. Mathias Morhardt is *not an honest man*, even though he claims to be. He is not my friend. He writes to Paul for information about me, and then uses what Paul tells him to betray me. Although he's arranged for a commission from *the Mercure de France* to make casts for my bust of you, I'm not interested, as the commission will cost me more money than I can earn from it. I understand he's writing an article about me, which he claims will do much for me and make me famous. I don't want it published. It will bring jealousy, anger and the wish for revenge down on my head, which I do not need, to say the least. As far as his wife is concerned, she, like most women, pretends to care about me. But you know very well these women all hate me and will use any weapon to get me out of their husband's way. As soon as a man comes along who is kind and generous to me, they'll take him in their arms and keep him from helping me. Because of them, I'm afraid I shall never be able to reap the fruits of my labor but will melt away in the dark forever. Please keep these things I tell you secret, as it would endanger my life for them to become public."

Rodin answered my letter, but it was of no help at all. I could have swatted him! That fool I used to love! Whatever was wrong with me, to have let that blockhead come near me? Believe me, I never will make that mistake again. He denied what he knows to be true, and wrote that in contrast to what I thought, the Morhardts were good friends of mine and I should remain faithful to them. Why, oh why, does no one understand that I live in constant fear for my life? Why won't anyone see the terrible hatred and jealousy women feel towards me, and they'll do anything to hurt me and keep me out of their husbands' lives?

Although these women hate and despise me, they talk about me all the time. Guess what they whisper about the most? Right, my sex life! Probably because they don't have any themselves and are jealous. ("Can you believe she sleeps with that old lecher? A married man, yet. And twice her age, at that. What a curse she is on her lovely parents! Pssst…pssst…listen to this I heard she had an abortion! What an abomination! A disgrace to the Catholic Church. She should be horsewhipped! Monique, Brigitte, isn't it pathetic she has a limp? It ruins her beauty. You disagree? You say it serves her right for having an abortion? The woman is positively crazy. Even her own mother says so. She lives alone with seventeen mangy cats!") You'd think if they hated me so much they'd want to forget about me, but no, they can't find enough awful things to say about me. According to them, I'm a witch who rides her broomstick at night, and my seventeen cats are my accomplices.

Unfortunately for Rodin, the public did not agree with my appraisal of his Balzac. In fact, the members of the Société des Gens de Lettres were so angry about what they called his "sketch" of Balzac that they demanded a refund of the 10,000 franc advance they had given him. Rather than bother to sue them, Rodin returned the money. But that was far from the end of the story. His friends were furious about the incident, and started a petition and a 30,000 franc subscription to purchase the sculpture.

I ordinarily hate politics, and usually ignore what the papers tell us is going on. But it was difficult for me to overlook the Dreyfus affair, which was on the lips of all Frenchman for twelve years and had a devastating effect on the sale of Rodin's magnificent creation.

Alfred Dreyfus was a Jewish captain in the French army who was arrested and court-martialed for high treason on charges of being a German spy. He was exiled for life to Devil's Island. His devoted wife and brother fought tirelessly for his freedom, however, and found documents that proved the condemnatory evidence had been written by an officer named Esterhazy and not by Dreyfus at all. Nevertheless, Esterhazy was acquitted. This split the Republic down the middle. Riots erupted in the city, anti-Semitism was rife all over France, and neighbors and families turned against each other with opposing beliefs. Discussions of art became a rarity among artists, who were too busy flagellating or praising Dreyfus to have time for creativity. Jules Renard and my brother almost came to blows about the case, which marked the end of their friendship. The novelist Emile Zola,, the most famous of Dreyfus supporters, sent his famous letter to the President of the Republic, entitled "J'accuse." The French government did not take Zola's propaganda lightly. They summoned him to court, where they found him guilty of treason, and imposed a fine on him and a year in prison. Zola chose to exile himself in England instead. Years later, Dreyfus was pardoned by a new French president. But Rodin, who was anti-Dreyfus, was embarrassed that Zola, the president of the Société des Gens de Lettres, and Dreyfus's most important supporter, had defended him. Rodin declined the subscription to buy Balzac and moved the statue to the garden of his home in the Villa des Brilliants in Meudon, where it probably rests to this day.

My family was against Dreyfus. Since I was always an apolitical person, I tended to go along with their political views, especially those of my father. Even though I was no longer a practicing Catholic, I tended to think of Jews and Protestants as strangers who were not to be trusted. I was bored with the affair and happy when it was finally settled, as I had a problem much closer to my heart.

Octave Mirbeau, one of the critics who had always liked my work, used the Champ de Mars exhibition as the opportunity to write me that he had invited Rodin to come visit him along with Mademoiselle Claudel to discuss an idea he had that would benefit me. Rodin answered it had been two years since he'd seen or written to me and he didn't know whether I would consent to visit Mirbeau while he was there. (You have that right, Monsieur Rodin!) According to Mirbeau, Rodin repeatedly professed his belief in my genius. Soon after, the critic wrote his greatest review of my work, saying I was "an anomaly, an astonishing natural mutation, a woman genius" and even though I worked passionately and tenaciously on my art, it still was not subsidizing me. He ended with a plea to the Ministry to purchase Claudel's work, as I was very discouraged and thinking of abandoning my art. Right, Mr. Mirbeau! That's exactly what I was thinking. Why should I keep spilling my life's blood on these beautiful works of art when many more people prefer to buy mawkish cupids sneaking around with their bows and arrows? When the only person who makes money from my work is that double-crosser Rodin?

I found a way to let out my rage at Rodin and have some fun at the same time in a series of sketches about him and Rose I sent to Paul. In the first one, a scrawny, hairy hag is in bed with Rodin, and with raised finger is prodding him to "perform." In another drawing called *The Confinement System,* a man (guess who) is sitting chained to a prison wall. A nude prison guard (female, of course) marches around shouldering a witch's broomstick. My favorite scene of this group is the one in which Rodin and Rose are sketched with their rear ends glued together. The man is seeking to break free by holding onto a tree, but doesn't seem too successful at cutting the cord. The sketch is called *The Collage*, which is a pun on *être à la colle*, the expression for unmarried people who live together. Paul had an interesting response to the drawings. He said I've always bullied people by belittling them. I can't argue with that one.

At this time I was working on *L'Age Mûr*. Rodin did not know anything about it. I hesitated to tell him because I knew he would be upset by a public exhibition of his most intimate problems. But I have to go where my heart takes me, and I cannot choose my subjects to suit Monsieur Rodin.

I first sent Paul a few small sketches of the proposed sculpture that would become *L'Age Mûr*, in which an aging man is snatched from the hands of a beautiful young woman by an elderly hag. It is, of course, the story of my love affair with Rodin, who was dragged away from me by the tricks of his concubine, Rose Beuret, just as my mother always tried to tear my father away from me. The sculpture is also an allegory of humanity itself, in which the relentless progression of time wrenches our aging bodies away from the passions of youth and beauty. The curve of the rocks in the front of the sculpture suggests the unfurling of the waves, which roll inexorably onto the shore to symbolize the indomitable destiny which rules our lives. This is a technical innovation I'm proud of. The traditional use of the pedestal as an inert lump upon which the statue stands is wasted space. In this work the curl of the rocks at the front of the base is an intricate part of the sculpture.

Miracle of miracles, an art inspector named Armand Silvestre was sent by the State in 1895 to offer me a commission for a bust. Much as I needed the money, when I'm involved in a sculpture, that's where my heart is, and I don't like to abandon it for another work. So I told Monsieur Silvestre I really wanted to finish my group of three, which I would do for five thousand francs, and asked him if he could substitute that project for the bust. He said he couldn't promise, but he would write to the minister and tell him of my request. To my surprise, Raymond Poincuré signed a decree instructing me to create a plaster of *L'Age Mûr* at the normal price for an original sculpture of two thousand five hundred francs. I accepted, but I should have asked for more, as my funds were rapidly dwindling and the State was in no hurry to pay me what they'd promised.

The larger than life-size *L'Age Mûr* was registered in 1895 as a work of art commissioned by the state. I used two models a day, a man and a woman. I worked on it seven days a week, twelve hours a day, until the light became so dim I no longer could see what I was doing. Even then I sometimes continued by candlelight, mainly using my sense of touch. I was often so tired my legs couldn't hold me up anymore and I fell into bed the moment I stopped sculpting. But despite all my hard work, the State continued to drag its heels about paying me. After many months, even though I rarely had enough money for a decent meal, I was happy to receive the two thousand five hundred franc purchase price. Although I'd already advanced two thousand francs on this group, I was relieved to collect the money, as I needed it badly to pay for new supplies, to say nothing of my long overdue rent. Six months later, the money was all gone, and I requested the State for a further advance. They sent Armand Silvestre to check up on me again. Apparently satisfied I wouldn't keep the money without supplying the statue and embarrass them, I received another thousand francs. This enabled me to continue working until the sculpture was finished in 1898, when I notified Henry Roujon, the Director of Fine Arts. Armand Silvestre wearily trudged in again to check up on whether I'd been a good girl and done what they demanded, which was to change the emphasis in the group of three from Rodin's treachery to a more abstract meaning. Silvestre informed Monsieur Roujon I had reworked the sculpture to symbolize a mature man who is carried away by his advancing years, even though a young woman tries unsuccessfully to hold him back. Despite Silvestre's recommendation, months passed by and still the State still did not come through with the money they owed me.

I was frustrated and angry and did not know where to turn for help to get what I was entitled to. I was afraid to ask Morhardt to intervene for me again because I was terrified he would tell Rodin about the sculpture, who would then do everything he could to stop the commission. I knew how sensitive he was to any public disclosure of his personal life, and *L'Age Mûr* is about as personal as you can get. Too bad! So I asked my dear father to step in and help me. He wrote a letter to the Director of Fine Arts, informing him of the horrendous expenses involved in creating such a work, including the cost of models, casting, and so forth. Would you believe, they never answered him! Papa, a man who's highly respected in Villeneuve, and who's been a trusted government official for so many decades! I was greatly aggravated they'd humiliated him in this way. By this time, I had nothing to lose, so I took matters in my own hands and wrote a scathing letter to the minister that said he'd commissioned me four years ago to sculpt *L'Age Mûr*, for which I was advanced one thousand francs, with the rest due when the work was completed. When I failed to receive the rest of the money, I continued, I had my father write him a letter, which his highness did not deign to answer. I said I'd spent two thousand francs of my own money on this sculpture, and insisted on being paid immediately, even though Monsieur Rodin disapproves. I ended my letter by saying I absolutely refused to wait any longer for what is mine by rights, even though an important personage like him decrees it.

I was vindicated when I was paid on January 5, 1899 and the Ministry of Fine Arts gave instructions for me to proceed with the bronze casting of the group. They stipulated neither the amount of money to be paid me nor the date it was due. Frankly, I was too angry with the treatment Papa and I had received to feel happy about it, but my temper was soothed a bit by the money. My relief, however, was short-lived. To my great shock, on June 24 I received an official letter from Henry Roujon in which the commission was canceled. No explanation was given.

I knew very well Rodin was behind their change of heart, and the loss of my commission was his answer to my letter written in plaster and blood. He certainly must have seen the work at the Société Nationale des Beaux-Arts exhibition of spring, 1899, where he was president of the sculpture section, and I'm sure was upset by it. I knew he would be, which is why I didn't let him find out about it in the first place. Still, one would think an artist who claims to love me would feel some compassion for the agonized girl in the statue, even if he could forget about the years I spent designing and molding it, as well as my desperate need for funds.

This incident taught me how right I was to refuse to have anything to do with Monsieur Rodin. I decided there'd be no further communication, no favors, no visits between us ever again. And I meant *ever!* I knew I would rather starve than to receive his "favors." To get away from him and his henchmen completely, I even left the Société Nationale and returned to the Société des Artistes Français, where I had not exhibited since 1889. But I still couldn't escape from the clutches of Rodin and his gang, as artists tend to congregate in the same places. Wherever I went, there they were, looking for more of my sculptures to steal. So after 1905, I stopped exhibiting altogether. If I knew Rodin truly was suffering from my abandonment and not just working to get my pity, I would be ecstatic. He deserved at least a taste of the anguish and desperation he had put me through.

My battle against the French government went on for a whole decade. I had tried to exhibit *L'Age Mûr* at the 1900 Universal Exhibition, but it was rejected. Now who do you think was responsible for that? Hint: Rodin was allowed to build his own pavilion there. In a rage, I withdrew all my other works from the exhibition. Despite the efforts of my friend Blot, who wrote to Dujardin-Beaumetz, the Under-Secretary of Fine Arts, for a follow-up of Silvestre's promise to purchase the bronze sculpture of *L'Age Mûr*, no satisfaction was forthcoming. Blot received a letter that said no promise for a commission had ever been given. Since Sylvestre was dead by then, there was no evidence such a commitment had been made. I had lost the last battle of the war. I had nothing left to fight with.

Fortunately, Rodin had introduced me at the Salon exhibition to Léon Lhermitte, the famous artist known for his paintings of harvesters. I was honored when the distinguished artist bowed and personally showed me his painting, *The Haymaker.* I told him I particularly admired the treatment of light in his painting, which reminded me of Rembrandt. He answered that Vincent Van Gogh had made the same comment. The painting suggested *L'Age Mûr* to me, in that it illustrates the three stages of life: youth, adulthood, and old age. Even the positioning of the ages is similar, with the young girl on the right, the couple in the center, and the old man holding a scythe representing death on the left. When I told this to Monsieur Lhermitte, he thanked me for the compliment and gallantly said he was pleased to hear it, as he thought I was a wonderful sculptor. The painting had been awarded the *grand prix* at the World's Fair in Paris in 1889, and incidentally, was an inspiration to Van Gogh, who emulated Lhermitte's technique in *The Potato Eaters*.

Monsieur Lhermitte did me a great service by presenting me to Captain Louis Tissier, a young officer in the French army. Like Monsieur Lhermitte, the Captain fell in love with my work. He immediately asked if he could purchase a plaster copy of *L'Abandon*, but I persuaded him to have a bronze made of *L'Age Mûr* instead. He was so taken with me he would have agreed to anything I suggested. In gratitude, I returned Monsieur Lhermitte's favor by sculpting a bust of his photographer son, Charles, and presenting it to the senior Lhermitte as a gift. I enjoyed sculpting the portrait of the young man because I admired his father so much. Charles himself I could have done without. In my opinion, he was a dilettante, and the bust's not one of my best works. Incidentally, I never saw it again. It seems to have disappeared. Maybe Rodin has it.

I personally oversaw the casting for Captain Tissier in the Thiébaut Frères Foundry, and that was one purchase which turned out satisfactorily all around. I was blessed to obtain the services of Monsieur Frères, who worked well with me, because everything is trial and error in the foundry business, and Foundry Masters are a rare find. The best thing about having a statue cast in bronze is that many sculptures can be made from the same clay model, whereas a marble version must be carved from scratch each time.

The metal casting process itself is quite simple, although the technicians work very hard at it. Imagine taking a simple wax candle, packing mud, mortar, or concrete around it, while leaving the bottom open. When the material hardens and dries, you place it in a very hot oven with the open end facing down. The heat melts the wax, which escapes through little cylinders called sprues, leaving the hard material hollow. What remains inside is a negative image of the original candle. The hard and hot material is then turned so the open end faces up, and is filled with molten metal, which replaces the "lost wax." Virtually any metal that will melt at a manageable temperature can be used. Following my candle analogy, you can shape the wax into anything you like, with similar results. A large sculpture like *L'Age Mûr* is divided into manageable sections and then reassembled like a puzzle to duplicate the original.

When the bronze is finished, it has to be polished and rubbed with special patinas. I did the finishing on *L'Age Mûr*, for when the sculptor does the work herself the finished piece costs much less. And, of course, is much more to her liking. At least this is how we did it at the Thiébaut Frères Foundry. I really don't know too much about the way most metal casters manage the process, as it's very difficult to get specific information from a Foundry Master about their technique. They all maintain a certain level of secrecy since they derive much pleasure from their work, and are able to advertise a skill when they can accomplish a specialized task other foundries cannot. Thank goodness I visited Monsieur Singer's foundry in Somerset a long time ago. Whatever I know about foundries I learned from that good man.

In 1903 I returned to the Salon des Artistes Français and exhibited the original bronze of *L'Age Mûr*. Here I experienced my usual run of bad luck. The critics disliked the sculpture intensely, and worse humiliation, compared it to Rodin's work. Naturally, the comparison was in his favor. He and his gang always stick together. One critic even wrote that I was imitating Rodin, I, Camille Claudel, who never copied anyone in my life! Thank goodness for Charles Morice, who wrote my bronze group was worthy of the reputation earned by "this talented and courageous woman."

My friend Blot came to my rescue again and purchased six reduced size bronzes of *L'Age Mûr*, which he exhibited in his gallery in 1907 and1908. Unfortunately, the reduced size statues were not as effective as the original, but I was in no position to complain.

The Ministry of Fine Arts finally broke down enough to give me a few handouts, but the amounts they gave me, one hundred fifty francs, one hundred francs, and another one hundred fifty francs, were so insulting I didn't even bother to thank them. In 1906, thanks to the efforts of Blot, the State finally awarded me a commission. It was for an original sculpture in clay and a bronze copy of it, for which they offered to pay a commission of one thousand five hundred francs. By this time my health had degenerated to the point where I didn't feel capable of beginning a large new statue. So I took the figure of a woman I'd sculpted for *Sakountala* and christened it *Niobide blessée*. There were some differences, however. In contrast to Sakountala, who was beloved by the king, the mythological Greek princess Niobide was abandoned by the gods. Like me.

Niobe, in Greek mythology, was married to King Amphion, a son of the god Zeus. Niobe bore him six handsome sons and six beautiful daughters. Niobe, a bit of a braggart, boasted of her procreative superiority to the goddess Leto, who had only two children. The gods on distant Mount Olympus heard her words and decided to punish her. Leto's children—Apollo, a master archer; and Artemis, goddess of the hunt—were selected to kill all of Niobe's children. The grief-stricken mother could not be comforted. In sympathy, the gods turned her into a block of marble that sprouted streams of water like tears. Like me.

You can read the downward spiral of my love affair with Rodin by following the changes in the figure of *Sakountala*. In the first one, Rodin and I were ecstatic in our joy of being together, where I was inspired by the lovely marble statue of Pomona in the niche of the wall of our love nest in the La Folie Neufbourg. Our passion and delight in each other was apparent in my statue of *Vertumne et Pomona*. Next I entitled the statue *L'Abandon* or *The Desertion*, because although I still could abandon myself to passion, I had already sensed an ill wind was blowing my way. The last in the series was *Niobide blessée*, in which the man has disappeared altogether, and the wounded figure of Niobide is dying of grief. Like me.

I wrote back to the Ministry to ask for an extra five hundred francs, saying I couldn't sell them the statue for so little money, as I had spent a great deal on a model who charged excessively high rates. They turned me down again, but I was so destitute I couldn't afford to be stubborn and accepted the commission, my first ever from the State. It seems I had to sculpt a wounded, asexual figure to get them to commission me. Anything even faintly sexual from a woman artist is given thumbs down.

But even then I didn't get paid. A month later, one inch away from starvation, I wrote and demanded a partial payment. They sent Art

Inspector Armand Dayot again to investigate whether I was working on the statue or was trying to cheat them. He reported the sculpture was remarkable, and recommended the State pay me eight hundred francs in advance for it. I soon received part of the fee, with three thousand francs still due. After the statue was finished, I informed the Ministry over and over of its status, and repeatedly asked them to send me the rest of the money. As they requested, I sent *Niobide blessée* to the Dépôt des Marbres, but the Ministry took their own sweet time about paying me the three thousand francs. I was furious, as well as hungry. To make matters worse, when I tried to get my plaster back from the Dépôt des Marbres, would you believe, they wouldn't return it to me! I know why they wouldn't. Rodin was keeping it to sell as one of his own, because he has never been able unable to come up with any original ideas of his own. I wrote this to the Ministry, and told them too that Rodin was responsible for the series of recent thefts going on in the Louvre. I said if they would inspect Rodin's home they'd find all the stolen artwork in it.

I commanded they pay me immediately for my sculpture, as was my right, and absolutely would not put up with any further delays. Of course I didn't receive an answer. I felt completely helpless and was so furious I ripped off the rest of the wallpaper from my walls. Since the Art Inspector Eugène Morand was supposed to send the Ministry a report on *Niobide blessée*, I knew he was to blame (probably because he was in the service of Rodin). I felt so helpless and outraged that I sent him a letter enclosing dried cat feces and some nasty remarks he deserved. I sent it anonymously, but apparently he suspected who the author was and refused to have anything further to do with me. In fact, he threatened to send a letter to the public prosecutor if nothing was done about it. *Tant pis!* Armand Dayot was immediately returned to my case. Three years later, the sculpture was given to the Bougie Museum in Algeria. Nevertheless, after the *Niobide blessée* fiascos, I determined never to go through anything like that again, and destroyed every subsequent work of mine with a heavy mallet. The destruction was partly a sacrifice to Paul's God, and partly to show the world how little I thought of it. Every time I pounded a statue to its death, I bellowed, "This is for Rodin! And this! And this! May he and his henchmen roast in Hell to the end of time!"

Part of my desperation was because my dear Papa, the only person in the world who always stood by me, was in financial trouble himself, and could no longer afford to help me as much as he had been doing. To my surprise, on one visit he gave me twenty francs, in place of the usual hundred. I said, "Thank you Papa, but I have no money at all and nothing to eat. Can't you spare any more?" He answered firmly, "I am sorry, but I can't give you very much this time." I looked away.

"Camille," he said hesitantly, "I've tried to keep this from you, but our financial situation has deteriorated badly. My estate has shrunk to where you wouldn't recognize it. We've had to sell almost all our land and we only have two fields of alfalfa and wheat left. The only property we still own is our home."

My heart was racing as I cried out, "Papa, I can't believe it! What has happened? You always had so much money. And you and Maman are so thrifty and never spend anything on yourselves."

"That's true," he answered reluctantly. "But we've had to help support Louise and Jacques, since de Massary died. And although Paul's career is very illustrious, the fact remains it took a lot of our capital to pay for his schooling and to prepare him for his diplomatic career."

"And me, Papa? What about all the money you've given me? Have I contributed to the problem, what with the money for rent, food, and so on?"

"I'm afraid so, Camille," he answered, "although it breaks my heart to tell you that. We pay your rent, your taxes, your butcher and grocery bills, and then there're the one hundred francs we frequently give you, even when you ask for less. To say nothing of paying to feed your army of cats," he added dryly. "It mounts up."

"Oh, Papa," I said, the tears rolling down my face. "I'm so sorry. But without it I would starve. What else can I do?"

"I know, daughter," he said wearily. "I feel the same way."

The Downhill Slide

1902–1912

Paul says my life history is in my work. I know he's right and I've sculpted an autobiography in art of the great moments of my life. Perhaps that's true of any artist, for how can anyone create anything if they've not experienced the emotion it's based on? *The Story of my Life in Sculptures* reads like this: It begins with the busts of my dear brother Paul at ages thirteen, sixteen, and thirty-seven. Then there's the bust of Rodin, from the days when my heart was young and hopeful; followed by the dream of my liaison with Debussy in *La Valse;* the passion of my life in *La Sakountala* or *Vertumne et Pomone; La Vague,* inspired by the overwhelming tragedy I shared with Rodin; *La Petite Châtelaine,* a record of the moment when I first sensed the story of my life had come to a close; *l'Implorante ou le Dieu envolé,* the heart-breaking rupture of my love affair with Rodin; *La Fortune,* in which a woman dances alone, in contrast to the ecstatic dancing lovers in *La Valse; Les Causeuses;* the gossiping women who exhibit the venom of my female relatives and neighbors; *Clotho,* the foreshadowing of my years in the asylum; *Persée*, a glimpse of the death of my soul while my body lives endlessly on, and my masterpiece, *L'Age Mûr*, a plea to Rodin to love me. My kneeling naked lady passionately reaches out to the man an aged woman is snatching away. She beseeches him to stay with her in a way that would have shamed me to say out loud. I had hoped through the statue to reach his heart, he whose life and mine had intertwined around our art.

Please, please don't leave me, she cries. I need you, I want you, I'm nothing without you. What have I done to keep you from loving me? Tell me, tell me, I implore you, and I will surely change. Is it because one of my legs is shorter than the other? I'm afraid that's the only thing I can do nothing about.

How could you, Rodin? Didn't I help you with your illustrious works so no one can tell where your creations left off and mine began? Did I complain when you got all the glory (and money) for the sculptures we worked on together? You know you couldn't have become the world famous Rodin without me, without my inspiration as well as my years of toil for you. *L'éternal printemps, Le baiser, Eternelle idole, Fugit amour*, I posed for one after another of these masterpieces, and I labored on them all alongside of you. Yet you have ascended the heights of Mount Olympus while I sit alone on the Quai de Bourbon on the Ile St. Louis among my cats and broken plaster.

Yes, you are the great genius, and I'm the nameless artist struggling to earn enough to buy her daily bread. But as I toss my way through the endless nights, I wonder which of us is the genius. How do you sleep, Rodin? I hear you're up all night. Is it because your conscience bothers you about stealing my work? Nothing would make me happier than to know you're as miserable as I.

Didn't I give over my sacred virginity for your lascivious, senile delights? Did you not ravish me for years and years, saying in the dark of the night, "You are the light of my love, the love of my life, the only woman I have ever loved?" And then you betrayed me to go off to Meudon with that awful, low-class creature. Our life together was so beautiful. How could you have abandoned it for her? Oh, Rodin, Rodin! Life is barren and banal without you. I have only my work, the work we loved together. But it gives me no joy now, for it's the graveyard of my dying heart. You must know who the little girl in my painting, *Little Girl with Doves*, is. Like her, I am dead, but there are no doves near my heart to bring me peace. Lover, my lover, come back to me now to my watery grave of a million frosty tears.

I want to disintegrate into the muck of the earth. I want to become part of the soil, so you can take the clay that was me and mold it into a new, a perfect being. Maybe then you'll love me. Oh lover, my only lover, take these hands, take my heart, take my body, take everything but my talent, only please come back to me!

Those were my feelings then: I'm embarrassed to read them now. I can see him before me as vividly as if he were here, a little old man in raggedy pants tied around his slim hips with a rope, always hitching them up when they slipped down to his buttocks. He smelled like a goat. In fact he looked like a goat, with his unkempt beard and long, greasy hair. He really was a disgusting creature, always ogling the naked women he kept running around his *atelier*. He said it was for his art. His art! Ha! Why didn't he have any naked men roaming around? He gawked at the women because he was a lecherous old man, and for no other reason. He could get away with it because he was the great Rodin. Anyone else who did what he did would be put in jail. Making them stretch one foot over their heads so he could gape at their twats! Ladies kissing each other or worse, sometimes three in a bed. Oh what I let him do to me! I will never tell anybody the things he made me do. I'm glad I got away from him. Even living in this dungeon's better than being in Rodin's whorehouse.

In place of my great love for him, I feel only a vengeful hatred that fills all my waking hours. He became an evil phantom that haunted me. He constantly hounded me, if not in person then by way of the henchmen he sent to ravage and rob me. He sold the works of art he stole from me for hundreds of thousands of francs, while I was lucky to have the money to buy a crust of bread. He hired a *bonne* to put sleeping powder in my sherry and steal my latest work, which he then sold for a million francs.

$\mathcal{I}$ thought things were as bad as they could be, but I was wrong. Not only did I not have any money for food or rent, but around the turn of the century I was brought to court for non-payment of bills. (Isn't that a great way to usher in the next hundred years?) A process-server named Adonis Pruneaux (what a name for a bailiff!) was constantly threatening me with jail if I didn't pay my bills. When Stanislas Margotin complained to Pruneaux for the umpteenth time that I never paid him for a few eggs he sold me, the process-server finally called my bluff and dragged me into court. I took my place in the dock, surrounded by an awe-inspiring number of magistrates, scribes, robed lawyers, armed police, and curious spectators, all seeking justice for the atrocious crime of owing money for three eggs. A brief account and hasty questioning completed the attempt to attain justice. The judge was completely unsympathetic.

"Mademoiselle Claudel," he said sternly. "Do you realize it's stealing to take food that doesn't belong to you and not pay for it? What a reflection on a fine family like yours to count a thief among their members! It is only because of consideration for them I am not sending you to jail." As if I were loaded with money and simply chose not to pay! Shades of Jean Valjean. I squelched the impulse to empty out my pockets and say pitifully, "But I was hungry, your Honor." The judge ordered me to turn over two hundred francs to my victim. I used my long overdue rent money my father had given me to pay the fine.

A man who could have been the artist I was waiting for was the great sculptor, François Rude, who unfortunately, died nine years before I was born. For me to love a man, he must be a great artist, and Rude was certainly that. Of all the sculptors who lived around my lifetime, he's the one whose works I most admire. In my opinion, his *Fisher-Boy Playing with the Tortoise* is on a par with the work of Michaelangelo. I love the joy with which the boy plays with the tortoise. His beautiful body makes me want to hug him (and Rude), as does the rhythm in its movement, his muscular balance, and the pleasure reflected on his face. It's one of the few sculptures by other artists I wish I'd created. In fact, it looks like my work

I love Rude's imagination and the way he (like me) could create a work of art out of nothing. The government had commissioned him to carve a bust of Philippe Picot, Baron de Lapeyrouse, botanist, geologist, and mayor of Toulouse, for the Marine museum. The stone they supplied was too large for Rude's project, however, so he hacked off a peculiar piece shaped like a prism, which he wanted to carve into another sculpture. Everyone thought he would never be able to make anything out of the strange shape, but he kept playing around with it until he came to the idea of the *Fisher-Boy*. As with me, there were many of his works no one paid any attention to, but for some unknown reason the public took to *Fisher-Boy,* and Rude soon became the most popular sculptor in France.

Rude was a great man as well as a great artist. Unlike some men we know (guess who), he was a wonderful husband and father, who was faithful to his beloved wife all their lives together. He was also a simple man, and worked not for fame or fortune or what people would think, but because of the joy he found in his art. He was an artist who was content to do the best work he could. We worked the same way. Most sculptors begin with small details like noses, hands, and feet, and then make them into the whole. Rude and I worked differently; we began with a study of the whole figure, and got to the details later. He always considered himself a workman, and never had the slightest desire to raise himself into a higher social class. Like me, he lived for his art and the few people he loved. And like me, he had a great disappointment in life. His beloved son died when Rude was forty-nine years old, and he never was happy again. From then on, he was tormented with severe physical and nervous ailments. But that didn't stop him from carving his beautiful statues. Yes, we were very much alike, Rude and I, and had we lived at the same time, he could have fit the role of *my artist* much better than Rodin. Too bad he's dead.

In the spring of 1905, my dear gallery owner Eugène Blot came to see me in my *atelier.* He was the first visitor I'd had in years, although we'd kept in touch by mail. He got in by kicking open the rickety door. At first I covered myself up in the drapes, because I thought another of Rodin's henchmen was trying to break in, but when I saw it was Blot, I rushed out to kiss him on both cheeks. To my surprise, he backed away and looked carefully around.

"What's wrong, Eugène?" I asked. "Don't you like me anymore?"

He paused for a moment and then looked straight into my eyes and said, "I'll tell you the truth because I love you, Camille. I'm horrified at the shape this studio's in." He strode around the room pointing to each item as he spoke of it. "Look up there, Camille. Spider webs cover the wallpaper, which is hanging down in large clumps. Over here, your armchair is broken and full of holes. The place looks and smells like an outhouse filled with cat muck, broken plaster, and the piled-up filth of years. How can you allow yourself to exist in such squalor? I've never known anybody to live in such a disgusting mess! The shutters are locked shut. When did you last see the sunlight or get any fresh air? Don't you ever go outside?" He strode toward the damaged door and flung it wide open.

I squinted at him in the dim light and answered, "I can't go out and get fresh air except to run to the grocers late at night when I have nothing to eat or drink."

"That doesn't answer my question. Why do you lock yourself up in this putrid excuse for an *atelier*? You've turned it into a fortress, with security chains and wolf traps behind every entrance. (Peering incredulously at a gaping metal-coated hole in the wall.) And what is that strange opening in the wall over your door, I'd like to know?

"It's a device used in early times to pour molten lead on the heads of one's enemies."

"You can't be serious!" (I don't answer.) "I don't believe it! Why did you put it there? It belongs in a torture chamber."

"You don't understand, Eugène. Nobody understands. I need to lock myself away from the outside world for protection because my life is in danger. Just last week, Rodin hired two Italian models to force open my shutters and climb into the *atelier* and kill me. It was only by keeping my chiffonier up against the windows I kept them out. And it's a good thing I did. Before I moved it, Rodin used to stand on a chair at my window and look through the blinds to see what I was sculpting."

"Don't be silly, Camille! You're carried away by your imagination. A man of Rodin's stature doesn't have to stoop to do such things!"

"You're wrong, Eugène! I've got to stand watch over my work because his murderers and robbers steal it as soon as it's finished. Every time I make a new statue everybody else gets rich from it. The casters, the *mouleurs,* the artists, and the gallery owners make a fortune; I make nothing. It's been going on for years. Last year Monsieur Picard, a neighbor who just happens to be a friend of Rodin's and the brother of a police inspector, broke in with a passkey. A statue of mine in a yellow dress was leaning against the wall. Since then Rodin has sculpted three women in yellow, all the same size as mine. Now everybody is making women in yellow and when I show mine they'll say I copied it."

"A strange coincidence, Camille. What's your proof they stole the idea from you?"

"A coincidence that *everybody* is sculpting women in yellow? You are naive, Eugène. Another year I used a boy to carry in wood for me. At that time, I was working on a sketch of a woman with a doe. He went to Meudon every Sunday to report what he'd seen here to Rodin. So that year there were three women with does shown in the Salon. Rodin made a hundred thousand francs on that statue alone, while I was lucky to afford a crust of bread. It was the same story with *La Petite Cheminée (The Little Hearth).* Everywhere I went that year I saw women sitting, standing, or kneeling near chimneys. The identical thing happened with *Maturity,* which got him decorations, ovations, dinners, and so forth. They even gave him an advanced degree! Rodin who couldn't put two words together without checking their spelling with me! I should have gotten that degree, for all the work I did for him. Still another time, they sent in a cleaning woman who put a sleeping potion in my coffee. I slept for twelve solid hours. When I awoke I saw a white rim around my coffee cup. What more proof do I need? While I was asleep she went into my dressing room and stole my figure, *The Woman with the Cross.* Then three figures of *The Woman with the Cross* appeared in the galleries. Are you surprised I refuse to have anything to do with that kind of a system? As long as they don't do anything about the situation, my *atelier* will remain sealed off from the world!"

Blot turned away and took out his handkerchief to wipe his forehead. He looked crushed. Then he turned back and said, "Camille, what can I say? I'm bewildered to hear such things come out of your mouth. You're an intelligent woman. Where's your good sense? And Camille, I heard you refused an invitation to exhibit your work in Prague. Why did you do such a thing? That's no way to advance a career!"

"You heard right," I answered. "That's exactly what I did. And I'm glad of it! In no way will I allow my work to be exhibited next to Rodin's. If I agreed, he would act as if he were my protector and pretend he inspired my works. Then he could take credit for any success that came to me. I'm not going to be cheated any longer by that charlatan and hypocrite, whose greatest joy is to swindle people! Would you believe he actually published my photograph on postcards and sold them all over France, even though I prohibited him from doing it?"

Blot began to walk in circles around the *atelier*. Then he abruptly turned to face me again, swallowed, and said, "Camille, I obtained a thousand franc advance for you to go to Puget-Théniers in the south of France to prepare a *maquette* for the 1905 centenary of the revolutionary Auguste Blanqui. You told me you were interested in sculpting a memorial for Blanqui because he was a rebel like you, and like you, fought constantly against a world poisoned by falsehood. I got you the advance because you said you had nothing to wear and needed to buy a few dresses and hats for the trip. Yet you never got to Puget-Théniers. What happened?"

"I wanted to work the statue in marble. The town representatives insisted on a cheaper version so I decided not to do the monument. I offered to do a bust instead, if money was such a problem for them. But they refused. So I stayed here."

"I gave you the money, but you never even bothered to tell them you changed your mind. What happened to the money?"

"I spent it."

"Of course. All right, forget about it! I got it from the Ministry of Beaux-Arts. But what about the memorial? Aren't you even going to do the *maquette*?"

"No, Eugène. I'll never again make a *maquette* for someone else to get rich from."

"All right, Camille," he said firmly. "I have nothing more to say. I will give the commission to Aristide Maillol." The anguish in his eyes turned to tears, which dribbled down his cheeks. Somehow, his tears got to me where his words had no effect and I began to sob. He took me in his arms and we cried together. We cried for lost health; we cried for lost youth; we cried for lost love; we cried for lost hopes. We cried because we loved each other. After a while he wiped my eyes and then his own with his spotless white handkerchief and tucked it into the pocket of my filthy jumper. We were silent, lost in the pathos of the moment.

Then he said, "I don't want to hurt your feelings, Camille, but I'm appalled at how you look."

"How *do* I look?" I hadn't bothered with a mirror for years.

He answered. "I'm your friend, but I have to tell you you look like…well, to put it as kindly as I can, like a derelict. The concierge just told me your neighbors keep complaining that the odor from your *atelier* infests the courtyard. They won't let their children come near you. You take absolutely no care of your appearance. You obviously don't wash either yourself or your clothes, which you've probably worn even to sleep in for months. You shuffle around in torn, unlaced boots, with their tongues hanging out. Your hair—well, a self-respecting rat would refuse to nest in it. You have sallow, wrinkled skin like an old woman of fifty instead of one who is not even forty, and you've gotten large as an elephant. It breaks my heart to tell you this, Camille, but frankly, the odor you give off is revolting."

He dashed over to my chiffonier and scrounged around in its jumbled drawers until he came across a broken old mirror Hélène had brought back from Alsace for me thirty years before. He charged back and held it up to my face. I tried not to look, but he grasped my head and held it in front of the mirror as if in a vise. I closed my eyes, struggled unsuccessfully for a moment, and then gave in. I looked, and then puzzled, looked again. I thought, "Who *is* that bedraggled old beggar woman in my mirror?" Then tears ran down my cheeks again as I understood what I'd done to myself. "Eugène's right!" I thought. "I've massacred my beauty, my art, my loves, my friendships, and my family ties."

That's when I got the idea for *Perseus and the Gorgon,* an allegory of Rodin's jealous destruction of my genius. Medusa's gaze was so powerful, so alarming, that anyone who looked at it would turn to stone. Grotesque snakes, symbols of female rage and creativity, crimped and twisted around her head. Her hair had once been a magnificent crown of radiant beauty, but the goddess Athena was envious of Medusa's dazzling beauty and transformed her into a monster of deformity. Despite her frightful appearance, Medusa had retained her brilliance and ingenuity. As jealous of Medusa's creativity as the goddess Athena had been of her beauty, the god Perseus found it intolerable that Medusa was more talented than he and was consumed with the desire to kill her. But he knew anyone who gazed upon the gruesome writhing snakes would go blind from the shock. By reflecting the abominable image in his highly polished shield instead of looking directly at the hideous twisting serpents, he slashed off Medusa's head and was able to preserve his own vision. In the same way, so long as I remained Rodin's pretty little helpmate, he did me no harm. But as soon as my art became greater than his, he cut off the fame and money that belonged to me, and murdered my art as surely as Perseus severed the head of Medusa.

But alas, I'm afraid that's not the whole meaning of *Perseus and the Gorgon*. Maman, like Eugène, always said I bring down my troubles on my own head. In the agony of the eternal nights, I hear her appalling words and recognize that Perseus is also me. Yes, Maman, it is I who have destroyed my beauty. It is I who let Rodin murder my unborn baby. It is I who lifted my ax time and again to relentlessly butcher the sculptures I loved. I, who do not deserve the joy of creation.

The horror of my destructiveness is reflected in the eyes of Medusa's dismembered head, in a face distorted by horror, grief, and madness, in a face whose features are my own. As Paul wrote in *L'Oeil écoute*, "What is this head of bloody hair…if not the head of madness?" I wanted to take my ax and chop up Rodin into little pieces. But I couldn't do such a thing, whatever my family might think, so I turned my ax to the sculpture I was working on, a statue in which Rodin and I were making love. Like the creations of the Lord, from dust it began and to dust it returned. Sometimes I'm sorry, as I think the statue was better than *The Kiss* of Rodin. *Tant pis!* Now no one can be jealous of me and harm me. Now no one can steal my work.

As he loaded some of the garbage from the floor into the bag he'd brought food in, Blot delivered his parting remark. "I'll give you six months to get yourself together. Then we'll have a show at my gallery."

ℛodin wanted to come see me last week again. See me, ha! The old goat still wants to sleep with me. I sent him a telegram that my father had come to visit and I was going home to eat and sleep. I felt so strong! I wouldn't have been able to say no to him five years ago.

The same yesterday. This time I sent him a letter saying "Do not come here! I do not need another scene." Why should I let him call on me when all we do is fight? Something very strange is going on around here. I think Rodin has gotten all the *praticiens* together and told them to make war on me. A *mouleur* he and I both use broke into my *atelier* last week when I was out with my father and destroyed a number of statues, in order to get revenge on me. I'll have to stay in here as much as possible from now on, and only go out when I have to pick up food and wine. Or better yet, I'll have the retailers put the food they bring in a box on my window. That's the only way to protect my work.

Mon petit Paul has abandoned me, too. I miss him badly, and still yearn for his forgiveness so I can forgive myself. His rare visits are the only rays of sunshine that ever come into my life. He's been gone so long, perhaps the longest time ever between his visits. He's been sent to China. I'm upset not only that I haven't seen him for so long, but because he's gone to China without me. I want to go there so badly. Of all the places in the world, I most want to see China.

I've wanted to go there ever since I was a little girl and looked at pictures of the Forbidden Palace in Papa's library. When we were little, Paul and I vowed we would tour China together one day. My dreaming about the country made you want to visit there, Paul. Don't you remember? And now you've gone without me. Do you ever think of your pathetic sister when you visit the Great Wall or the treasures of the Forbidden Palace, and realize you've broken your promise to her? Will I ever get to China? Will I ever get anywhere in my lifetime but this freezing, rat-infested chamber of horrors I call an *atelier*? It's bad enough to live a nightmare, but it's even sadder to know the pleasures I yearn for the most will never be realized.

It was around 1905 (although it's hard to keep the years straight in my head, as they all run together) that Paul came back from China and took me for a little vacation in July to Eaux-Chaudes, near Lourdes, in the Pyrenees. Was he hoping for a miracle "cure"? I refused to go to Lourdes with him, as I wasn't sick. People like Rodin kept doing horrendous things to me, and I'm the one they called sick! While I enjoyed being with Paul after such a long time, did he really think one little trip was going to make up for all the years he'd abandoned me? He told me he was leaving for China again next year. His new wife was to go with him. I wasn't even invited to the wedding. When I got home, I destroyed all the work I'd done that year. The Lord giveth and the Lord taketh away.

Paul and I never again mentioned the terrible scene in which I told him about my abortion and begged his forgiveness. But he must have noticed the fourteen Stations of the Cross cut out from a newspaper from rue Bayard and pinned up on my wall with tacks, my one concession to his Catholicism. Anyway, if Paul was right and I'm headed for Hell, I need all the help I can get. The Stations moved me so much since Paul's disastrous words, I read them all the time, especially the following passages:

The Stations of the Cross
AN ACT OF CONTRITION

From the bottom of my heart I am sorry for all my sins...save me by Thy death from that eternal death which I have so often deserved. My Jesus, the heavy burden of my sins is on Thee...I loathe them, I detest them; I call on Thee to pardon them; by Thy grace aid me never more to commit them...My Jesus, Who didst comfort the pious women of Jerusalem...comfort my soul with Thy tender pity, for in Thy pity lies my trust...Ah, my Jesus, rather let me die than ever offend Thee again...strip me of love for things of earth, and make me loathe all that savors of the world and sin...My Jesus...make me crucify my flesh by Christian penance...O Mary, Mother most sorrowful...obtain for me hatred of sin and grace to live a Christian life and save my soul.

In December of 1905, Blot gave the exhibition of thirteen of my works that he'd promised. I looked forward to it as if it were Nirvana and hoped to make a dent in the mountain of bills that had piled up. I dressed up for the occasion for the first time in years, wearing the striped red velvet dress I'd pinned together from old drapes the night I gave the dinner party for Paul. I even put chalk-white powder on my face so I wouldn't look like a Moor, and circles of red paint on my cheeks. The gallery was crowded with well-known people from the art world. But Rodin must have gotten to them all. Although everybody raved about the statuary not a single person bought any. Fine! The sculptures are too good for the lot of them. I thought I behaved very well, talking loudly and laughing uproariously with the guests, when all I wanted to do was to shriek, "If everybody thinks my statues are so great, why is nobody buying any?" The next evening at my family's home, somebody mentioned the exhibition and they all began to laugh. I threw a horrible fit, screaming and cursing and kicking and slapping whoever came near me. They were all too stupid to understand why I was so angry.

"Poor crazy Camille, she's sick." Paul said condescendingly. Sick, my rear end! Couldn't they see it was the ebbing away of my life's blood they thought was funny, and that I yelled to keep from sobbing? I will never again give an exhibition or go to a party.

1905, the year of my great disappointment in Blot's exhibition, marked the beginning of the end of my career as a sculptor. It had to do with Rodin, of course. When I tell people he was a thief who stole my works, nobody believes me. They say, "Oh, that crazy Camille is imagining things again." Well, I have proof now nobody in their right senses can deny. My marble version of *Clotho* had been exhibited at the 1895 banquet given for Puvis de Chavannes. It was received so well that Morhardt and Rodin raised money with a subscription to donate the statue to the Museum of Luxembourg. Against my better judgement, I allowed them to proceed.

It was a big mistake to let Rodin do anything for me. That swindler said the museum needed time to decide if they would accept the piece, and in the meantime he would keep it at his home in Meudon. Years passed, and still the museum had not accepted the sculpture, which remained in Rodin's keeping. When Morhardt wrote to Léonce Bénédite, the director of the museum, to ask him to accept the sculpture for the museum, Bénédite wrote back that he would have to ask the Conseil des Musées if they wanted to accept the gift.

"In the meantime," he added, "please send the statue temporarily to the museum." Morhardt then asked Rodin to ship the sculpture to the museum. Rodin said he already had. Years later, the museum still insisted they'd never received it. Nobody ever heard of it again. Never heard of that heavy marble sculpture, which Rodin said he sent to them? Maybe you believe it; I don't. My beautiful *Clotho* has disappeared from the face of the earth. Now I ask you, where else could it be but hidden in Rodin's *atelier*? Can you blame me for giving up sculpting shortly thereafter? Wouldn't anybody?

Paul wrote to say Madame de Vertus asked why I don't sculpt any more. I answered to give Madame de Vertus my best wishes and tell her I can no longer make my beautiful marbles because I'm crazy and my intellectual faculties have lost their balance.

Autoportrait avec coiffure de feuilles et de fruits (Self-portrait with a headdress of leaves and fruits), one of my last works of art, was a bust of myself which was left in my *atelier* when the attendants dragged me off to the asylum in 1913. I have no idea what happened to it; probably Rodin stole it and made a fortune selling it. I don't have a photograph of the bust, but I see it as clearly in my head as if it were right in front of me. I think I looked quite pretty for a woman of forty-nine, although there was a touch of sadness under my slight smile. Maybe I sensed what was coming. What I can't understand now I'm old and have worn the same antiquated hat and coat for decades is how I could ever have sported a monstrous hairstyle of leaves and fruit. I guess it was my mood. Sometimes I feel as high as a floating cloud. That's when I made strange clothes in my younger days, such as the dress of red velvet which I later folded into a bed for my cats. When I came down from the heights after designing the coiffure, I cut it into bits and threw it into the courtyard. *Je me plumerai la tête, je ne me plumerai la tête!*

I did a few more little sculptures after that, as I sat looking out the window into the courtyard and sculpting the daily little dramas that took place there. My favorite of this period was *Vieil Aveugle chantant*, the blind man sings. When I sculpted it, a circle of children surrounding him were laughing at him. His face is in great pain. He's crying as he sings and wiping his nose on his sleeve. It makes *me* cry now to think of it. How right you were to cry, Monsieur l'Aveugle! Life is long and life is hard, even for those of us gifted with sight. How ghastly it must have been for you to grope your way through the endless night!

Le Peinture (The Painter), a little statuette that was cast in bronze is of the same order. It's a portrait of a painter grasping his paintbrush in his right hand, his palette held by the thumb of the left hand, joyfully mixing his colors before applying his brush to the canvas. It reminds me of better days when I loved Rodin and had hopes for our future together.

Little did I know in 1913 when I modeled the two little singers holding their hats and looking up at the closed windows that it would be the last time I would put fingers to clay. I had tried to design the head of a dying man the day before, but was so hungry I couldn't concentrate. I hadn't eaten for days. WHATEVER HAS HAPPENED TO PAPA? I asked myself. He never stayed away this long before. It wasn't like him. Regardless of the stresses and strains in his life or mine, he was the most reliable person on earth. I was terrified he was sick, and didn't dare imagine what would become of me if he were.

My hunger was ceaseless by this time. There was scarcely a moment I could forget about it. I felt like *The Starving Dog* who was tearing his meat to shreds, a statue I sculpted in 1893. I had only two sous in my pocket and was so famished I crept out into the courtyard at midnight when I thought everyone was asleep. I could hardly recognize it. The tree-lined square that was so lovely in the daylight had become a vast forest filled with frightening shapes and unknown boundaries. Nevertheless I was so famished I had to continue. Although it was still freezing winter, I didn't even feel the cold. I silently inched my way in the fearsome darkness to the row of garbage cans, looking around carefully before each step so that if the concierge was still around he wouldn't hear me. With fingers strengthened by years of sculpting I pried the frozen lid off the closest garbage can. Then the single most gruesome incident of a lifetime of horrors happened. As I removed the lid, a large rat leapt out of the can, making me drop the lid. and causing a deafening clatter as it hit the ground. I screamed and apparently scared him away, ramming my hands over my mouth to keep from screaming more. When I stopped shaking enough to look around, I was grateful no one seemed to have heard my outcry or the racket made by the falling lid. I was so ravenous by this time that nothing mattered but putting some food in my stomach. Gone was my pride, my arrogance, my dignity. I hastily dumped the contents of the can on the ground which was still spotted with dirty remnants of the winter snow, and passionately rummaged through them. It was nauseating to touch the stinking meats alive with bugs, the slimy fish bones, rotting vegetables, and the half-eaten carcass of a cat. Clenching my nostrils, I tried to keep out the stench which was making me retch. It didn't help. I persevered nonetheless, as I knew if I didn't put something in my stomach right away I would be too weak to get out of bed, if I didn't actually die from hunger. Finally I came upon a piece of moldy bread, wiped it off on my ancient woolen jumper, and stuffed it into my mouth then and there. Although I did everything I could to keep it down, I gagged and threw up. Stumbling back into the *atelier,* I cried for hours. Abominable as the experience was, I hadn't even gotten to keep the bread. For hours afterward, everywhere I looked—behind the door, through the blinds of the window, on the top of the chiffonier—I saw rats leaping at me. I couldn't sleep all night, as every time I closed my eyes the image of the hurtling rodent leapt into my mind. How the mighty have fallen! Camille Claudel, sculptor *par excellence*, daughter of a distinguished family, sister to one genius and lover of another, has been reduced to stealing the dinner of a rat!

I was sitting rocking in my wicker chair the next morning around eleven o'clock, reading The Stations of the Cross on the wall and stroking five of the army of loudly squawking cats that surrounded me. The stroking didn't help; if anything it made them screech even louder. The poor animals were starving and of course I didn't have any money for food for either them or me.

"Sorry, kitties," I said. "I'm hungry, too. I can't understand why Papa hasn't brought us food for a week. I hope he's all right. Maybe he'll come later today, to spare me the horror of raiding the garbage cans again."

Suddenly there came a knock at the door. I knew it wasn't Papa, because we had a secret signal of three short knocks and one long one. I ignored the thumping as I always do, but the banging grew louder and louder until I got scared and hid behind the window drapes. The knocking stopped for a few minutes. Then just as I began to relax I heard a thunderous crash as the door was knocked off its hinges. Two burly policemen in helmets and boots pushed their way in. They marched around the room until one man came to the bulge in the curtains I thought concealed me.

"Here she is, Joseph!" he shouted. "Come and get her." Joseph stumbled forward, tripped on three cats, and cursed loudly. Then he pushed the drapes aside and yanked me out of my hiding place among the spider webs. The men held back my arms and dragged me off kicking and screaming over the howls of the cats to a carriage waiting outside. At first I thought, "This cannot be happening! It's only a nightmare and I'll soon wake up." But it didn't and I didn't. The nightmare went on and on and hasn't ended yet.

Terrified as I was, I kept hoping there was some mistake, or that this was some ghastly joke someone was playing. When they pulled me into the carriage with barred windows, the driver began to beat the horses, who bucked and whinnied under the whip. I shrieked at the attendants.

"Why are you doing this to me? I never did anything to you. Let me out of here!"

They answered, "You're crazy, Madame. We'll take you to a place that'll help you."

"Help me?" I cried. "I don't need any help! You're the crazy ones. Isn't it crazy to break into a law-abiding woman's home and lock her up just because her place is a little dirty and she has a few cats? I demand my freedom!" They didn't answer, but continued on our way to the Ville-Evrard Asylum for lunatics, near Paris.

Part III

The Asylum Years

1913–1943

$\mathscr{A}$s if being carted off to a lunatic asylum wasn't enough for one week, my dear Papa passed away. No wonder he hadn't come to see me for a whole week! He never would let me down that way. I wasn't told about his death or even allowed to attend his funeral. I found out about it in a letter my cousin wrote me. How could my family do such a thing? They'd always treated me badly, but never in my worst nightmares would I have thought that my father would die and they wouldn't even tell me about it. My father was the only person among them who loved and supported me. Now he was gone. My beloved father was buried without me, the one person he loved most in the whole world. How incredible! I wouldn't do such a thing to my worst enemy. I can't bear to think that Papa on his deathbed asked to see his daughter and I didn't come. He called for me on his deathbed and they didn't tell me. Yes, even on his deathbed, they tried to steal him away from me. I hope he knew I *couldn't* come, and nothing would have kept me from being there if only I'd known. Father, forgive me, for I knew not what they do.

Those sneaks who call themselves my family! Not only did they not summon me to my father's deathbed or tell me about his funeral, but no sooner had he taken his last breath than they had the attendants break into my *atelier* and haul me off to the lunatic asylum. There're some dirty politics going on here I have to investigate. He should have lived to be a hundred. I suspect Maman poisoned him, and needs me to be declared insane so nobody will believe me when I say she murdered him. Papa died without knowing a thing about the catastrophe that's overtaken me. The family's wanted to institutionalize me for years, but he'd have none of it. He loved me unconditionally and wanted for me whatever I wanted for myself. He wouldn't have tolerated having his favorite child locked up with screaming lunatics!

In the translucence of the freezing nights, I cry out to him, Papa, oh Papa! What have you done to me? Why have you abandoned me? You left me just when I need you the most. Papa, dear Papa, if only you had lived I wouldn't be entombed in this house of catastrophe. They wouldn't have had the gall to do that to me if you were around to protect me. Papa, sweet Papa, when I was little you carried me on your shoulders down to the sea and made me taller than you. Before that, I was just a tiny little girl, the smallest in the whole world. And isn't that what you did for me all my life, carried me on your shoulders? And didn't that make me bigger than all the others? Now you're gone and I am little again. You were always so proud of me, Papa. How proud of me would you be now? I am woe. Woe is me. The Oak of Villeneuve has died, and I'll never see his like again.

In my quieter moments, I try to make sense out of this whole ordeal. I think Louise is at the bottom of it all. Her greedy fingers are clutched around the family cookie jar. She's in cahoots with Rodin, who I saw kissing her on the mouth in the woods. He wants to keep his work in the number one position by not having to compete with mine. I spend very little money on myself, but they want to keep even that pitiful amount for themselves. Most of all, Louise is scared I'll claim my share of the inheritance, thus diminishing little Jacques' pile. I wrote Maman that she needn't be afraid I'll claim any part of the Villeneuve house. I've no such thought in mind. I would rather deed my share to little Jacques and spend the rest of my days in freedom. It's agonizing to know I've worked so hard all my life with my great talent, only to end up like this without a penny, cursed in every aspect of my life and deprived of everything that makes me want to stay alive. Deep down inside me, I've given up. My life no longer interests me. All I can do is wait for death to release me from

Montdevergues. Nobody else is going to liberate me. As someone said of King Lear leaning over the body of his beloved daughter Cordelia, "Is this the promised end?"

I've been doing a little reading on the legality of my abduction, and have discovered the infamous law of 1838 which is still in effect. It says patients can be institutionalized on the basis of one simple medical document. They're then under the jurisdiction of the doctor of the institution, who has the power to release or hold them behind barred windows forever. How unjust that one person who barely knows me has the power to ruin my life! The only proper means of revenge against such a person is a revolver, which would be a just and fitting punishment.

The Catholic Church is also in on this heinous transgression against me. It can do whatever it wants because the religion is beyond the reach of the law. I'm sure Maman and Louise told the Church about my abortion and my outlaw moral code, and it's belatedly seeking revenge. This is an unspeakable clerical crime which should not be allowed to continue. My mother, brother and sister are all under the evil influence of Rodin, and will do nothing to help me escape. I write them constantly, but they pay no attention to my frantic pleas. I'm very frightened. My friend, the Marquis du Sauvencourt from the Château du Muret, died just a short while ago, after being locked up here for thirty years! Can you imagine anything so horrible? Things can only end that way for me. Sometimes I just want to bang my head against the wall until it splits wide open. Everything's grey and dreary, grey, bleak, and far away. I can't eat anything, just lie in bed all day long. When I feel like this all I can do is lie under the covers, day after day after day. I can't even let myself feel how horrible life is or I would surely die. I had a dream...A skeleton head...It turned to black. Every night I go to bed praying I won't wake up. Every morning I cry that I'm still alive. It's hopeless. The greyness will never end.

*I*n August, 1914, Ville–Evrard Asylum was directly in the path of the German advance. The three armies of the German invasion's northern wing were sweeping south towards Paris, and the French 5th and 6th Armies and the British Expeditionary Force were forced to retreat. When

General Alexander von Kluck, Commander of the German First Army, was ordered to encircle Paris from the east, I, along with a group of other refugees, was temporarily evacuated to Enghien, north of Paris. Two days after the beginning of the Battle of the Marne in which France halted the advance of the Germans, we were sent to the horrendous Montdevergues, near Avignon in the south of France. We arrived after a frightful train trip that lasted forty-two hours. There was barely room to sit down and we had only a little dry bread and dirty water to last the entire trip. The future inmates screamed and howled all night long. The only way I could get a few minutes of sleep was to put my fingers in my ears. The trip was a fitting introduction to Montdevergues, where I've spent the rest of my life.

The mountain was first named Montdevergues in 1442. Before that it was called the "Mont de Vierges," the mountain of virgins, sometimes known as the Mountain of the Roses. The mountain is very beautiful, which is more than I can say for life in the asylum. The estate includes the mountain, much land, and a vineyard. The asylum itself was established in 1839, right after the law of 1838 made each province responsible for the care of its own mental patients. Before that, paupers, criminals, and madmen were all mixed together. The asylum is on a hill, and resembles a small village built around a chapel in a large garden. The homes of the doctor, the director, the concierge, and eight two-story pavilions for the inmates surround the chapel like a wheel. Crossing a courtyard, one comes upon two infirmaries, a pharmacy, a kitchen, the nuns' quarters, the laundry rooms, two workshops, the waiting rooms, and two bathrooms, each of which contains ten bathtubs. The location was selected because it was thought by the sages that its beauty would have a therapeutic effect on mental health. Take my word for it: It doesn't! The word "asylum" is taken from the Greek "asulon," meaning refuge. I leave it to you to judge how much of a refuge Montdevergues is.

They hold me prisoner here, despite my loud protestations and tears. They won't allow me to have any visitors besides Paul, Maman, and Louise, who never come here anyway. They take away the letters I write and won't let me receive any, except from the three of them. Letters from anyone else can be destroyed if the officials deem it "beneficial" to my health. I can have absolutely no communication with the outside world. They call it sequestration, and say it's to keep me from getting any information that would upset me. Exactly! And I'm the Queen of Siam. Why don't they call it what it is, solitary confinement?

I'm watched night and day like a criminal. I've managed until now to find a way to get my mail posted, away from their ever-watchful eyes. There's a woman who worked here who (after having her palm greased, of course) was good enough to mail my letters and bring back the answers. I gave her address to the people I wrote to and asked them to place a small envelope with my name on it inside of a larger one they send to her. Now she's sick and may never return. I don't know how I'm going to send or receive any more mail. I don't know what to do, because anyone else I could approach to do her job would report me to the doctors like a criminal, and I would pay the price.

The punishments here are dreadful. They're supposed to be therapeutic, or contain those who are violent or otherwise uncontrollable, but all too often they're used to serve the cruel instincts of certain members of the staff who're in the employment of Rodin. There's the camisole, a long robe made of thick white linen closed in the back by laces. It has long sleeves that are crossed over one's chest and tied around in the back. Sometimes the "offender" is given hydrotherapy and put to soak in a tub of warm water, camisole and all, for the whole day. The unfortunate captive rests on a wooden plank with a hole in it for his or her head, which is encased in an iron collar. The baths are supposed to calm the culprit. I'll bet! An order to put a person in a camisole must be signed by a doctor, thank goodness.

Then there're several kinds of leather shackles that are bolted around one's waist, wrists, or ankles. Repeated lawbreakers have their chairs chained to a radiator and enclosed in a small space, which would drive anyone crazy who already isn't.

Then there're the very agitated, old, or incontinent people who are shackled in their camisoles to an iron bed bolted to the wall. Mornings they're awakened, unscrewed, washed, and have their excrement cleaned up.

Sometimes the "criminals" are put in a solitary cell, with nothing in it but a straw mattress. That punishment is only an exaggeration of daily life for anyone sequestered in Montdevergues Asylum. Worst of all there's the dreaded *La clef* or the key, in which wet, soapy rags are placed around the necks or over the faces of victims. It supposedly stifles their breathing so they become more tranquil. I've heard it rumored that some offenders have suffocated under the "treatment." These implements look like instruments of torture dreamed up by the Spanish Inquisition, which were probably not much more painful. I've been lucky in that I've never been punished. But then I've never been caught breaking any of their rules. I'm worried they'll catch me this time for my "offense." Imagine being punished like a disobedient child just for writing a letter! Even Maman's punishments were kinder. I would rather work around the clock as a maid in Villeneuve than continue to live behind bars in fear and desolation. I have nowhere to turn for help. In a country that considers itself civilized, is there no one who will rescue me from this catastrophic situation? I keep hoping it's some odious nightmare I will awaken from at any moment. But this is one nightmare from which there's no waking up.

This place would be right at home on Rodin's *Gates of Hell*. Winter lasts seven months and this year it's been particularly harsh. The sleet and wind have never stopped blowing, as if the icy Arctic Ocean had moved in on us. It cuts into your face like a handful of shattered glass. It's so cold I can hardly stand up.

To write this, I should go to the common room, but it isn't much warmer than my own, as only a niggardly little fire burns there. The commotion made by the screaming, singing, yelling, cursing inmates in the common room from morning to night and then from night to morning is so distracting it's difficult to concentrate. They holler and make faces all day long and can't put together three words that make any sense. Their own parents sent them away because they couldn't stand them, so why should I be forced to live with them? I can't bear their shrieks anymore. They tear me apart.

My room is so frigid my fingers shake and are so numb I can barely hold my pencil. I've been freezing all winter long and have a terrible cold. One of my friends here, a lovely young teacher from Lycée Fénélon, was found dead in her bed where she literally froze to death from the cold. She was the only person here besides Dr. Brunet who I could talk to about my sculptures. During the last conversation we had before she died, she asked me which of my statues had been the most difficult to sculpt. I told her the last one I did was the hardest for me, because the muscles were so difficult to get right. I will miss my friend. There aren't many like her in Montdevergues. I mourn her doubly. She was the age my daughter would have been, had she lived.

In the dining room, the patients sit all squeezed together at a tiny table, which is in a direct draft. Everybody has dysentery all year long, an apt comment on the filthy food served here. The soup consists of poorly cooked vegetables in water with hardly any meat. All year round, we get an old beef stew in an oily sauce which is always sour, dried-up macaroni swimming around in fat, or a dish of rice drowning in plain grease. For hors d'oeuvres, there're a few shriveled slices of raw ham or a moldy piece of goat cheese. To drink we're served wine-turned-to-vinegar and chick-pea water which they have the nerve to call coffee. And oh, I forgot—for "dessert" we get some dried-up dates or figs and a couple of stale biscuits. For this they have the nerve to charge twenty francs a day. The only thing good about the so-called cuisine is that I don't have to go scrounging around for it in rat-infested garbage cans. There're no spoons, forks, or knives, of course. Some poor souls who sleep in the dormitories don't want their dishes (made of iron) washed with all the others in the community kitchen, so they carry them around all day concealed under their clothing. I don't want my dishes mixed up with all the rest either, so I hide them under the mattress in my room. That's where I eat most of the time, in my room, as the odious smells, the noise, and the confusion in the dining room are unbearable. I ask for baked potatoes and hard-boiled eggs day and night and that's what I live on, except for the food Maman, and later, Louise and Paul, have sent me, like Brazilian coffee, butter, sugar, flour. tea, and a few bottles of white wine. There's one more good thing about being here—I don't have to worry about paying the rent. There're no process-servers in Montdevergues.

My room is as reprehensible as everything else here. There's practically nothing in it, not even a quilt or a sanitary bucket, only a narrow iron bed low to the ground, in which I shiver from the cold all night long, and perhaps (if I'm lucky) a hideous cracked chamber pot. There's no hot water. The nuns have to lug water for us from the men's pavilion. Obviously, not much washing of persons or clothing is done by the inmates. Occasionally—very occasionally—I wash out a few clothes on some stones I brought into my room. I don't remember the last time I did that.

I can't leave my description of "hygienic" procedures without describing the primitive toilet facilities at Montdevergues. There're no water closets or running water in the latrines. There're simply huge community pipes in which one defecates and urinates, with no means of siphoning away the grossly unpleasant odors. The latrines cover one wall. There's no separation between them: It's simply one giant outhouse. Worst of all, there're no doors for privacy. I'm not a particularly modest person, but there's all the difference in the world between posing nude for a sculptor and defecating in the presence of insane women who stand there and stare, pointing their fingers and laughing like hyenas. Many were the times I waited in discomfort, rather than have my "performance" watched by these crazies. Wash basins in the community room face the stalls, in which a few spouts of cold water are available in the morning for ablutions. There's no possibility of washing oneself well or still less of taking a bath in these quarters. Not that I would use them if there were. Once a week, fifteen or twenty of us are herded like sheep to the "big bath." There's only one bathtub for the whole pavilion. It offends my dignity. Sometimes I hide in the park and hope they'll forget all about me. Unfortunately, they keep a written record of all those who have taken baths, so they often note my absence and insist I accompany them.

After taking care of their morning hygiene, the only thing most of the non-paying inmates from the dormitories have to do is to sit in an immense room called The Court. It's thirty meters long and six feet wide, paved with black and white tiles with walls painted in deep grey three-quarters of the way up. Attendants guard the inmates as if it were a prison. The healthier ones come and go, but the halt, the crippled, the blind, the aged, and others in various states of deterioration sit around in a circle all day on benches cemented to the floor. When a rare visitor walks by, they reach out with fragile, shaking hands and plead in quavering tones for attention. If I have to walk through the room, the body odors of the old people and the stink of urine and feces shock me so I gag, while the toxic smell of the harsh disinfectant sets off a choking fit that lasts for hours. Needless to say, The Court is not a place I frequent.

*T*he sequestration policy naturally continued in Montdevergues, just as it had in Ville-Evrard. After I'd been imprisoned for years, an incident happened which illustrates the cruelty and senselessness of the rule of "protection."

Dr. Brunet, my psychiatrist, said to me, "Mademoiselle Claudel, I've been looking over some of the early papers in your file to see if I can find anything there that can help me to understand you better."

Can you imagine, a doctor who actually wants to understand me!

"I found this letter," he continued, "and see no reason why you shouldn't have it, even though it's very old. It's from a dear old friend of yours. It can only make you feel better."

"What friend? Who's it from?" I said, feeling excitement for the first time in years.

"Here, you take it," he said as he stood up. "We have to stop now. Read it and if you want, we can talk about it next time." I wanted to give him a kiss when he handed me a crumpled, yellowed letter, and escorted me to the nurse waiting outside the door to bring me back to my room.

I held onto the letter for a long time before opening it. I get such little news from the outside world that I wanted to savor it as long as possible. I also was afraid I would be disappointed, that the letter would be from somebody who wants money (not that I have any) or a favor I was in no position to grant. I try not to look forward to anything, so it won't hurt so much when I'm disillusioned. Unfortunately, the technique doesn't work very well; I still am disappointed. Finally, that night before I went to sleep—or perhaps I should say before I went to bed, since I rarely sleep—I opened the letter. My first reaction after I read it was a shock they'd kept the letter from me. Even I, who've known excruciating brutality, have rarely experienced anything so cruel.

Dear Camille (it began):

Before refreshing your memory about me, I would like to tell you how I remember you. I see you as clearly as if it were yesterday, the brilliant pupil at the school of the Sisters of the Christian Doctrine in Epernay.

When you recited your history lessons to Mère Marie-Colombe in so perfect a manner, one could already see in your huge eyes the clarity of genius. I admired you and told myself you were beautiful and gentle. Mère St. Joseph, your drawing teacher, showed the beautiful heads you had drawn to everybody. You were only about twelve or thirteen years old; I was seventeen. We talked together sometimes at recess. Our parents all lived in Tardenois and we exchanged news about our relative in common, Mère Marie-Louise of Villeneuve. I also remember your beautiful mother. There are many such things I would like to tell you.

Most of your *chef-d'oeuvre* are known to me. I am familiar with the beautiful careers you and your brother forged. I have wanted to write to you for years, but my shyness always stopped me. You remember Marie Dazois. She was an older student when I was one of the little ones. She has been married for thirty years to a merchant, is the mother of three children, two boys and a girl. The last one is very much in love with art and is already a comedienne. She would like very much to know you. How often I have spoken of the great sculptor, Camille Claudel! Should you wish, Madame, to receive us at this very moment, we are at your disposal. Any day or hour would be fine. A great thank you in advance from your admirer.

M. Montavox

How dreadful that I received so beautiful a letter and never got the chance to tell Mademoiselle Montavox how much I appreciated it. How I needed her warmth and admiration, when everything that made me Camille Claudel had been taken away from me. She surely wondered why a person wouldn't answer such a complimentary letter, and I imagine her feelings were badly hurt. And now she probably is dead and I can never let her know what a lovely gift the letter was and that I admired her, too, as one of the "older" students in the school, when I was a child.

 *T*here was no logical reason for the "sequestration," except the wish to be cruel and punishing. The letter would have made me feel good about myself and helped me remember a time when I was a free, valuable member of society, and that there once were people who loved and respected me. Why wouldn't any so-called doctor want me to feel that way? Dr. Brunet's a different breed and I'm grateful to him for giving me the letter. Perhaps some day all asylum doctors will be of his ilk. It's always painful for me to sit and wait for answers to letters that never were mailed, but not receiving Mademoiselle Montavox's letter is one of the most excruciating incidents of my life. It was almost on a par with the family not letting me know when Papa was dying.

The only joy of my life besides my cats is visitors. Unfortunately, they come very rarely, sometimes only once every five years. I sit and wait for them anyhow. That's what my life is, waiting, waiting, waiting. Waiting to go home, waiting for a far-away brother, waiting for a sister who hates me and doesn't want to bother with me, and waiting for a mother who never comes. In 1913, the year I was abducted and incarcerated in Ville-Evard, Paul was appointed the Consul General of Hambourg. He was too far away to come and see me, of course. Never mind that his visits were all I lived for. He was too busy taking care of his constituents who were strangers than to look after his own sister. When I was moved to the hospital of Montdevergues, near Avignon, which was much farther away from Villeneuve than Ville-Evard, it gave my loving family a better excuse to stay away. Otherwise, I was more fortunate than most of the other inmates. Maman's packages eased for me the wartime shortage of food that left most patients frantic with hunger.

In 1920, I got the news I'd been waiting for since 1912. Dr. Brunet told me I'd improved very much (Improved? From what, I'd like to know!) and he was writing to my mother to recommend that she take me out of the hospital and return me to the bosom of the family. What a wonderful doctor! I couldn't believe I finally had a physician who was a human being and not a stick. Whenever I want something very badly in life, just the opposite is sure to happen. As I've said, I ordinarily try to play down my hopes so I won't be too disappointed when they don't come about. But this was no ordinary situation. Dr. Brunet was handing me the only thing I wanted in the whole world. To make sure I wasn't making it up in my head, I glanced at him and asked him to repeat what he'd said. He looked directly at me with his candid grey eyes and said again, "I have written to your mother to recommend that she remove you from the hospital and take you home."

I looked at him again briefly, and saw pleasure, admiration, honesty, hopefulness, weariness, and strain on his face. There was no mistaking what he had said. I shrieked. I stomped. I cried. I clapped! I even threw my arms around him. After eight years of prison, I was going to savor the delicious air of Villeneuve once more, to climb up the hill and sit in the lap of my old friend, *Le Gèyn*, to promenade around the fragrant town square under the shade of the lime trees, to visit my beloved Presbyterie again where I spent so much of my youth, to hear the sweet sound of the church bells ringing out the hours. My heart beat to the rhythm of the church chimes. The Camille Claudel that was had come back to life! I rushed to my room, grabbed my grubby little wooden chair, and lugged it down to the front door where I began my wait for Maman.

I waited a day. I waited a week. I waited a month. I waited so long I lost all track of time. Finally I realized Maman was not going to come at all, the whole thing was a hoax, and Rodin had sent that letter to the doctor. He did it so I couldn't demand my sculptures back and take away the millions of francs he and his henchmen collect from all over the world.

As soon as I understood what had happened, I demanded to see Dr. Brunet, but was told I had to wait six weeks for my turn like everyone else. The six weeks felt like Chinese water torture, so slowly did they drip away. When I finally got to his office I immediately asked him about the letter he said he had written to my mother.

He said in dismal tones, "I'm sorry, Mademoiselle Claudel. I can't understand it. If I'd known what her response would be, I never would have told you I'd written her."

I felt the walls balloon outward and then cave back in on me.

"Response? What response? What did she say?" I asked hoarsely, although I already suspected what his answer would be.

He paused. "I'm going to tell you the truth, Mademoiselle Claudel, because I believe that dealing with patients honestly is therapeutic."

"Yes, yes, I'm sure," I said hurriedly, although I could hardly talk by then. "What did she say?"

He said in a despondent voice, "Your mother answered my letter to say she's old and sick and unable to take care of you." He paused to wait for my reaction. When he saw I was unable to speak, he continued, "Frankly, Mademoiselle Claudel, she said you hate her and are eager to do any evil in your power to your family. She added you have caused her so much grief she couldn't possibly open herself up to seeing you again."

I felt punched in the stomach. All the wind was knocked out of me and I could hardly breathe. When I finally was able to catch my breath, I wiped away my tears with my knuckles, and angrily demanded to see the letter. He had the gall to say it was lost. Of course he said that! It's obvious there never was such a letter in the first place, and he was only protecting himself from a lawsuit. And he had the audacity to say honesty is therapeutic! How could I ever have thought he was a person with feelings? What kind of doctor is he, anyhow? He should recognize a hoax when he sees one. He could have spared me the agony of disappointed hopes by keeping his "information" to himself. As far as I'm concerned, I'm never again going to wish for anything. It's too painful to want something and to be thwarted over and over. Nor will I ever again talk to Dr. Brunet or any of the other doctors. What's the use? What's the use, when they only break my heart?

I guess Dr. Brunet really did feel bad about my mother's letter. He wrote me a note the next week. He said in it he had written Maman again that if she couldn't take me home, she should at least try to bring me together with the family, since I missed them so much. He told her I was much calmer with fewer ideas of persecution, and he thought seeing them would help my mental state. The note made me feel a little warmer towards him, but this time I was under no illusions that his letter to Maman would do any good. I did the right thing for myself, as my skepticism kept me from being broken-hearted again. Nobody in the family came to see me until Paul's visit five years later.

Six weeks passed and I met with Dr Brunet again. There're so few people I could talk to in the asylum that despite my anger with him the last time, I found myself looking forward to seeing him. Unlike the other doctors, Dr. Brunet took the time and interest to discuss my case with me and even to read about it. He's a nice gentle man, who looks a little like Papa when he was young. He even talked about my sculptures every time we met. He liked that I was never afraid to portray my emotions and said very few artists have that kind of courage. He really seemed interested in me, and didn't go through the motions of interviewing me just because he was supposed to. I must say I enjoyed our meetings, unlike those with some doctors who, in my opinion, should find another line of work.

"Mademoiselle Claudel," he said at our next appointment. "You walked through that door as if you were looking right through me. Why did you do that?"

"So I won't get hurt," I answered. "I turn off first. When I reached out to my mother she pushed me away. It tore me apart. That's what people do when they know I care about them, they rip me to shreds. You might do the same. I'm not about to let that happen again: It would kill me."

"You've been badly hurt by many people," the doctor said. "But you have my word I won't be one of them."

We had a different kind of discussion at our next meeting, maybe because he'd been so nice to me. I really talked to him, the first time I'd spoken with anyone about feelings in many years. He was standing at the door as I came in, in such a position that I had to meet his glance.

"Is the eye maneuver for all patients?" I asked him, as I sat on the patients' little black chair.

"No," he answered. "It's especially for you."

"I can't look at you."

"I know. Thou shalt not see. What would happen if you did?"

"I have a pain in my heart that never goes away. If I looked at you it would shoot out through my body into every nerve I've got. I think it would kill me."

"Try. I'll help you live with it."

"No! I can't! It would open up too much pain and longing. Why should I?"

"You looked at me briefly on your way in today. Nothing awful happened."

"That's because I can look and not see. I keep everything foggy."

"And if you let yourself see clearly?"

"I'd scream and scream and not be able to stop. Everybody would hate me even more than they do now. Once I was scared during a thunder storm and began to cry. My mother shouted, 'Louis-Prosper, why is that child screaming? Make her stop. I can't bear it another moment!' Nobody ever wants to hear about my feelings."

"*I* want to hear about your feelings."

"Even angry ones?"

"Even angry ones."

"Suppose in my half-conscious state I broke your ashtray, pulled down the drapes, and cracked up the photograph of Montdevergues?

"I don't believe you would. You told me about it first."

"But suppose I couldn't help it. Would you retaliate by being mad and throwing things back at me?"

"No, I'm not scared of your anger. I'll help you control it."

"You don't care what people think, but only what they do. Is that right?

"That's exactly right."

"Suppose I said I wanted to jump at you with a knife?"

"It's only a fantasy and you haven't hurt me at all."

"Well, suppose one day all your patients leaped at you with knives? What would you think then?"

He laughed. "Do you want to know what I'd really think?"

"Yes."

"I'd think I was in the wrong profession!" He laughed again. We laughed together until it was time for me to leave.

The time dragged before I saw him again, though I was relieved we didn't talk about eye contact this time. With my eyes still averted, I said, "Dr. Brunet, I wrote a poem about you." He seemed surprised.

"Yes? And what is it?"

My doctor is like a field of wheat
blowing in the wind
this way and that way
however it blows
is the way the doctor will bend.
My doctor is a finger
held to the wind
ever alert
to which way
it blows.

I dared to look straight into his eyes. He was looking at me intently, and his eyes widened almost imperceptibly as they met mine. Then he smiled a big smile from the inside out, and I knew he liked my poem and that I'd really looked at him. I guess they would say in this asylum I'd made progress. Progress, my rear end! I don't want to make their kind of progress and submit to tyranny. The man was more genuine with me than any physician had ever been, really liked me and tried to understand me, and often gave me gave me a new way of looking at things. So of course I could drop my guard with him more than the others. I also decided I'd try to consider the picture of me he painted and compare it with the way I see things myself.

First of all, he asked if I knew why am I here. I know I'm here only because Rodin's gang, who've stolen all my work and become millionaires from it, keep me here. Of course the doctor disagreed. He makes more money off my family that way. But just once, I played devil's advocate and examined my case as objectively as Dr. Brunet himself.

"Here I am 79 years old and still in a mental institution after thirty years of interment," I said. "Is it possible there's any *good* reason why I'm still here?" The doctor nodded. He liked that kind of thinking.

I told him my balance is not as good as it was, and while walking with the nurse lately I had to hold on to her in order not to fall. Is it because of my age? I was almost as old last year and it wasn't so bad then. I said it's caused by people who're trying to poison me with arsenic and curare, a plant used by the South American Indians to paralyze the motor system. The kitchen staff, who are part of Rodin's gang put the curare in my food. It poisons the muscular system so I can barely move. "Don't you think so, Doctor Brunet?" The doctor made no comment. His unusual silence made me anxious, and I rushed to fill in the gap.

"Sometimes I think I walk like the drunks I see in the streets," I continued quickly. "Could I have guzzled down too much wine over the years? It's true I like a little snort every day and sometimes more. In fact I often lose count of how much I've drunk, but I never thought I was an alcoholic. I know you think I am. Don't you?" I felt him gazing at me steadily with his quiet eyes.

I blurted out, " I know you think I'm an alcoholic, Doctor Brunet, but you're wrong! I'm just old, and I would be the same age outside of a lunatic asylum as inside it." I peeked at his face. No expression on it betrayed any reaction.

"My tongue and my fingers tremble, Doctor. I see a lot of that around here. I think it's because of the freezing weather." I went on, trying to goad him into speaking. Again he was silent. Just as I was about to succumb to despair, he spoke. He didn't spare my feelings one bit.

"You *are* an alcoholic, Mademoiselle Claudel. After so many years of drinking, alcoholism causes tremors. You see things in your head that aren't there."

Who, me? What is he saying? That I suffer from delirium tremens, as he has had the nerve to insinuate since I first came here? I? No! I'm an artist and that's the way I see the world. I always pictured my statues in my head, and nobody ever thought that was reason to institutionalize me. If they're looking for a rationale to keep me here, they'll dredge up anything they can think of to justify their crime.

The doctors have always maintained I'm paranoid because I persist in thinking people are trying to poison me with arsenic and curare. Well, they are! How can I be called paranoid if people are really doing what I think? Only an insane person would stop thinking what they know to be true. If anything, they're driving me berserk with their lies. Anybody who can't see that is crazy. And much as I like him, that includes Dr. you-know-who!

Then he said he thinks something is wrong with my thymus gland. Maybe, whatever that is. I'm going to look it up in the medical reference book in the library when I feel stronger. But even if my thymus is diseased, does that mean I'm insane? If a gland is malfunctioning, isn't that a physical and not a mental illness? I think he's way off the track. It's clear the shaking is the result of the curare they put in my food. That's why I don't eat anything they prepare in this den of debauchery. They *are* trying to poison me! That's what makes me crazy, when they say it isn't true. There're a lot of crazy people here, but I'm not one of them.

The nuns told the doctors I don't sleep, and walk around my room all night. They say I'm hyperactive and manic. Could *you* sleep if you'd been endlessly locked up in a lunatic asylum? What else is there to do in the wee hours of the morning but walk around the room? How many hours can one lie in bed waiting for the first beams of the rising sun to lighten up the sky?

And then there's the cave. I'm very scared of the cave. At night I think about it. A bottomless dark cave is somewhere deep inside of me. It keeps calling, calling, calling. Suppose I go inside of it and never come out? I'm afraid to go to sleep.

I'm growing weaker and weaker. Never mind the traipsing around at night, there're many days now when I can't get out of bed. Is it my age? My father was much older than I am now when he died and he still was walking around as well as when he was young. Dr. Brunet says I suffer from malnutrition, that one cannot eat only baked potatoes and hard-boiled eggs for years and years without paying the price. Well, if he's right, it's better to be weak than dead, which is what I would certainly be if I ate the food Rodin's henchmen prepare for me in the kitchen. Then again, sometimes I think I should eat their poison and let them finish the job.

I wanted to be open-minded about the catastrophe that has befallen me. So looking at the whole picture, I came to the conclusion that, yes, I'm getting old and may drink a little too much, but that doesn't mean I'm crazy or an alcoholic. Now that I think of it, I was wrong to allow Dr. Brunet's fabricated warmth and interest to seduce me. He's the insane one, as well as an incompetent. He can't tell the difference between physical and mental illness. He colludes with my family, veils the truth, and shamelessly inters me for his own gain. As I've stressed over and over again, I've been kept here all these years by Rodin and his henchmen who scheme with the doctors so they can all get rich off my sculptures. The workers in the kitchen may not have to keep trying to poison me. Dr. Brunet may be doing it for them. When I was in his office last time I smelled something funny in the air. I stopped breathing deeply and took in only a few little wisps at a time, just enough to keep going. It made me dizzy, and I was glad when it was time to leave. I think he put poison in the air to try to kill me. And he promised he'd never hurt me! That's what I get for trusting him, against my better judgment! I'll never trust anybody again. I wonder if he's one of Rodin's gang? These doctors are all the same. None of them believe I know what I'm talking about. May they rot in Hell with all the rest of Rodin's thugs, and take the whole asylum with them!

I got up and stamped out of Dr. Brunet's office, determined never to return. But I was robbed of the satisfaction of getting even with him. He never even knew I didn't come back. He was replaced by Dr. Charpenel, who was followed by Dr. Clément, and Lord knows who else. I got along well with all the doctors and felt they mostly protected me against evil influences. But I determined to listen to my own instincts after that and never again talked so intimately to anyone as I had with Dr. Brunet.

Dr.Clément's cousin, incidentally, was a sculptor who'd studied in Paris and frequented the finest artistic circles. This cousin was horrified that I was wasting my life in Montdevergues. and tried to talk the doctor into forcing me to sculpt. Dr. Clément brought me clay and did his best to make me work with it. That did not convince me to sculpt, rather the reverse. I just let the clay sit there until it all dried up.

Everybody always asks why I destroyed my finished statues. To them I say, if I bother at all to answer, I reacted morally with the only weapon left to me against a malicious world. I don't think anyone would understand I was consumed with a rage so great it seemed monstrous flames were blasting their way through my body, until every organ, every aperture, every crevasse seemed to be burning up in oil. I became the fire. Camille Claudel as a person ceased to exist. The torture was agonizing, and there's nothing I wouldn't have done to stop it. The fires blazed on and on until I felt I was roasting in Hell. How well I understood Dante's emotions when he wrote the *Inferno*! Nothing helped until I raised my ax high in the air and chopped chopped chopped to tiny bits every plaster sculpture in the *atelier*, coming down progressively harder with every stroke. I chopped up *L'Age Mûr*. I chopped up *Sakountala*. I chopped up *La Petite Châlelaine*. I chopped up *Giganti*. I chopped up *Clotho*. I chopped up *Perseus and the Gorgon*. I kept chopping until every plaster statue lay in bits at my feet, when I collapsed from sheer exhaustion. I destroyed the statues for the same reason I sculpted them, for pure pleasure. But the pleasure of destruction is the sheer joy of relief, in contrast to the godlike pleasure of creativity. It's a moot question which I enjoyed more, making the sculptures or breaking them. Is this crazy? I don't think so. I loved to create them, but I didn't want Rodin stealing them, so I destroyed them, getting pleasure and relief in the bargain. Then, too, my dear Paul says to punish myself for my sin I must give up what's most dear to me. Nothing's more dear to me than sculpting. I sacrificed my genius to appease Paul and my conscience.

Have I given up anything else, along with the sculpting? Yes. I've given up all meaning in life. I've disowned myself, abandoned my identity, for who was I but a sculptor? I've given up all excitement, anything that has significance, any reason to get up in the morning. I've given up what marks the dissolving of morning into afternoon, the merging of afternoon into dusk, and dusk into night, so I hear the church bells chiming all night long, one o'clock, two o'clock, four o'clock, five. When I yielded to Paul's demand, I severed all feelings from their source inside me, including the intuition that fueled my artistic achievements. I amputated my center like Hélène cored apples, so I no longer have a set of values to guide me. I can't distinguish between what's good and what's evil, unless someone like Paul tells me the difference between them. I've lost the ability to evaluate the art of others, as well as my own. I've given up all hope of leaving anything of value to remember me by when I leave this earth. I can no longer experience the beauty of nature, or any other beauty, for that matter, for nothing that exists is beautiful to me now. I've no wish to be with people, let alone love anyone. I've given up what soothes me, what stimulates me, what makes me happy. I only know when I'm cold or hungry and not always then. I live in an immense void, as if in a coffin, sitting in a corner of my room on my little wooden chair with my cats meowing at my feet. I sit there day after day, year after year, waiting, waiting, waiting…All I have to look forward to now is the end of the road. Dear God, please make it soon. I've been in this House of Hell for almost thirty years now. Haven't I punished myself enough yet? Do you think Paul—and God—will forgive me?

My only recreation is a long walk I sometimes take in the hospital park when the icy wind abates a bit or an occasional errand I'm given permission to run with the nuns. Most patients work in the fields, on the farms, or in the workshops. Another group works as servants for the doctors and officials. Many a child has been raised in the complex by inmates. Dr. Clément had at least six working for him and his family. One patient grew the vegetables, another polished their shoes and scrubbed their clothes, and two or three took care of the garden. From the looks of it, they did a wonderful job. I do not work. I refuse to be herded like an inmate. There's a theater set up in the Women's Boarding facilities. I don't go there either. Nothing they could show me would interest me. Patients also can receive visitors on Sunday. Since Paul, and only Paul, comes to see me about once every five years, I don't get to do too much of that, either. I miss having visitors. Strangely enough, I miss my mother most of all. Not once in all the years I've been here has Maman or my dear sister come to see me. I wrote to Paul to please try to persuade Maman to visit me, that I would love to see her. I said she can come on the Express train. She can do that for me, I told him, it should not be so tiring, even at her age. But my plea went unheeded. My mother did not come to see me because she was held hostage by Rodin's gang.

When Paul came to see me in June, 1915, for the first time since I entered this den of depravity, I was so angry he hadn't come before I barely spoke to him. He spent most of his visit talking to the nuns about Catholicism. When he left, I realized he was still the same old Paul, maybe a little older and fatter, and I still loved him very much. I could have kicked myself around the asylum because I'd spoken so little with him. I promised myself I'd never do that again. I suspected it would be years before I got another chance.

When his little girl Renée was born in 1917, I tired to make amends to Paul for my sulking behavior. Then too, I thought I'd try to love Renée to replace my own lost baby, and also, I must admit, to get Paul to forgive me for my sin. So I made the baby a festive blanket from pieces of silk I cut out of old dresses. It was full of large, vibrant flowers and wild, tropical birds with green, yellow, and red plumage. Even though the nuns helped me by rounding up some old clothes from the townspeople, it took a long time to find enough silk to make a whole blanket, and my hands were often numb with cold. Nevertheless I persevered until my fingers were bleeding, until I finally finished it. I was thrilled when I was able to ask the director to send it off to Paul and his wife, and then waited patiently for their response. To my great disappointment, nobody even thanked me for the gift. The only thing Paul wrote me about it was, "It's kind of bright for a baby, isn't it?" I decided that was the last present I'd ever make for a member of his family. Or for anyone else, for that matter. For all the visits he makes to me, there isn't much to lose.

I was right it would be many years until I saw Paul again. In 1920, he finally got around to seeing me. Since it was five years since his last visit, I was so happy to see him I forgot my pride and fell into his arms in tears. I stayed there sobbing, when he began to blubber, too. I almost didn't recognize him. He had gotten fat, and with his big bald head looked like a swollen mallet. Whatever happened to my beautiful golden boy? Time has not been kind to the Claudels. Of course I don't look all that great myself, having lost most of my teeth and with my hair all grey, but Paul was kind enough not to mention that. The visit was over like a flash of lightning, and I didn't see him again for—yes, you've guessed it—another five years.

In 1925, I received another low blow. Paul told me Maman had sold our Villeneuve house to her grandson, Dr. Jacques de Massary, and Jacques had changed its structure so much the house was virtually unrecognizable. I fell down onto a chair and thought I'd never get up again. What? Never to see my beloved house again? *Never?* Can it be that it exists as I remember it only in my dreams? How could Maman do such a thing? How could Paul have allowed it? I've experienced great disappointments in my lifetime, but this is the ultimate calamity. They won't even allow me to keep my dreams.

In 1928, Paul came again. It only took him three years between visits this time. He'd aged a lot in those years and looked even worse than before, with a head like a big fat parakeet. He told me about the dramatic oratorio he's writing, *Joan of Arc at the Stake*, which he believes will be produced in Basel, Switzerland. Oh how I wish I could be there! Am I never to see my own brother's plays? How much deprivation can one person endure and stay alive? Then I experienced another feeling along with my genuine happiness for Paul. A sneaky little sensation slithered through the barriers I'd built to keep it away. I couldn't help but remember all the years I'd talked to him about Joan of Arc. She was my interest and never his. Does he have to take everything? Does he have to have it all? Couldn't he leave anything to me? Except for one of the versions of *La Petite Châtelaine*, I never got to sculpt the statue of Joan I always intended to do. With all he has in his life, couldn't he at least allow me to keep for myself the one saint I loved? Paul is living for both of us. He has two careers, a wife and children, while I have nothing but my cats. I might as well be in the ground, for all the pleasures I have in my life. Nevertheless, it was good to have Paul with me again. I cried when he left.

My ever-more successful brother wrote me that Jean-Louis Barrault was acting in his play, *Soulier de Satin*. Paul told him he should seek inspiration for a scene in the play from my sculpture, *L'Age Mûr*, which he can find at the home of Madame Berthelot. Perhaps I'm ungrateful, but I've mixed feelings about it. I'm flattered Paul believes my creation is superb enough that even a great actor can learn from it, but doesn't Paul have enough success in his life without stealing the little left in my own?

When Paul came to visit in 1928, he let slip that Rodin had died long ago, on November 12, 1917, as a matter of fact. Since they won't let me read the newspapers here, I'd no way of knowing about it before. That was all right. For me, he was dead from the beginning of time. I had no feeling of regret about it at all. Why should I, when he stole my life's works from me, sold them for millions of dollars, and got rich and famous because of them while I was rotting away in this hell hole of doom? Although I wonder why I found it so hard to fall asleep after Paul gave me the news, harder even than usual for a long time afterward.

Then I had a little dream about Monsieur Rodin the night I was told about his death. I was a beautiful young woman again, exactly as I used to be, and he of course was much younger, too, as he was when we were lovers. He was sculpting *The Kiss* and running his hands over my body, as he so often did when he sculpted a statue of me. I was carried away with rapture. Just at the moment when I reached the peak of pleasure, I awoke drenched in sweat. No wonder I can't sleep, if I'm going to have dreams like that! My head had more sense than my body. Never again! I'd rather give up sleep altogether than have another dream like that. How could I ever let that old goat smear his hands all over me? I must have been out of my mind.

Funny about that dream. It was certainly Rodin's face I saw in the dream, but when I woke up and thought about it he looked like my godfather Uncle Nicolas who died so long ago. I loved Uncle Nicolas very much. He was one of the few people who believed I'd be a great artist some day. I still remember the wonderful box of yellow pencils he gave me and how he used to fool around and make us laugh. When I woke up from the dream I forgot all about that monster Rodin and cried and cried for Uncle Nicolas.

1929 was an eventful year, in this life of non-events. It was the year Jessie Lipscomb and her husband, William Elborne, visited me. It was nice to see her, but we had very little to say to each other. Who is this old woman who thinks she knows me? I wondered when I first saw her. How dare she sit holding my hand? William took a lot of photographs of us, in which we look like two old ladies who happened to sit next to each other on a park bench. I think we had so little to say because our lives have taken such different paths. I followed the tempestuous road to becoming an artist, fighting discrimination against women, narrow-mindedness, and poverty every inch of the way. Yes, I lost the battle, and have ended up here in this hell on earth. But didn't I put up a great fight, though! I sculpted some works of great beauty, even of glory, and found infinite pleasure in the sculpting that not many people experience. I believe creativity is the closest we humans will ever come to knowing God. I console myself that my work received many fine reviews, and I've been called the finest sculptor in the country, finer even than Rodin. Perhaps my statues will live on after I'm gone. And perhaps my struggles will make life easier for women artists in the future. Then it all would have been worthwhile.

Jessie, on the other hand, followed the more conventional path for women of marriage and raising children. She has a loving man by her side and four apparently wonderful children. Unlike me, she's a respectable woman in the eyes of society. She seems happy enough, although William never made much money. She's even built a little studio at the back of her garden, where she modeled some busts of her children when she could get away from her household tasks. It sounds as if she's far better off than I.

Would I choose her life, if I had it to do over again? I probably could have married Claude Debussy and been a normal wife and mother, whatever that is. If I'd made a baby with him, I wouldn't have had to kill it. With the two of us for parents, our child would have been a demigod. Would I have led a happier life if I'd married Claude? Would I follow Jessie's path another time round and be happier? No, I wouldn't follow the route Jessie chose. William Elborne's been a good friend to me and I like him very much, but I couldn't imagine being married to him. He bores me. Except for the years with Rodin, I never wanted any life but that of a sculptor. I followed my passion and no doubt would do it again, if I were given the chance. The happiest moments of my life were those I spent creating my sculptures in the company of my cats. I never wanted to do anything else. This's what I've learned in a lifetime of misery and bliss: For a real artist, the sun only shines when one lives in one's art.

But I feel nothing for this stranger who says she's my friend. Is it possible we once loved each other? She says we did, but all I can remember is standing by the sparkling Seine and vowing to think about each other whenever we saw glistening water. Since I never see any rivers here, glistening or otherwise, I don't have to worry about that. Oh, now I remember what happened. She wanted to cheat me out of the rent money. I didn't let her and threw her out of my *atelier*. I can't abide cheats. She also said some strange things about being a go-between for Rodin and me. What a meddler she was! No wonder I feel nothing for her. That chiseler Rodin! Why would I need anyone to connect me with him? I only wanted him to leave me alone.

Funny, I didn't feel anything for Jessie when she was here, but after she left, I cried. I can't say exactly why, although it obviously had something to do with her visit. Maybe it's because nobody else comes to see me.

*O*n June 20, 1929, my mother passed away in Villeneuve. She was eighty-nine years old. Paul wrote me she died of an enormous ovarian cyst, that Dr. Jacques said could not have developed recently but must have been growing for many years. She refused to have it removed by surgery, as she knew such operations generally are fatal to people her age. Maman was given the simple ceremony she asked for, conducted by the pastor of Villeneuve with the kind of service he gives the villagers. In her last instructions to Paul, Maman made it clear she didn't want chimes to ring out for three days when she died, but only on the day of her funeral. Nor did she want her death to be announced in newspapers anywhere else than Villeneuve. She was buried beside my father near her parents in the little churchyard, as she wished, and asked that Paul give a small contribution to the church.

When I read the letter, I cried out in pain. The nuns gathered around me and tried to comfort me, but I pushed them away. I didn't want them with me. The most important things in life one must do alone. I went to my room and for the first time in my life, I talked to my mother.

You died without saying goodbye to me, Maman. You died after not seeing me for thirty years. You did terrible things to me, but you died without giving me a chance to tell you I forgive you, that I know you couldn't come to see me or take me home because Rodin always interfered. You died before I could tell you how sorry I am, Maman. I'm sorry I caused you so much sorrow, sorry I couldn't be the kind of daughter you wanted, sorry we never understood each other. You died without giving me one last chance to make you love me. Now it's too late and you're gone forever. I wish I could've told you you weren't such a bad mother, Maman. For thirty years you kept me alive with packages of delicious food and warm clothing you sent me, even during the war when you had little of your own to spare. No one else here received such gifts and many died without them. Surely that showed your maternal devotion. It's just that we were terribly mismatched as mother and daughter. You were a good mother to Louise and Paul, but you weren't the right one for me. How characteristic of you to want so simple a funeral! You needed a simpler daughter like you, another Louise who would follow in your footsteps without giving it a thought. And I needed a compassionate mother who understood the compulsion to create, no matter what the cost. It really wasn't anyone's fault. It's just that we were so different from each other. You "joked" that I was so unlike the rest of you I wasn't your baby at all, but a Moor who'd been left on the doorstep by the gypsies. You said that's why I'm so dark.

I painted a picture of you a long time ago in which you were sitting in the shade of our garden. Remember that portrait, Maman? Whatever happened to it? You looked beautiful in the painting. Your large eyes concealed a secret sorrow, and your entire posture drooped, as if life itself had been a terrible disappointment to you that you were resigned to. Every thought, every action of yours was dedicated to your sense of duty. In the eyes of society; you were a good woman, Maman. Even though I didn't know it then, the picture glows with my hidden love for you. Remember the time you fell against the table and passed out? When you came to, you were surprised at how upset I was. You said that was the only time you ever felt I loved you. Well, I know it now, Maman, now that it's too late. Too bad I didn't know it then. Something like that happened to me, too. Remember when the little grey mare ran away, dragging me behind her? You said you thought if I was killed you wouldn't want to live. I was surprised to hear you cared for me that much. Oh Maman, I wanted to hold you in my arms just once before I die, you, the little orphan girl who didn't have a mother to cuddle her. It might have changed your life. Now that can never be. We suffered not from hatred of each other, but from disappointed love. And the most painful cut of all, Maman, is that you died before I could tell you I love you. I love you, Maman. Maybe you can hear it now.

In 1930, I received a pleasant little surprise. I was summoned to the sitting room, where I found my nephew Pierre, his daughter Chouchette, and her husband Roger waiting for me. I recognized Pierre right away, as he's the image of Paul. He seems like a very kind person. He set off nostalgic memories of the days of *Le Géyn*. I was ready to take his hand and walk him up the hill, as I did his father so long ago. Chouchette is very pretty, just as she was as a little girl. She looks like her mother. I was delighted to meet Roger, who's nice as could be and ran to Montfavet to buy me fruit and whatever else I wanted. They were all dressed very nicely, and made me feel quite shoddy in my dilapidated coat and squashed hat which fell down nearly to my chin, as I hobbled around with rheumatism-on-the-knee. It was wonderful to see them, but then they left, and I felt more alone than ever. Maybe it's better not to have visitors at all: It feels so bad when they leave. I doubt if I'll ever see them again.

Speaking of visitors, in 1932 my still-loyal gallery owner Eugène Blot came to see me. Eugène's the best friend I ever had. I think I would've died of starvation many times or killed myself if it weren't for him. How lovely he hasn't forgotten me after all these long years! He looked old and weary, and said he's been ill or he would've come sooner. We spent the all-too-short time allotted to us talking about my sculptures. He said Monet had told him I and Rodin brought truth and genuineness to the world of sculpture, and with my work the viewer left the hypocritical world of pretensions for one of truth and beauty. Monet regards the *Implorer* as the symbol of modern sculpture. Blot himself thinks the original piece is one of the finest in his gallery, and says he never passes it without being overcome by a surge of powerful emotions and stopping to stroke its head.

"At last," he continued joyfully, "you totally outgrew the influence of Rodin and became absolutely yourself!"

"Oh Eugène," I said weeping. "I've been waiting twenty years to hear those words. No one else has ever understood that after I left Rodin, becoming free of him was the motive behind every work I sculpted." I threw myself into his arms and wept anew.

When I stopped crying, Blot told me Rodin had paid his gallery a visit fifteen years ago and stopped in front of a portrait of me. He looked at it, rubbed his cheek against it, and began to sob.

"He really loved you, Camille. He never loved any other woman as much. I know how much you suffered because of him, but time will make everything right."

I answered, "After I'm dead, maybe."

"Maybe." Eugène said.

In the thirties, I experienced another loss. Up to that time we'd been taken care of by nuns, which made me feel rather at home, as I had been taught by sisters when I was five to twelve years old. In 1936, several events led to the shrinking of their ranks. There were a number of strikes on the popular Front and as a result forty-hour work weeks were established throughout France. Young women no longer wished to work lengthy hours for no pay. After all, God was not an equal rights employer. As the sisters grew old and died, there were very few girls who wanted to become novices and replace them. As of 1938, the number of sisters fell from forty to twelve, and continued to drop. When the nuns left or died off, they were replaced by lay people. It was a great loss to me, as some of the nuns really went out of their way to spoil me and make me comfortable. For instance, on the feast day of Joan of Arc, who they knew I loved, they made festive draperies. Behind the altar, which was perhaps six meters high, they hung a beautiful tapestry of Joan by climbing a step ladder they'd built themselves. Sisters Sylvie, Saint-Cyr, and Sainte-Blandine never failed to attend the celebrations. In the effort to comfort us, there was always a spot of brandy to lighten our souls. I've always admired creative people, and the nuns were the most creative artisans in the asylum.

Sister Odilia was also a generous woman. She took the inmates for a special walk once a year into the woods, where she prepared a wonderful picnic with wine, fresh fruit, and all sorts of goodies. She was a sweet, gentle woman, who looked at me with love in her warm brown eyes. She reminded me both in appearance and manner of Mère St. Joseph of the Sisters of the Christian Doctrine in Epernay, who encouraged my drawings so much when I was little. I remember thinking as a child, "If I had a mother like Mère St. Joseph, my life would be much happier." I felt the same way about Sister Odilia. The nuns were replaced by nurses, who often were quite nice. But it wasn't the same thing. They weren't familiar-looking and didn't bring back memories of my childhood. I miss the sisters dearly.

Shortly after Sister Odilia died, a new catastrophe overtook me. My stomach had been swollen for days, and I had terrible cramps with diarrhea and was nauseous all the time. The spasms got so bad I couldn't get out of bed. I knew I shouldn't have eaten that stew the nurse said she made especially for me a few days ago. It probably was full of poison. Anyway, two men in white suits came in early one morning and shocked me out of my sleep. They lifted me out of my bed, held down my arms, and shackled me to a stretcher with leather straps. I thought they were kidnaping me, as when they carted me away to the lunatic asylum. I knew there was nowhere they could carry me that could be worse than this place, but they could take me to an isolated spot and torture me. I was on to them! They were members of Rodin's gang and were planning to kill me. I yelled "Fire! Fire! Help! Murder!" And tried to bite one of them, until he clamped my mouth shut. I jerked and tugged at the straps to try to get loose, paying no attention to the awful pain in my stomach. I didn't realize I had that much strength left in me. I kept hollering, "Put me down! Put me down! Why're you doing this to me? Where're you taking me?" I figured I might as well fight them as hard as I could, since I was sure I would end up dead anyway.

"Be quiet, lady." The attendant I tried to bite answered. "And stop thrashing around, will you? Otherwise, it'll be worse for you! There's nothing wrong here. We're taking you to see the doctor."

"See the doctor?" I shouted. "Patients have to go to his office to see a doctor. I just saw one yesterday. He didn't help me with my stomach at all. You don't fool me. I'm on to you. You're part of Rodin's gang. Let me off this thing! My brother's an ambassador. He'll see you go to prison for this. Get me off of here, I tell you! Let me down!"

But of course they didn't. They didn't even bother to answer again. They wheeled me into a room painted all in white, with bright lights overhead. Dr. Roget, who had been seeing me for my cramps, was waiting there.

I cried out, "Dr. Roget, why're these men bringing me here? What're you going to do to me?"

He said. "You know you've been having severe pains lately, Mademoiselle Claudel. We have to look inside you and see what's wrong before we can help you get better."

"Look inside me?" I screamed. "You're going to cut me open?"

He tried to reassure me. "It's just minor surgery, Mademoiselle Claudel."

My heart was pounding like a mallet on marble. "I'm feeling much better, Doctor," I lied. "I'm sure surgery is unnecessary and time will heal my stomach completely."

When he smiled and moved a knife from one hand to the other, I knew it was a lost cause. I had nothing more to lose than my life, so I decided to play for time. "Can you at least tell me why I need surgery, Doctor?" I said. "I'd feel better if I knew."

"All right, Camille, if it would make you less frightened. We think you're suffering from something doctors call an Epiploic Hernia. That means you have a little sac on your colon that has ruptured. If we're right, and I'm almost certain we are, we'll remove it and you'll be fine in the morning." If he said anything else, I didn't hear it, as at that point I passed out from fright. I suppose they did the surgery, because I woke up the next morning with a bandage over a cut. To tell the truth, I was surprised to wake up at all.

The doctor wasn't exactly right about my feeling fine, either, because it took several days before I felt better. And the pain did go away. But they can't fool me with that medical gobbledygook One doctor told me it's a disease common to horses. I was not reassured when he said the horses usually survive. Regardless of what an Epiploic Hernia is, I don't believe I had one at all. It's obvious to me I was poisoned by the kitchen workers, who're part of Rodin's gang. I was right not to eat their food for years. The gang gave the doctors instructions to cut me up, to make sure I never get out of this place alive. Dr. Roget and I get along well, thank goodness, and he couldn't find it in himself to carry out their orders. He pretended to go along with them and only cut me up a little bit to fool them. I hope the gang doesn't find out and make him pay for defying them.

There were no further events worth recording until 1934, when the Salon of Modern Women Artists had an exposition which showed my sculptures, *L'Imploration*, *La Valse*, and *Le Buste de Rodin*. I was glad to be remembered, but if any money was made, I never saw it. They probably sent it to Rodin's gang.

*I*n May of 1935, my sister Louise died. My baby sister, who was two years younger than me. That's against the law of nature. Older sisters are supposed to die before younger ones. Why did she have to die before me, when I would've been happy to go first? We never liked each other, dead or alive. I'll never forgive her for taking my mother away from me, for not visiting me in all the years I've spent in this den of debauchery, and for consorting with that scoundrel Rodin to steal all my money. May they continue to consort in Hell! After Maman died, Louise took over the job of sending me packages of food and clothing. I would've liked to return them, but then I would've starved or frozen to death. Maybe that wouldn't have been such a bad idea. Whatever will I do without the packages? Life has so few pleasures for me I can't afford to give up even one. I hope Paul or his wife takes over that job.

Funny, I didn't think about Louise very much when I first heard the news, but somehow her death seemed to set off a chain of memories. I really treated her badly. She had an inane sweetness that made it almost impossible for me not to be cruel to her. I remember a photograph taken of the two of us when we were little. Louise looks lovely as usual, but I'm scowling. On the back of it Papa had written, "Camille has always abused her sister."

Once when she was little, I did the worst thing I ever did to anybody. I said to her, "Close your eyes and open your mouth and I'll put something good in it.' She closed her little eyes, puckered up her face, and opened her mouth like a hungry fish. I dropped some cat poop the size and shape of a chocolate bud into her eagerly awaiting mouth. I can still hear the screams when she discovered what it was. But to her credit, she didn't tell Maman on me, who would've made me pay until Hell froze over.

Despite my abuse, Louise still did nice things for me once in a while. I remember her coming to my rescue when we were quite young. Amalie, the fattest girl in the Catholic school, always called me "Gimpy"—"Hey, Gimpy, do you have a peg leg?" she'd shout so loudly in the schoolyard the whole school could hear. "Show us your peg leg!" Once Louise happened to be passing by during a tirade of Amalie's, and even though

Louise was smaller and younger, she leaped on Amalie's back and kept passionately pummeling her on the head until we had to pull her off. I was surprised she was that strong. When we got Louise off her back, Amalie ran home grasping her ears in her hands and yelling her head off. But my little sister's revenge paid off. Amalie never called me Gimpy again.

How beautiful my sister was as a young woman! She posed for me many times, without complaining nearly as much as Paul. I have to admit that besides her beauty, she had a certain sweetness I could see when I wasn't busy tormenting her. It came through in the statues of her I sculpted. Poor Louise! It must've been awfully hard on her to have a sister who mistreated her so. It wasn't her fault she wasn't very bright.

I'm aging fast, and seem to get weaker every day. But I didn't realize I looked so old until Paul's visit in 1933, when he looked shocked at the sight of me.

I said, "Paul, what's the matter?"

He answered. "It's nothing, Camille."

I said, "Oh come on, Paul, you forget this is your sister you're talking to. I know you better than that. What's the matter?"

He hemmed and hawed a while.

I said, "Well, out with it, Paul!"

He said with tears in his eyes, "It's just…that I'm not used to seeing you without teeth, with just stumps in your mouth." I thought I had no vanity left, but I burst into tears, too. We cried together in each other's arms. When it was time for him to leave, I couldn't bear to watch him go out the door, so I dropped my eyes and turned my head to the wall.

My health is very bad, both mentally and physically. It seems I can't remember two words from one moment to the next. I'm afraid I'm getting senile. I started to write a letter to Paul and then realized I'd written him the same thing that very morning. I've gotten very thin, thinner than I've ever been, so that it feels like a strong Montdevergues wind could blow me away like the spores of a dying dandelion. The doctor says my heart's nothing to brag about either. *Tant pis!* That's fine with me. Why prolong the agony? The sooner I leave this place the better. Even worse are my terrible digestive problems. The doctor has diagnosed me with Enteritis, an inflamation of the intestines, and says my condition is caused by extreme malnutrition. I've just about stopped eating. Attacks leave me weak with nausea, vomiting, and cramps, and a certain malaise, so it's even harder to care about anything than usual. I've slowed down so much the hare has turned into a tortoise. I also have muscles that ache all the time. How ironic that I who knew more about how muscles work than anyone should be unable to cope with my own aches. Of course, the pain makes me limp worse than ever, so it's getting more and more difficult to walk at all.

My Enteritis is getting so bad my dear doctor assigned me last month to bed rest. I suffer from Edema, which means my legs and arms are swollen, and my digestive system is hardly working at all. I'm so weak now and it's so hard to walk I'm satisfied to stay in bed. I can curl up like a baby in the womb, as I lay once in my mother's womb, as my baby lay in mine. It relieves the pain a little. The nurses are very nice to me and are quite friendly. They keep me company, and often sit by my bedside knitting when they've finished their work. I have a lady doctor now who seems to like me a lot, too. She drops by my room often and stays there a long time. It's very nice to feel surrounded by friends. Once a nurse stuck her head into my room and said, "It sounds like a party in here!" I haven't had so much loving female companionship since my English friends shared my *atelier*.

The way people regard me here seems to have changed over the years. For some reason, whether it's because I was a sculptor, or my brother an ambassador I don't know, I'm greeted in respectful tones and treated with consideration. For instance when Paul comes to visit he's always received by the director. I don't have to entertain him in the community parlor where inmates usually bring their guests. We're taken instead to a special salon where very important guests are accommodated. Another instance is the way I'm treated in church. When the chapel clock calls us to services, I put on my old black coat and pull my hat of black felt down over my ears. I carry my missal, which I covered in black cloth, under one arm, as the nurse accompanies me to the chapel. People move aside to let us pass. I nod to the doctors, the director, and my particular nurses when they greet me. I rarely speak to the lesser employees and never to the inmates. There's a special pew I always sit in, although places are not reserved. And there's a little *prie dieu* I use, which no one else ever takes, although they often fight among themselves to claim ownership of other positions in the chapel. I haven't been able to go there lately, as I'm so weak. The nurse told me nobody sits in my place or uses my *prie dieu*. It seems they're all waiting for my return.

Once I was failing so badly they called a priest to administer Last Rites. I fooled them, though! I'm not ready to die. Paul says he's coming to see me and I want to be around when he does. Then, too, I'm not ready to go until I finish my autobiography, such as it is. I haven't done all this work on it only to turn out to be a shirker at the very end. Sometimes I'm so weak I can hardly lift my pencil. I write a few words, or if I'm lucky a few sentences, fall asleep for a while, and then when I feel stronger pick up the pencil again. I'm determined to finish it so at least one thing in my lifetime will have a positive ending. Perhaps the record of my life will help future generations to understand the horrors in the life of a woman artist who was betrayed by her times, and keep it from happening again. Who was it who said people who refuse to look at catastrophe are doomed to repeat it? Look on my catastrophic life, oh ye women of the future, and take heed you do not repeat it.

To add to my life of horror, war clouds were looming again. As of January, 1939, there were one thousand nine hundred and forty-nine inmates at Montdevergues. By January 1943, when Hitler invaded Poland, France became involved in the struggle, and the number of occupied beds dropped to one thousand seven hundred and sixty-three. Despite the large number of patients who'd been moved here from psychiatric hospitals in occupied or threatened war zones, more and more of the inmates were dying of the freezing weather and malnutrition. Paul, who was the French Consul in Hambourg, wrote he and his family were booed by a crowd in Germany, which threw rocks and spit at them. They were crammed into a train bound for Copenhagen, with only a few cans of food and a little water to last for the endless, miserable journey. When Paul finally arrived in Paris, he found my beloved city was "deserted, silent, and purified."

What a wonderful surprise! A special guest came to the area especially to see me and visited every day for a whole week! Paul was not able to get away yet and sent in his stead Nelly Méquillet, the mother-in-law of his daughter, Chouchette. I'm especially grateful to her, as she had to travel twenty-four hours to reach Montfavet. Her train arrived at the village at 3 a.m. (Wouldn't you know? Nothing works well at Montdevergues, especially during wartime) and had to wait three whole hours in the station before the gates of the asylum were opened. Even though I was very weak and went in and out of sleep much of the time, I was so happy to see her I seized both of her hands and wouldn't let them go. She brought me delicious eggs, grapes, and milk that she'd saved from her own breakfast. I grabbed the food and gobbled down every last bit. Nelly apologized because no butter was available, but I wasn't in a position to complain. It'd been a long time since I'd enjoyed food so much. In fact I often was unable to eat at all, even on the rare occasions during the war when decent food was available.

My doctor asked Nelly to have Paul send me some butter, eggs, sugar, jam, and cake, as food is easier to get in rural Bragues than in the cities. The thought of tasting butter again made me weep for joy. We get very little to eat here, as the Germans have requisitioned most of our supplies. An ordinary dinner roll is cut into quarters and served to four people. Dinner usually consists of the equivalent of one slice of bread, with a bowl of fatty water they call soup. The women at my table wait for crumbs to fall off the bread, and wet their fingertips so as not to miss any when picking them up. You have to be careful and watch your food, because one inmate here goes around grabbing food off people's plates. There's no point in protesting, because she pops it right in her mouth before you can slap her face. People eat beet roots, leeks, boiled carrots, whatever they can find. Some of the aids and patients climb the mountain to search for any edibles and wood to heat the freezing rooms. No one here, whether inmate or staff, escapes the terrible deprivation.

It's clear asylums do not rate very high on the government's priority list. Last July I was so weak from hunger Dr. Izac ordered me to stay in bed. Many patients have died of starvation, as many as eight hundred out of two thousand, almost one out of two! Every day I hear about four or five more who've died. Besides the lack of food, we have a scarcity of all supplies, such as medication, soap, disinfectant, clothing, and means of transportation. We sleep on straw mattresses, and there rarely are sheets to cover them. The first thing we do in the morning on waking up is to look for bugs. The lice in our clothing are so large they're frightening, sometimes reaching the size of a centimeter. When inmates ask for clean linen, they must return the dirty ones first. Many wash their own things, as underwear and handkerchiefs sent to the laundry often are never seen again. Almost everyone here has scabies, and the itch is dreadful. People scratch so much they become infected and develop abscesses, which must be cut open. Since there's no proper remedy available, they have to take pliers and alcohol to lance them. The infected areas resemble burns. Many people die of tetanus, who could be saved with proper medication. It's a terrible thing to see. Look upon our faces, oh ye mighty, and despair.

The wartime transportation is as horrendous for other travelers as it was for Nelly. Some attendants were sent to Rodez at the frontier of the occupied zone to pick up one hundred ill Parisians. The returning train trip took a night and a day. They had to ride in the baggage car from Avignon to Rodez. There was no place to sleep in the hotel at Rodez for many of the patients, and some even had to bed down in bathtubs. The group had to leave at five o'clock the next morning, to make room for the next group of clients of the hotel. The sick patients arrived at Montdevergues filthy, exhausted, and emitting a group roar the wind carried all the way into the village.

I told Nelly about all the shortages here, and she will do her best to send some supplies. It made me sad to have her leave, as I probably will never see her again. She hugged and kissed me affectionately and gave me a special kiss from Paul.

Speaking of Paul, I still have certain matters concerning him to clear up in my mind. Of all the people I've ever known, Paul for better and for worse had the greatest influence on me. He always encouraged my art from childhood on, and remained my only confidant all my life. As a highly creative person, he always understood what I was trying to say in my sculptures. I don't know if I could have become as great a sculptor without his constant support. As children we loved each other dearly. I never stopped loving him, although I suppose it's strange I'm not angry with him, seeing he did nothing to get me out of this prison which he says I deserve to expiate my misdeeds. Even though I adore him, I'm afraid I sometimes think his fierce fanaticism has clouded his judgement about sentencing me to this purgatory. I still can't believe my loving and beloved brother could do such a thing. It's easier when I feel he's acted under the influence of Rodin. When Paul was criticized in a Parisian newspaper for allowing my sentence of life imprisonment, he wrote he endured the scandal as a punishment for his sins, and catastrophes were good for him and were the common fate of Christians. Good for *you*, Paul? How about for me? Despite my abiding love for him, I think—at least at this moment—he's a man without a heart.

Although Paul's a rich and famous man as well as a devout Christian, there're many people who have similar reservations about him. They consider him an abominable human being who frequently surrenders to fits of violence, prejudice, and, strangely enough for a devout Catholic, exhibits a complete absence of Christian charity. For example, he was so pig-headed and merciless about the Dreyfus affair his longtime friend Jules Renard refused to have anything more to do with him. Paul literally threw his good friend Jacques Madaule out the door of his home. His crime? He'd requested Paul's signature for a petition demanding Franco's bombing of Guernica be stopped. Paul "explained" in a letter that he considered the petition an outrage against the priests who'd been massacred by the Basques, whom he loathed and considered traitors. In his favor, Paul's always very upset when he has an outburst. He wrote me it's very sad that at seventy years of age he still can't stop himself from exploding with fury, as he did in his youth. He said he feels bad for many months afterward and the guilt interferes with his creativity.

André Gide also had some unkind words to say about Paul. The famous novelist disliked Paul intensely, and wrote that he talks constantly and can't be stopped by any protest a listener might raise. Gide added that if Paul's interrupted, and it's necessary to intrude upon his monologue unless one wishes to remain part of the scenery, he politely waits until you're finished, and then picks up where he left off as if you hadn't said a word. He doesn't value or even listen to any opinion besides his own. Strange, it never occurred to me before how much he's become like Maman! He's even getting to look like her.

One thing I'm grateful to Paul for. Even though he thinks it an abomination I had an abortion he's never let it end our relationship. For a Catholic with his severe conscience, that's saying a great deal. It's the only time I know of he's put the needs of a person before his religion. It means he really loves me and has never stopped doing so. It's true he doesn't come to see me very often, but he's always written and never abandoned me to the asylum as Maman and Louise did. There's no doubt in my mind *mon petit Paul* is the love of my life.

With the money he made in his two successful careers, Paul just bought himself his first home, Le Château de Brangues, which he said looks like a castle. He's now a famous poet, playwright, diplomat, husband, father, grandfather, and land owner. I picture his estate looking like a newer version of La Folie Neufbourg. How I wish I could see it, even for a visit! Paul's worked hard all his life and deserves his new affluence. I'm happy for him. Nevertheless, it's a bit difficult to keep from making comparisons. Here's my wildly successful brother the lord of a castle, while I, at least as gifted, am not permitted to have even a small attic room of my own. I'll never understand why.

And then there's the matter of the sexual play we had as children. I really can't blame him, as I was the older sister, who not only let him go ahead but even encouraged him in his explorations. I have no regrets for myself, as we found a lot of pleasure in each other. I believe our sex play made it possible for me to discredit the thinking of the times that "good" women never enjoyed sex and only submitted for the pleasure of their husbands. I'm glad I didn't fall for that line, thanks to Paul and his groping, which made it possible for me to enjoy ten years of wonderful sex with Rodin. And yet I feel guilty about the effect our activities had on Paul's development. If I'd known what our actions would do to his character, that they'd make him so rigid, unforgiving, and opposed to pleasure of all kinds, I never would've permitted our explorations to take place. They've crippled him for life with a perverted conscience. I suspect that's a greater crime on my shoulders than the abortion, and why I deserve to be incarcerated for so many years. I'm sorry Paul, so sorry, although I can never tell you that. Mea culpa! Mea culpa! Perhaps that's why I've never blamed him for my incarceration.

The night after I wrote this I had a dream. It was so real I couldn't believe it really hadn't happened. I was maybe the age I was when Paul and I...played together. A young and handsome Papa and I were in his library, sitting close together on his favorite brown leather chair. He stroked my forehead, as his soft mutton-chop beard brushed against the top of my head. Papa hugged me to him and said, "Camille, forgive yourself for what you and Paul did together." I couldn't believe my ears and said, "You mean what we did was...all right?" He answered, "No, Camille, it wasn't all right. But after all, you were only a child, too." I sat there on his lap sobbing loudly and woke up soaked to my armpits in tears. Papa, my dear Papa! Thank you, thank you! You've always been there for me and now you're here when I need you to help me make peace with my guilt before I die.

I'm so weak now I sleep most of the time. I'm very tired, and ready for a good, long rest. But Nelly said Paul's coming to see me soon, and I'm waiting for his visit before I take my departure from this vale of tears.

He's coming! He *is* coming! I received a letter from him today saying he'll be here in September! Can I hold out for two more months? I'll fight with my last breath to do so. There's no way I'd miss my chance to say good-bye to the person I love most in the whole world.

He's here! He really is here! I was asleep when he came into the room and woke up to see his face leaning over mine. Tears were running down his face. I didn't cry, but lit up like the sun had broken through a month of cloudy skies. I didn't have the strength to talk, but muttered over and over again, "*Mon petit Paul. Mon petit Paul.*" Then, holding his hand, I fell into a happy dream state in which all are united with those they love, and everyone is happily engaged in work they care about. I don't know how long he stayed there beside me but when I awoke he was gone. It was all right. I already had said good-bye. I had made peace with him in Papa's dream.

*T*his dying process is very interesting. I seem to have resolved my problems with Maman, my sister Louise, and now even Paul. Only Rodin remains a nail in my coffin. (I'm happy to see they couldn't knock out my sense of humor, even after thirty years of purgatory, when I'm knocking at death's door.) What about Rodin? I ask myself. Can I possibly forgive him for all the atrocities he's committed against me? After all, Christ said to turn the other cheek. Can I stop hating Rodin just this once before I die?

No, I won't! I refuse to give up my rage at him. It's mine and I choose to keep it! It's become clear to me in recent days there's some bizarre comfort I get from detesting him. Sometimes I think the hatred is my entire emotional life and consumes me as much as my love for him in years past. While he was alive, I could hardly wait for another of his letters so I could rip it up into tiny pieces and watch them blow away in the icy wind. It gives me great pleasure to imagine him waiting for my answer in Hell, as I waited all those years for him to marry me. My loathing of him keeps me warm at night when the frost of the bleak winter chills my bones. I wrap myself around the feel of him like a baby at her mother's breast until it lulls me to sleep. When I wake in the morning, I check to see it's still there. It keeps me company during the unending days at Montdevergues, as I yell and scream at him in my head. Much as I despise him, I'd be desolate without my rage, for then I'd be truly alone. And when they carry my mortal remains to their final resting place, my soul will envelop itself around my hatred for him. It will keep me warm for eternity, as it has done for so many years.

Now, Monsieur Rodin, now! I'm coming...I know you've been waiting a long time for me. Are you ready?...Are...you...ready....

Addendum

1. A candy available in Alsace-Lorraine.

2. A distorted form of *géant*, the French word for giant.

3. Alma Bond, as derived from Psalm 139.

4. Easter.

5. European women of the times called their men by their last names.

6. A French Christmas celebration in which little figurines are hidden in a cake.

7. Bond, Alma H. in *Aspects of Psychoanalysis*, Exposition Press, Smithtown, N.Y., 1984.

8. Why so Pale and Wan? Sir John Suckling (1646). *The Viking Book of Poetry of the English Speaking World*, Ed: Richard Aldington, The Viking Press, 1941, P. 423.

9. Algernon Charles Swinburne, The Garden of Proserpine (1866), *Swinburne's Collected Poetical Works*, 2 vols. London: William Heinemann, 1924: I, 169–72.

10. In sculpture, even two people comprise a "group."

11. The old-fashioned term in which an artist invested all of his life knowledge and talent in a work in a bid for professional recognition of status.

Bibliography

Although I have consulted numerous books and articles, those which have proved most useful to me in writing this book are:

1. *Dossier Camille Claudel* by Jacques Cassar, nouvelle éd, 2001, Maisonneuve and Larose, 15, rue Victor-Cousin 75005 Paris, France.

2. *Camille Claudel, Catalogue Raisonné* by Anne Rivière, Bruno Gaudichon, and Danielle Ghanassia,c 2000, Société nouvelle Adam Biro 28, rue de Sévigné, 75004 Paris, France.

3. *Montdevergues, Les mémoires d'un hôpital,* Oeuvres Sociales Locales, Coordinator: Lyne Valente, Historical research: David Chauvet, 2000 Centre Hospitalier de Montfavet, France.

4. *Camille:* The Life of Camille Claudel by Reine-Marie Paris, translated from the French by Liliane Emery Tuck, 1984 by Editions Gallimard, Translation copyright1988 by Seaver Books, Arcade Publishing Company, Inc. New York, Little, Brown & Co. by arrangement with Seaver Books/Henry Holt and Company, Inc.

5. *Camille Claudel, a Life* by Odile Ayral-Clause, 2002 by Harry N. Abrams, Inc. 100 Fifth Avenue, New York.

6. *Alfred Boucher Catalogue,* 2000, Musée Paul Dubois—Alfred Boucher, Nogent-sur-Seine, Aube, France.

7. *Paul Claudel and The Tidings Brought to Mary* by Kathleen O'Flaherty, 1948, Cork University Press, B. H. Blackwell, Ltd., Oxford, England.

8. *Paul Claudel,* The Eye Listens, 1950, The Philosophical Library, Inc., 15 E. 40th Street, New York.

9. *Rodin, a Biography* by Frederic V. Grunfield, 1987, Henry Holt and Co., New York.

10. *Rodin:* The Shape of Genius by Ruth Butler, 1993, Yale University Press, New Haven and London.

11. *Round My House* by Philip Gilbert Hamerton, 1888, Roberts Brothers, Boston, MA

12. *The Life of Debussy* by Roger Nichols, 1998, Cambridge University Press, 40 W. 20th Street, New York.

13. *Old Masters:* Great Artists in Old Age by Thomas Dormandy, 2000, Hambledon and London, London and New York.

14. *Le Pays Des Coûfontaine ou Le Tardenois de Paul Claudel,* Catalog of the Exposition "Le Pays des Coûfontaine."

15. *Paul Claudel* by Bettina Liebowtiz Knapp, Modern Literature Monographs, Frederick Ungar, 1982.

Glossary

atelier: an artist's studio or workshop
au naturel: nude, in a natural state
baiser: kiss
bonne: a maid
cerveau: brain, mind
chat: cat
château: castle, manor
Châtelaine: lady of the Manor
ciel: sky
clef: key
école: school
écoute: listens
enfant: child
femme: woman
fille: girl
folie: madness
format d'éole: school curriculum
grand: great
hôpital: hospital
imploration: entreaty
jeune: young
lycée: college
maître: teacher
maquette: a small clay model created as a guide for a larger sculpture

mémoires: memories
mère: mother
mouleur: moulder, caster
mûr: mature
oeil: eye
ondeur: founder, smelter
otage: hostage
pain dur: dry bread
patois: dialect
père humilié: humiliated father
petite: small
practicien: technician
prie dieu: a stool for kneeling at prayer
printemps: spring
sculpteur: sculptor
soulier: shoe
tant pis!: too bad, so much the worse!
tête d'or: golden head
valse: waltz
veille: old

Breinigsville, PA USA
20 December 2009
229551BV00001B/149/A